The closet door knob latch g door itself began to slowly accompanied by an ominous creaking noise better suited to some door within a haunted house.

Icy spiders of panic skittered up my spine as I watched the clothes hanging inside my closet draw away like stage curtains to reveal the wall of blackness behind them. Normally, that blackness would've merely been the shadowed rear of my closet. But this was somehow different. The darkness behind my clothes seemed to possess a tunnel-like depth. One that my fear-fueled imagination insisted belonged to the throat of a monstrous dragon.

Then something moved within the shadows.

THE BOOGEYMAN
A Monstrous Fairy Tale

by Shane Berryhill

OTHERSIDE PRESS

For James Clayton

Where do they come from? The dust. Where do they go? The grave. Does blood stir in their veins? No, the night wind.

—*Ray Bradbury,* Something Wicked this Way Comes

1

A MONSTER RAIDS MY CLOSET

I guess this is the part where I should tell you my name. But like my dad often says when he's in a hurry, there'll be time enough for pleasantries later. The important thing for you to know right now is that the Boogeyman is real. I know. I've seen him. He came out of my closet only a few hours ago!

This is what happened: I went to bed the same time I always do, and then waited for Mom and Dad to follow. They watched the news for a while first. I know this because I could hear the TV anchorman's familiar, smarmy voice talking about how several children from our town have gone missing over the past few days. According to the news anchor, the police now thought the disappearances might be connected. He ended the story by saying the police were pursuing all leads to their fullest extent.

I'm old enough to know that when adults say such things, they're covering up the fact that they're clueless. Like the time I asked my fifth grade science teacher, Mr. Swanson, what made the universe. He said, "The Big Bang." When I asked what caused the Big Bang, he said, "Ultimately, another Big Bang."

As if that answered anything. There are just a lot of things out there we simply don't have explanations for. Case in point, the Boogeyman appearing in my closet. There's absolutely no logical reason for it. That's why I can't say anything to Mom or Dad.

Don't get me wrong. I love my parents, and they love me. More than anything. But, at my age, if I told them or my teachers that the Boogeyman was living in my closet, at best, they'd think I was teasing them. At worst, they'd call Dr. Stuart's emergency line. He'd just say it's my *condition,* and place me back on medication. That'd mean more teasing and name-calling from my classmates if they found out (*And they always do*). And I go through enough of that already.

So, that leaves me on my own where the Boogeyman is concerned. But I'm getting ahead of myself.

Back to a few hours ago…

It wasn't long before I heard the TV switch off, and the sounds of Dad's snores echoing through the house. Confident my parents were asleep, I took out my flashlight and began reading the latest offering I'd taken from Dad's bookshelf. I've always been a night owl, and reading is one of the few quiet activities I'm able to engage in despite my *condition.* I get a sense of peace and calm when I read. Anyway, the book in question tonight was a paperback titled *The Master Mind of Mars.*

I know Tarzan gets all the buzz, but if you ask me, when it comes to Edgar Rice Burroughs, his Mars series is where it's really at. There are creatures within its pages unlike anything here on Earth—kangaroo men, synthetic golems, and coolest of all, giant, four-armed apes. Everything you could want where monsters are concerned. And being a boy of twelve, monsters concern me a lot. Much more than Dr. Stuart considers healthy for me (*Now do you understand why I don't want to see him?*).

Truthfully speaking, I *do* like monsters a heck of a lot more than the other boys and girls in my class do. While the few friends I have are crazy for baseball and Reality TV, I prefer horror comics and Godzilla movies. It's just another one of those unexplainable things I was talking about, I guess. Monsters have simply always *called* to me.

At least until I saw a real one come out of my closet.

That was definitely what my sports-nut pals would call a "game-changer."

Anyway, I guess I've avoided telling you about the Boogeyman long enough. Please forgive me for failing to get to the point, but it really gives me the willies to think about what went down earlier. But as my dad would also say, time to put up or shut up.

So, here it goes: like I said, I was sitting in my bed, reading with my flashlight. The dim glow of the moon coming in through my room's sole window illuminated my drawing desk, comfy chair, and monster-postered walls. I was deep in a chapter about a mad, Martian scientist conducting a brain-transplant between a beautiful, young princess and an ugly, old hag when, all of a sudden, a feeling of great dread came over me.

Everything got very quiet. Even for that time of night. Dad's snores had stopped. There was nothing unusual about that. He has his quiet spells throughout the night. But those times are always filled by the tick-tock of the antique cat-clock hanging on the wall in our kitchen. You know the kind—the black one whose faux eyes and tail rock in time with the ticking seconds. But it too had grown quiet.

This eerie silence was merely the first precursor to the Boogeyman's appearance.

Next, I noticed that the air in my room seemed to have taken on a tangible weight. One that pressed down on me in waves and made it difficult to breathe. It felt like I was drowning, though the closest body of water is the pool of my next-door neighbor, Mr. Korn.

This pressure seemed to be coming from my closet. The white paint adorning its closed door appeared pale blue in the moonlight. How exactly I knew that was where the negative energy was coming from, again, I can't explain. I simply knew without knowing. And as I stared at the closet door, it abruptly rushed toward me, filling my field of vision.

I threw up my hands and shut my eyes in reflex. I waited, frozen. After a time, when the closet door failed to slam into me, I dared a peek. My closet door was there in its proper place and size, same as it had ever been. Even the suffocating pressure filling the air had vanished. For a moment I thought I must have been dreaming, and that everything was perfectly normal.

But I thought that only for a moment.

I looked on in disbelief as my closet's brass door knob began to slowly rotate all on its own. It was as though some invisible ghost was turning it. Or worse—as though there was a living, breathing person who had no business being in my house, much less my room, twisting it from the door's other side.

I flicked off my flashlight and dived backwards into my bed, pulling the covers up to the twin boiled eggs my eyes had become. I was too frightened to call out. All I could do was lie there shivering.

The closet door knob latch gave way with a click. Then the door itself began to slowly swing open. Its movement was accompanied by an ominous creaking noise better suited to some door within a haunted house.

Icy spiders of panic skittered up my spine as I watched the clothes hanging inside my closet draw away like stage curtains to reveal the wall of blackness behind them. Normally, that blackness would've merely been the shadowed rear of my closet. But this was somehow different. The darkness behind my clothes seemed to possess a tunnel-like depth. One that my fear-fueled imagination insisted belonged to the throat of a monstrous dragon.

Then something moved within the shadows.

I gazed in horror as the darkness at the rear of my closet began to take on shape and substance. It was as though something as dark and horrible as the shadows themselves was pressing through into my bedroom. Then I realized this new blackness for what it was: a silk top hat. One like the hat you've probably seen President Lincoln wearing in the pictures of your history text. Only this top hat was crooked to the point of being cartoonish. In fact, that is exactly what it looked like—the hat of some cartoon villain bent so far forward it was comical.

But seeing such a hat here in the real world was anything but comedic. It was disturbing. Especially when I saw the pale, fanged jaw jutting out from beneath its down-tilted brim. The jaw was grotesquely long, and as bowed as the black top hat cresting above it. Taken together, they formed the shape of a forward-facing crescent moon. But this was the least horrible thing about the creature invading my room.

The thing looked up, the brim of its dark hat leveling out, and I saw its gruesome, white face in its entirety. A pale, hooked nose curved down like a smaller, opposing version of its chin to divide a mouth full of black fangs. Two sharp ears worthy of a Vulcan from *Star Trek* bookended either side of its long, narrow face. And worst of all, two eyes of crystalline night rode atop cheeks so bony and sunken you would swear there was no flesh on them at all.

The creature drifted out of my closet, having to duck so that the length of its crooked top hat missed the lintel. The darkness the creature sprang from followed after, swirling around it in the form of a broad cloak with a high collar of undulating shadow. The cloak ebbed and flowed as though it were sewn together from the writhing shadows of living snakes. Considering everything I saw, perhaps it was.

Terrified out of my mind, I shut my eyes and pretended to sleep, hoping this vile, shadowy thing would leave me alone and move on to whatever dark business had brought it into my room—*into this world.*

A moment later, I felt the awful pressure from earlier once again fill the air, and I knew that the creature was hovering over me. It made a sound like the low growls of the lions on *Animal Planet,* and it was everything I could do not to scream and make a break for my bedroom door.

What happened next came as a surprise. The creature sniffed me. Just two quick inhales of air through its nose. But when the nose of the thing smelling you is the size and shape of a giant cockatoo beak, being sniffed is like being directly beneath a vacuum turned on high.

I sensed the creature abruptly pull away. This sensation was followed by that of the thing's terrible presence fading from the room. I opened my eyes and looked up. The creature was gone. But I felt a cool autumn breeze on my face and saw that my room's sole window stood cracked open.

Much to my own surprise, I got out of bed and went over to the window. It was more than my condition or simple morbid curiosity that caused me to do such a ridiculous thing. I guess I was just too out of my mind with fear to behave in any reasonable fashion.

Anyway, my heart pounding, I peered out the window. At first, I didn't see anything out of the ordinary. Just the big tree in our fenced-in backyard standing still and silent in the moonlight, its fallen leaves resting around its base, waiting to be raked. Then I looked down and gasped at what met my eyes.

The creature that had emerged from my closet was climbing head first down the side of our two-story house. Except, climbing is too crude a word to describe what it was doing. The thing *glided* on its belly down the length of our house, the swirling blackness of its cloaked torso pulled along by two clawed hands attached to long, spindly arms sheathed in black.

It reached the yard and hovered across to the fence, moving like a ghost in the night, its cloaked body barely brushing against the ground. It was up and over the fence in seconds flat, traversing the fence as easily as it did the side of our house, the bottom of its cloak disappearing from view with a final swoosh of inky darkness.

It was at this moment that my mind decided I'd seen and experienced enough strangeness for a while. My eyes rolled back in my head, and my body crumpled to the floor. I was already fast asleep and having nightmares about the creature before I landed.

2
THE BOOGEYMAN ACCESSORIZES

The Boogeyman!
That was the first thing that popped into my head when I awoke.

The creature that came out of my closet was the Boogeyman!

I've been lying here on the floor, gazing up at the movie-monster posters lining my walls (the moonlight making them appear in shades of black and blue), going over it in my mind now for several minutes.

What I'm saying is, the creature being the Boogeyman makes sense. It certainly fits all the Boogeyman criteria. For instance,

Appearing out of a dark closet.

Check.

Looking like a shadow-cloaked, crescent-moon-faced, top hat-wearing monster.

Double-check.

Scaring the living daylights out of me!

Check, check, and triple-check!

It *must* be the Boogeyman. It's just too much of a coincidence otherwise. I mean, there has to be some reason why practically every culture has a myth about a monster-man who invades the rooms of children at night? Some truth behind the myth?

Granted, I never dreamed that truth would come slinking out of my own personal closet. But the Boogeyman had to have appeared out of someone's closet somewhere at some time—more than likely a lot of somewheres and some times—for the legend to be so widespread. As much as I hate to say it, my closet was just as likely a place for the Boogeyman to come out of as any. *Obviously.*

The question is, what am I going to do about it?

But, before I can even begin to think about the answer to that question, I notice that the house has become eerily silent once again. I feel the air in my room begin to take on what is now a familiar, oppressive weight.

The Boogeyman is coming back!

I scramble to my feet and leap into bed. In the back of my mind, I realize I would've been unable to do this during the seconds immediately leading up to my first encounter with the Boogeyman. The negative energy heralding his first coming would've frozen me in place. But, somehow, this incident of his preceding aura is not quite as nasty. Either I'm getting used to the Boogeyman, or he isn't as threatening as I originally thought. Still, saying the Boogeyman is less threatening the second time around is like saying you have already faced an angry grizzly, and now all you have to worry about is a rabid Pit Bull.

I stare at the window, waiting.

And waiting.

At last, the top of the Boogeyman's jagged black hat crests the windowsill, rising against the night like a dark, crooked flower. Fear reaches up from my gut and seizes my heart in its cold fist. I will myself to breathe slowly and remain calm. If I panic, I know it'll mean my end.

I pretend to be asleep again, but this time, I keep my eyelids cracked just enough to see what the Boogeyman is up to. He opens my bedroom window the rest of the way and climbs inside. Only, he doesn't climb so much as *ooze* into my room, the billowy, sentient blackness of his cloak carrying him inside, one shadowy piece at a time.

The Boogeyman stands before the window, a corona of moonlight around him, studying me with the twin eight balls he has for eyes. Although he remains hunched over, the top of his crooked hat and the swell of his cloaked shoulders brush against the bedroom ceiling. If he ever decides to stand up straight, I imagine he'll reach at least nine feet in height.

I doubt there's much chance of that, though. Him standing

up straight, I mean. The hunched look certainly gives him more of a predatory bearing. And my guess is the Boogeyman is definitely a predator.

I want to hold my breath. But I know if I don't maintain the steady rise and fall of my chest, the Boogeyman will know I'm only feigning sleep. So I keep my breaths even and slow.

It's amazing what you can do when you have to.

After a time, the Boogeyman turns toward my closet, apparently satisfied I'm asleep. Gazing at his profile, I'm able to see that he's now carrying a brown, threadbare sack held together by numerous patches and stitching. The sack is full of something, and distends from the Boogeyman's cloaked back like a large hump. Standing there with the sack, the Boogeyman looks like an evil Santa Claus from some insane parallel universe—an *Anti-Claus*, if you will.

Then, unable to stop myself, I gasp as the outline of what is in the Boogeyman's sack—an outline that appears humanoid in shape—moves.

The Boogeyman is on me in an instant, his approach so fast that my bed seems to lurch toward him rather than him toward it. He leans over me, his dreadful presence now back in full effect. His low, measuring growl once again issues from deep inside his throat.

Fighting my terror, I pretend to be asleep for all I'm worth, playing off my gasp with some dramatic stirring, making it appear as though I was merely having a bad dream before at last settling back into what I hope looks like a peaceful slumber.

The Boogeyman lingers at my bedside for several eternity-long minutes. He growls again, but this time the sound is dismissive. He turns away from me and glides toward my closet. I open my eyes to watch him go and see the brown sack at his back twitching with movement. I'm not certain, but I think I can also hear faint cries coming from inside it.

The cries of a child.

The Boogeyman reaches my closet door, and it opens before him as if by magic. The clothes hanging inside the closet part once again to allow his passage. He ducks his head and slides in. The shadows at the rear of the closet swallow him and his sack. The aftermath of his presence drains from the room, and I exhale in relief.

Then I begin to cry.

I lie in my bed sobbing quietly for some time, upset and yet also numb.

Why was this happening? Have I done something to deserve such a fright? I'm a bit of an oddball, I admit. And my *condition* often gets me into trouble. But have I done something so bad that I deserve to have the pants scared off me in this way? I just don't get it.

I wish I could just go to sleep and pretend nothing has happened. Or just dismiss the Boogeyman as a dream. Heck! Even believing I have at last gone off the deep end would be somewhat of a relief. At least my condition is something that happens on a regular basis here in the real world—something that can be dealt with.

But I know I'm not crazy. My open window and closet door tell me without question that I'm as sane as can be. And if I still have any doubts about the Boogeyman being real, I have none whatsoever about what he carried in his sack.

Once again, it all adds up. The wriggling, human shape in the sack and the cries coming from it tell me my bedroom isn't the only one the Boogeyman has visited tonight. If I were old enough to gamble, I'd bet the Boogeyman is behind the recent disappearances of several of the town's children.

I sit up in bed and swing my pajama-clad legs out over the floor. I hop up and go over to my open closet. Moving tentatively, I step inside and push back my clothes with a sweep of my arms. The closet's rear wall stands before me, a sheet of blackness. I swallow hard and reach out and touch it.

I whimper when it gives beneath my hand.

Rather than feeling hard to the touch, it's syrupy, and sticks to my hand for a moment before snapping back into place when I pull away. Whatever magical passageway the Boogeyman used to enter and exit my room still seems to be in place. He must plan to keep using my bedroom as his gateway into our world and the means by which he can continue his kidnapping spree.

That tears it.

I have to tell my parents about this. Whatever the cost to me, it would be wrong to keep quiet if saying something can prevent the Boogeyman from taking any more children.

I run out of the room, yelling for my parents when a horrible thought occurs to me: *What if the grown-ups can't stop the Boogeyman? What if, instead, I'm leading them to their doom?*

3

I INTERRUPT MOM AND DAD'S BEAUTY SLEEP

"Mom! Dad! The Boogeyman was in my room!"

I burst into my parents' bedroom and flip on the light. Mom sits up in bed, sleepy-eyed, her dyed-blonde hair standing in a thousand directions, each one of them different and comical. She's dressed in a faded pink nightgown. Her face is covered in a pale-green paste she calls her "beauty cream," but in truth is anything but.

Dad starts awake with a fit of clipped snores that sound like the grunts a hog makes. This is funnier still as he is no hog at all, but skinny as a rail.

"I'll have those reports on your desk first thing tomorrow, sir!" he yells. Then his eyes flutter open, and he shakes his head in confusion. He rubs his whiskered jaw, and then runs a hand through his dark, matted hair. The V-neck T-shirt he's wearing is soaked with sweat. Apparently I'm not the only one in the house having a rough night.

"Are you all right, honey?" Mom asks.

"What's the matter, son?" Dad mumbles.

"Mom! Dad!" I rush over to Dad and take him by his wrists, trying to wrench him from bed. "You have to come quick! The Boogeyman was in my room!"

"The what was in the who?" Dad asks groggily.

"The Boogeyman!" I shout. "He came out of my closet! Come! You have to see!"

"Goodness gracious," Dad begins, annoyed. "I knew it was going to be rough when we took you off your meds, but—!"

Mom lays a hand on Dad's shoulder. *"Charles."*

That's all Mom does—speak Dad's name. Yet, he stops in mid-sentence, and his entire demeanor changes. It's as though she has cast a spell, that one little word giving her complete power over him.

"Dad, please," I say, frantic.

Dad looks at Mom from the corner of his eye and sighs. "Oh, all right. Let's go have a look."

Dad gets out of bed and dresses in his fluffy, blue robe. He leads me out into the hall and then into my bedroom. He flips on the light.

"Are there any Boogeymen in here?" His voice is loud and full of sarcasm. "If so, you're about to get the butt-kicking of your life!"

"Dad, don't," I chide. "He's not here now, but he still might hear you. The passageway into my closet is still open."

"Passageway into your closet, eh?" Dad says. "Let's have a look."

I sink back against my desk, watching with renewed fear as Dad strides toward the open closet. He steps inside and eyes the clothes hanging there. Slowly, cautiously, he reaches for them.

Sweat pops out on my forehead. My heart becomes a jack-hammer inside my chest. I look down and see that I'm gripping the edge of my desk so hard my knuckles have turned a white even more stark than my skin's already unhealthily pale shade. Suddenly, Dad seizes my dangling pants and shirts and shoves them aside. I yell in terror at the sight of...*a blank white wall?*

Dad turns to me, a single eyebrow cocked in Spock-like fashion. "You see, son? Nothing there."

Mystified, I walk over. Dad steps aside. I reach for the back of my closet. Paint and hard drywall meet my fingers.

Then the answer dawns on me.

"It's the light, Dad." I say. "The Boogeyman's passageway was pitch-black. To travel into our world, he must need it to be dark. He must use the shadows."

"Um-hum," Day says. "Whattaya say we test your hypothesis?"

Before I can stop him, Dad reaches around the door jamb and flips off the closet light. Then he closes the door, sealing us in total darkness. Panic seizes me in its claws, and I begin searching frantically for the door knob.

"Dad? What are you doing? No!"

"Look here, son. It's okay. See?"

He takes one of my struggling hands in his and pulls it toward the rear wall of the closet.

"No, Dad! No!"

My hand brushes against wool and cotton and then, surprisingly, the solid surface of my closet's rear wall.

The closet door opens. The interior light comes on, and I see Dad's hand returning from beyond the door jamb.

"You see?" Dad asks. "Nothing to be afraid of. Lights on or off, no Boogeymen or spooks anywhere. You were probably just having a nightmare."

I shrug in defeat. Maybe the Boogeyman was just a figment of my imagination? Maybe I dozed off without realizing it?

Or maybe I'm crazy after all?

We exit my closet, shutting the door behind us. Dad takes a long, hard look at all the posters of monsters wallpapering my bedroom.

"Son, I know I'm the guy who got you into this stuff in the first place, but maybe Dr. Stuart's right? Maybe it's time you spent a little less energy on monsters and a little more focusing on things here in the real world?"

Dad sees the depressed look in my eyes, and his expression softens. He reaches out and musses my hair.

"Now don't be sad. I know how much you—heck, *we*—love this kind of thing. I just want you to realize there's other stuff out there, too, kiddo."

Dad places his hand on my shoulder and gently ushers me into bed. I pull the covers up to my chest and look him in the eyes.

"Are you guys going to have Dr. Stuart place me back on medication?"

Dad winces as though punched and shakes his head. "No, son. I'm sorry about what I said earlier. I was half-asleep and running off at the mouth before I was thinking straight.

"We took you off the medication because we wanted *you*

back. No one likes how those drugs make you. Least of all your mother and me.

"But it's going to be an adjustment. One we have to help each other through. Okay, pal?"

I give a small smile and nod. I hate it when my condition causes my parents grief, but I'm so thankful they love me anyway.

"You going to be okay?" Dad asks.

I say that I will, though, at best, I'm unsure.

"All right then. Let's hit the hay."

We hug and then Dad gets up and turns off my bedroom light. The hall's light frames his silhouette in the doorway for a moment. Then he's gone, and my room is bathed in pitch once more.

The darkness's return brings that of my fear along with it. And the absolute certainty that the Boogeyman is real, and that if someone doesn't do something, he will come back, and more children will disappear.

Your dad was here, an annoying voice inside my head says. *That's why the passage was closed.*

You're wrong, I argue back.

It ignores me. *It won't open with him here. Only you.*

Why? I think back.

You know.

No I don't.

Yes you do.

No. I. Don't!

Apparently, I win the argument. The annoying voice in my head keeps quiet.

I stare at my closet door, chewing on my bottom lip, my instinct for self-preservation battling against my desire to do what's right.

I could just go check the rear of the closet, I think. This time it's only my proper self forming words in my noggin. *If the wall is solid like it was with Dad present—which it will be—then that settles things, and I don't have to worry about it anymore. I will know I'm merely having a 'spell,' and will ask Mom to make me an appointment with Dr. Stuart myself.*

My eyes adjusting to the darkness, I gaze at the door to my closet.

But if the wall isn't solid…

My mind refuses to finish the thought.

A thin stream of air pushes its way through my lips. Then I throw off the covers and swing my bare feet over the edge of the bed without ever taking my eyes off the closet. It remains still and silent.

I take my flashlight in hand. I flick its switch and a concentrated beam of soft, yellow light cuts through the darkness and sparse moonglow to illuminate my objective. I walk over to the closet door and reach for its brass knob. My hand hovers, shaking above it. My breathing speeds out of control, and the room beings to spin around me.

"Itwilljustbeawallitwilljustbeawall," I repeat in a rush, my words a ward against evil.

Before I can let good sense get the better of me, I seize the knob and throw open the closet door. I step inside and sigh in relief as my flashlight shines upon my clothes and the white wall peering out from behind them.

But my relief is short-lived.

My flashlight flickers and dies, leaving me in near-total darkness.

Forcing back panic, I fumble around the door jamb for the closet light switch. My fingers locate it and flip it on. Once. Twice. Three times. Nothing. My closet interior remains cloaked in shadow.

I stand speechless and frozen with fear as, in the moonlight seeping into my closet, I watch my clothes draw themselves away to reveal the swirling pool of pitch that has once again taken over the back of my closet.

I perceive a "deepening" occur among the shadows, and, sure enough, wind rushes by me to fill some unseen void.

This is the part where I should run.

And I want to. More than anything.

And yet, I don't want to either.

I know the smart thing to do would be to hightail it out of here.

But the blackness at the rear of my closet calls to me, just as the monsters adorning my walls have called to me my entire life. Only this is a hundred times more powerful. As wrong as it is, it feels right. Again, it's just one of those things I can't explain.

The annoying voice in my head takes this opportunity to speak up again.

It's the children. At least, that's mostly the answer. You must protect them.

Why? I counter. *They've never been big fans of mine. Apart from a few guys and girls I can count on one hand and have fingers to spare, most of them have never wanted anything to do with me—other than to make fun of my small size and pale skin, that is.*

That's because you're different, the voice answers without hesitation. *They don't understand you. And what people don't understand, they fear.*

You're not exactly making a case for them here, I think in response.

Now, now, the voice continues. *Don't judge your classmates so harshly. They may be a little rough around the edges right now, but most of them will grow up to be kind, loving people just like your mother and father.*

Not all of them, admittedly. But enough.

More than enough.

That's why you have to help.

Help where all others cannot.

Why me? I think. A single tear I didn't realize was swelling in the corner of my eye rolls down the side of my face. *Why is this happening to me?*

Much to my anger and frustration, the voice inside my head chooses this moment to go silent again.

I curse and stare at the wavering darkness before me, at war with myself. Then, moving with something older than thought and deeper than instinct, I reach for the shadows. My hands touch something. In the sparse moonlight, I see the membrane of darkness at the rear of my closet ripple around my fingers. Then my hands vanish, swallowed up by my closet's inky depths.

I will my hands to ball themselves into fists. I'm unable to tell if I succeed or not. There's no sensory feedback coming from beyond the veil of shadow. Not even a tingling numbness. It is as though my hands have simply ceased to exist. For all I know, they have.

The Boogeyman exists on the other side, the voice says, its imaginary lips apparently loose once again. *And he's got the children with him. You can count on it.*

I give the world's biggest sigh and then steel myself, knowing what I must do—and that there is probably no going back once it's done.

Defying every reasonable fiber within my being, I step forward into utter darkness and absolute unknown.

The last thing to cross my mind as I leave reality is that I wish I'd thought to change out of my pajamas and slip on some shoes.

4

OUT OF THE FRYING PAN

I'm either the world's bravest boy or its dumbest one. I've followed the child-snatching monster known the world over as the Boogeyman through my bedroom closet into whatever world he calls home. Traveling through a wardrobe or not, somehow I doubt the Boogeyman's home will prove to be Narnia. (Yes, that's sarcasm you just read.) Judging from the Boogeyman's hideous appearance, I certainly don't expect there to be any kindly little fauns there to greet me when I arrive.

As my body passes completely into the shadowy void at the rear of my closet, I go blind. Or rather, darkness covers my entire field of vision. I'm overtaken by a sense of vertigo that makes a ride on the world's biggest, fastest rollercoaster seem like a stroll around the block on a warm, sunny day. It makes the pizza I had with my parents earlier in the evening rise in my throat. (Pizza. I'll probably never taste its gooey, cheesy goodness again—at least not the way you're supposed to.)

Then abruptly the feeling of the ground beneath me returns, and the darkness before my eyes recedes. What I see when it does defies description. However, I'll give it my best shot.

I now stand on an endlessly branching walkway that hangs unsuspended in the middle of all-encompassing darkness. This darkness isn't like that of my room, where you can still make things out in the moonlight if you squint. This dark is complete and utter. It's like being on the inside of a giant glass bottle painted black.

I shouldn't be able to see this at all. There's no obvious light source here, yet I'm able to see the walkway and its doors as clear as day.

Each branch of the walkway I stand on ends at what I'm guessing are interdimensional portals (judging by the one I just came through), their number unquantifiable. Most of the portals are the rectangular shape of the rear wall in my bedroom closet back home. The rest are every size and shape imaginable.

I turn around and, sure enough, a dark rectangle is there behind me, my clothes partially visible through the shadowy veil separating me from its other side—my side.

I face forward and stare up at the twisting pathways and their portals. Looking at them as a whole is like looking at the biggest fruit tree in the universe—the walkway being the tree's innumerable branches and the portals being the fruit they bear.

Speaking of looking at the walkway as a whole, doing so causes my vertigo to intensify. The pizza that had already started to come up my throat finishes its climb. I drop to my knees and the remains of my dinner go over the edge of the walkway to disappear into the pitch beneath me.

I never hear it land. Either the bottom of this place is an incredibly long way down, or there's no bottom at all. Looking at the uncompromising darkness below, my guess would be the latter.

I glimpse movement off in the distance from the corner of my eye. I raise my head and catch the tail-end of the Boogeyman's billowy shadow cloak disappearing into one of the portals.

You're lucky, I think. *He could've gone into any of these portals. Good thing you looked up just in time to see which one.*

"Lucky?" I say. "Are you kidding—?"

My words are eclipsed by a noise I first mistake for the echo of distant thunder. But then another sound coming from the opposite direction answers the first, and I realize what I'm hearing isn't thunder at all.

It's a roar.

Or rather, roars. Sounds that could only be made by creatures large beyond imagining.

A cold, clammy sweat covers me as my heart begins doing laps inside my chest. I will myself to move, but my feet remain fastened to the ground, my terror serving as their securing glue.

A faint screeching sounds from behind me, and I slowly turn

my head in its direction, willing my eyes to divide the pitch. At first, I see nothing. Just empty space. Then suddenly, there's movement everywhere.

The screeching rises in volume, no longer one shriek but a chorus of thousands.

Then I see them.

The sight of the grotesque, bat-winged creatures that come flying out of the blackness shaves at least five years off my life. But they're not what get me moving. It's the tentacled, planet-sized thing I see following behind them that causes me to scream in terror and bolt for the Boogeyman's exit of choice.

What these creatures are—what they truly look like—I can't express in words. While the walkway defies description, my mind flatly refuses to process the things rising out of the darkness behind me.

The sound of their screeching grows louder in my ears. The monsters are closing in on me!

Finding a speed reserve I didn't know I possessed, I zoom and even *leap* across the winding walkways to reach the portal last taken by the Boogeyman.

I can safely say I never in my life thought I'd be running away from monsters only to reach another one.

I feel hot, fetid breath blow against the back of my neck just as I reach the portal. At the last second, I kick myself into a higher gear still and plunge through, a thousand enraged shrieks and roars echoing after me.

I burst out of the portal's shadowed veil and fall through an open doorway to land upon a spiraling, stone staircase. The impact knocks the wind from my lungs. Gasping for air, I roll onto my back and watch as the doorway I came through closes on countless grasping claws and tentacles. One of these appendages is unable to withdraw in time. Its owner pays the price as the door slams shut, severing the gnarled claw.

The severed claw drops onto the cold stone steps I lie on and bounces toward me. It brushes against my left ankle and seizes me in a grip like an icy vice. I scream and kick at the thing, wishing I had at least thought to put shoes on before chasing after the Boogeyman.

I win the day by knocking the severed claw off my ankle and over the stairway's edge. It drops for what seems like forever before landing somewhere below with a satisfying *splat*.

I exhale in relief and lie back, taking a moment to catch my breath. I survey my surroundings. The staircase continues circling upward, supported and surrounded by a concave wall made of the same dark, moldy stone. Large wooden doors like the one I entered through are positioned at each level. Flickering wooden torches bookend every other door, lighting the stairwell. Lying here gives me the feeling of being inside the tower of some ancient, medieval castle.

I'm taking all this in when something brushes against my leg. Something warm and furry. I leap to my feet, stifling a scream. I look down and, much to my relief, no monsters or severed claws meet my eyes. This time, the creature before me is a nice, normal, black molly cat with a red collar and large, intelligent eyes.

She brushes the length of her body against my leg and purrs warmly. I grin and kneel so that I may pet her. She arches her back in pleasure as I do.

"Hey there," I say. "What's a nice kitty like you doing in a place like this?"

A clatter echoes below me. I peer over the edge of the staircase, gazing down the tunnel formed by its receding spirals. I just catch the Boogeyman slinking out of sight on the bottom floor, the wriggling brown sack still slung across his hunched back.

"What am I doing here?" I whisper, my voice full of fear.

I feel the cat move from beneath my hand. I look down and see her treading farther up the staircase. Several spirals above me she stops, stretches, yawns, and lies down. She's instantly lost in a purring, carefree sleep.

If only I'd gone to sleep when I was supposed to. I never would've seen the Boogeyman, much less followed him here to this dreadful place.

I hear a door slam below and jerk my head back over the edge of the staircase. I see nothing. The Boogeyman must have entered a room on the ground floor.

"I've come this far," I whisper. "I might as well go all the way."
Resigned to action, I begin tiptoeing down the stairs. The stone is icy cold beneath my bare feet. The stairs' downward spiral seems to never end. When at last it does, I find myself within a circular chamber of dark stone. More burning torches and wooden doors circumvent its walls. Surprisingly, there's no greasy spot marking the severed claw's demise.

Maybe the cat licked up its remains? I think, and almost chuckle. There's no way the cat would've had time to slurp it down and then scamper up the stairs to meet me. Nothing's that fast.

I approach one of the wooden doors and press my head against it, trying to see through one of the gaps made by its old, worn slats. I see a flash of canine teeth glistening with saliva, and thunderous barking erupts on the door's other side. I scramble backward just as something slams against the opposite side of the door with the force of a locomotive. The door creaks and bows outward, but holds.

A voice like exploding dynamite booms from behind a door on the room's other side, shaking the ground and knocking me off my feet.

"QUIET!"

The barking from behind the door in front of me becomes a defeated yelp before ending altogether.

I should go back, I tell myself. *I should just get up and get the heck out of here.*

Fat chance of that, the annoying voice in my head says. *The monsters on the other side of the door you entered seemed pretty angry.*

I hate it when he's right.

Having little choice, I get up and walk over to the door that produced the booming voice. I press my eye to a gap in its slats, trying to see what's on the other side.

The Boogeyman is there, standing before a stone hearth and a chair of scratched wood and moth-eaten cloth with a ridiculously high back. He gestures to the hearth and fire springs from the blocks of wood lying within. He motions to a bent coat rack in the room's corner. It straightens as if alive and marches over to him, cantering along on three clumsy wooden legs badly in need of repair.

The coat rack halts a few feet behind him. The Boogeyman lifts his crooked top hat, exposing a bald, forward-curving head that completes the crescent-moon shape begun by his chin. Without turning around, he tosses his hat at the rack. It lands perfectly on target.

The Boogeyman lifts the shadowy cloak from his shoulders, and it leaves his hands to flutter onto the rack all on its own.

The absence of his cloak and hat causes the Boogeyman to diminish somewhat in size, shape, and bearing. I now see that he wears a ruff-collared jacket, doublet, breeches, and high riding boots that could've belonged to a young Henry the Eighth. All his clothes are black, of course, and contrast greatly against his cue-ball-hued skin.

He sighs like my dad often does after a long day at the office—though the Boogeyman's sigh is more like the guttural purr of a tiger—and begins to sit.

The high-backed chair slides forward of its own accord to move under him just before he can fall to the ground. The Boogeyman lifts his feet, and an ottoman in worse shape than the chair slides across from the other side of the room to serve as his footstool.

The Boogeyman closes his eyes. I can hardly believe my luck when snores on par with Dad's begin sawing their way out of his nose. I exhale in relief and move on to the next door.

At first I don't see anything. A second later, I recoil when a razor-toothed shark glides across my field of vision, a trail of bubbles following after it. The room is flooded with murky sea-water! Crazier still, the water somehow stays in place rather than pouring out around the door.

I'm in a madhouse.

I peek through two more doors—one revealing an upside-down room with gravity-defying furniture, the other showcasing a blue forest beneath a violet sky with twin green moons—before finding the room that holds the reason I came here.

Between the slats of the third door, I see a little boy even younger than myself sitting with his knees hitched to his chest as he sobs. A wagon wheel of candles hangs suspended on chain above him, revealing a set of crumbling stone walls with strange markings scribbled all over them. The Boogeyman's now-empty sack hangs on an iron spike pounded into the wall directly behind the boy.

Jackpot!

Now if I can just get us out of here without waking up the Boogeyman, we should be home free. One of the doors in this place has to lead somewhere safe, surely.

I grasp the iron knocker hanging on the door and pull. It doesn't budge. I take hold with both hands and tug again. The door groans in protest then abruptly pops open. Startled, I freeze, waiting for the door to the Boogeyman's room to burst open in a fury. I sigh in relief when, after several moments, it remains shut.

I tiptoe inside the room. The boy has stopped crying. He looks at me, his face full of hope. I gesture for him to remain quiet.

"Who are you?" he whispers.

"I've come to get you out of here," I reply.

"I can't leave," the boy says. He gestures to a thin chain of dull metal hung around his neck. "It's enchanted, and holds me to this spot. I can't remove it." He shrugs. "Maybe you could—?"

I nod and creep over to him. The chain appears simple enough. Just a chain and a clasp. Much like that of my mom's necklaces. If it's magical, its appearance gives no indication.

I give the doorway a quick glance. Seeing the chamber outside still empty, I begin trying to open the chain's clasp.

"Have you seen any other children?" I ask.

He shakes his head. "I'm afraid they're gone."

The clasp opens within my hands, and I lift the necklace away. I glance back over my shoulder, willing the Boogeyman to stay in his room.

"How do you know?" I ask.

"I know because I ate them."

"*You what—?*"

I turn around and see that the boy is gone. In his place stands a giant, clawed monster with hungry, serpentine eyes and an enormous fanged mouth dripping with slobber.

We both scream—the monster in triumph, me in absolute terror.

5

THE KID I CAME TO RESCUE TRIES TO EAT ME

Why oh why did I ever think it would be a good idea to follow the Boogeyman through my bedroom closet into an insane world brimming with horrendous monsters?

One of them stands over me here and now within the bowels of the Boogeyman's lair, its child-disguise shed to reveal dark scales, black claws, and glistening fangs. The thing looks like a giant, walking snake. Case in point, as it seizes me in its grip and lifts me screaming from the ground, the broad hood of a cobra flares out from the sides of its head. The monster hisses and begins shaking the rattle at the end of its long, whipping tail. Then its jaw unhinges, all but dropping onto its chest as it prepares to swallow me in one huge gulp.

That's when the Boogeyman appears in the doorway, once again dressed in his crooked top hat and cloak of living shadow and looking as mad as a charging bull. I'm able see to his reflection in the snake-monster's glassy, serpentine eyes.

The creature hisses at the Boogeyman in challenge. My unending scream rises in pitch as the snake-monster hurls me at the room's stone wall. I spend what I expect to be my last seconds tumbling through air, knowing the unyielding surface rushing toward me means my end. Then everything lurches to a halt—my tumbling, my screaming, and seemingly time itself.

I look up and see that, amazingly, I'm not dead. The Boogeyman is cradling me in his long, spindly arms. He scowls down at me and the corner of his upper lip rises into a shark-toothed snarl beneath his hooked nose. Much to my surprise, he doesn't eat me with his black, serrated teeth or wring my neck with his long, clawed fingers. He simply drops me. I smack the floor with a thud. I'm sure I'll have a nasty bruise on my rear end, but I'm otherwise okay.

I notice the snake-monster is gone from the room a split second before the Boogeyman does what I can only describe as "go smoky." His torso elongates into a pillar of boiling shadow that snakes out the door at incredible speed. His lower body follows microseconds later, leaving a few small stray wafts of shadow behind in its place.

I scramble to my feet and run out of the room after him. Exactly why, I don't know. I guess my *condition* is interfering with my impulse control. Or maybe my ambulance-chasing instinct simply gets the better of me.

I spot the snake-monster slithering up the spiraling stone staircase, moving every bit as fast as the Boogeyman. The Boogeyman races after him, his black cloak trailing after him like the exhaust of a fighter jet.

Suddenly, out of nowhere, the black cat that greeted me upon arrival comes bounding down the steps toward them. My jaw drops as the cat changes shape while in mid-run, morphing before my eyes into a roaring, panther-shaped shadow with gleaming, red eyes. The frightening, 3-D shadow that was the cat leaps at the snake-monster.

I'm flabbergasted by what happens next. The snake-monster changes shape yet again. It shrinks into an actual, slithering cobra and drops onto the stairs, just evading the shadow-panther. The cobra that was a monster who was a child slithers up the stone wall and over the stairs onto the next landing, placing itself well out of the shadow panther's reach.

This places the Boogeyman directly in the shadow panther's path. The Boogeyman jerks to a halt, but he's unable to react quickly enough to prevent the two of them from colliding. The shadow panther crashes into him, and they tumble down the staircase in a mass of roaring, yowling blackness.

They land at the bottom and are immediately up and moving again, both of them heading for the stairs. However, they abruptly end their pursuit as the cobra disappears below one of the many doors along the stairs.

The Boogeyman yells in frustration, his voice shaking the entire stone structure serving as his home.

"Oh, stop showing yourself," the cat, already having returned to its original form, says. I'm as taken aback by her tone as much as by the fact she can talk at all. Her voice is a sultry, Southern drawl, and causes me to imagine a beautiful, dark-skinned lady with long, thick eyelashes and bright red lipstick.

The Boogeyman whirls on her. "It's your fault the changeling got away!" His voice is full of deep bass. It sounds like what you would expect to hear coming out of Count Dracula's mouth. If Count Dracula wore kilts, that is. The Boogeyman's accent is a thick, Scottish burr. "I almost had him!"

The cat yawns. "Just like you almost had him last night? Or the night before? Or the night before that?"

"That's different!" the Boogeyman counters. "We were in the Mortal Lands. My magic isn't as strong there as it is here in Shadow Tower—a tower you are supposed to be guarding, I might add. Where the heck were you?"

"Ah, excuse me—" I say, my voice sheepish.

"You know where I was," the cat says, ignoring me. "This place doesn't stay vermin-free on its own. Darkness knows your cleaning skills don't help in that regard!"

"Excuse me," I repeat.

"Don't try to change the subject!" the Boogeyman argues, also ignoring me.

"Besides," the cat interrupts, "my job is to protect the tower from all things external, honey. Anything you bring inside is your domain. I was just trying to help you out. I wouldn't have bothered if I had known this is the thanks I would get!"

"Well," the Boogeyman says, pointing a skeletal claw in my direction, "this never would have been a problem if it wasn't for…for…what is your name, boy?"

The Boogeyman grimaces and throws up a hand in warning. "Wait a minute! Don't tell me! True names carry power. Best not to share them when you can help it."

"We have to call him something," the cat says.

"We'll call him Puck," the Boogeyman spits. "He's caused about as much trouble as that trickster ever did."

"EXCUSE ME!" I yell.

When I realize both of them have stopped talking, and that they're now staring at me with extremely intimidating gazes, I slouch, trying to become as small as possible.

In my mind, I see a much braver version of me demanding to know what the Boogeyman has done with the missing children. However, with my fear squelching my anger, all that comes out of my mouth is a timid, "N-N-Never mind."

"If you are protecting the tower from outside threats," the Boogeyman says to the cat without taking his eyes off me, "how do you explain Puck, here?"

The cat rolls her eyes. "Please! I wouldn't purposely attack him any more than I would you."

The Boogeyman nods as though she's answered his question. I, on the other hand, am completely lost.

"What did you think you were doing, Puck?" the Boogeyman asks. It appears my new nickname is here to stay. "Why in the Night Lands did you release the changeling? Now he's free to steal more children from the Mortal Lands!"

Waaaaait a minute.

What's going on here?

"B-B-But," I stutter, "y-y-you were the one who was taking those kids…w-w-weren't you?"

The Boogeyman's dark eyes go wide. "You think that—? Oh for darkness's sake!"

"Calm down, Boogey," the cat says. "He wouldn't know your purpose any more than the other mortals." The cat spots a dirty smudge on her fur and begins giving herself a bath.

The Boogeyman huffs and rubs his face as though he had a very bad headache. My mom does the same thing when she's been called into the principal's office because of my problem-causing condition.

His composure regained, the Boogeyman looks me in the eye. I get squirrely looking my neighbor Mr. Korn in the eye, and he's about the nicest guy around. So you can imagine how uncomfortable I am holding the gaze of a monster like the Boogeyman.

"I was not the one taking children from your town," the Boogeyman says. "It was the changeling. The changeling you set free, Puck. I had been tracking him in your world over the past several nights. Tonight I found him, captured him, and brought him back here to Shadow Tower."

The Boogeyman oozes toward me and hunches down even farther so that his horrible face is only inches from my own.

"That's my job as Boogeyman. When the things that go bump in the night escape into your world, I bring them back here to the Night Lands where they belong. In accordance with the terms of the ancient Pact between our worlds, I make sure that they don't cause any harm to mortals or themselves when they stray to the Earthly realm. At least, I try to. But it doesn't always work out that way."

"S-s-so," I stutter, "y-y-you're like a bounty hunter? Or in this case, a *bogey-hunter*—?"

The Boogeyman's top hat-wearing head slowly rises and then falls in a nod.

"I was trying to get some sleep so that I would be at my best when I performed the extraction spell upon the changeling."

The cat halts her bath and interjects. "The changeling holds the children missing from your town in its belly. Hence the need for an extraction spell."

Oh no!

"He ate them? Just like he was trying to eat me?"

"Relax, Puck," the cat says. "He didn't *eat-eat* them. Just swallowed them for safekeeping."

"You mean they're not dead?" I ask. "How is that possible?"

The cat rolls her eyes dismissively. "Anything's possible when you're dealing with magic. And make no mistake about it, sugar. You *are* dealing with magic."

"I was getting to that, Cat," the Boogeyman says.

"Not fast enough," the cat—or rather, *Cat*—counters.

"The children are fine for now," the Boogeyman says, ignoring Cat's slight. "But an extraction spell needs to be performed soon, and those things are tricky if you don't know what you're doing. Or even if you do, but aren't giving the incantation your full attention."

The Boogeyman resumes his normal ominous size and shape. "That's why I was trying to rest up for it when you went and let the very monster holding your peers escape."

My gaze drops to the ground under the weight of the Boogeyman's accusation.

Wow! If he's telling me the truth, then not only is everything the world thinks about the Boogeyman completely wrong, the misinformation has caused me to screw up. Royally so!

"I—" I say, no longer stuttering but at a loss for words. "I'm sorry. I didn't know."

"Sorry isn't good enough, Puck!" the Boogeyman thunders. "More kids might disappear because of you!"

I raise my hands to stall for time as my mouth catches up with my mind. "Well, why didn't you chase after him? That's what you said you do, right?"

The Boogeyman shakes his head. "There wasn't time. It will be dawn soon on the other side of the door the changeling entered."

"So?"

"So, unless he quickly finds a place completely free of sunlight to hide in, he's a statue of stone right now. The same would happen to me if I followed him."

"What?" I ask, my head spinning.

"You've probably seen gargoyles on churches and in graveyards," Cat says. "That's what happens to night fae when we are exposed to sunlight. We turn to stone. The process is extremely painful. And that's if you're lucky. If you're something like a vampire or a night shade, sunlight will destroy you outright."

"When the changeling went through that door," the Boogeyman continues, "it was an act of desperation."

I scratch my head in question. "Uh, you mentioned night fae?"

"Fairies from the Night Lands," Cat says, "like Boogey and me."

"You're fairies?"

Cat approaches and takes a seat at my feet. "Generally speaking, yes. The Boogeyman, the changeling, myself, and every other legendary monster you've ever heard of are from the Night

Lands, which is merely a sub-realm of the Fae Lands, aka Fae, aka Fairy."

"But I thought fairies were things like tree elves and little butterfly-winged pixies?"

"Aren't you listening, Puck?" the Boogeyman spits. "Those things *are* a part of Fae. But so are trolls, goblins, and countless other monsters."

"One group resides in the Day Lands, and the other here in the Night Lands," Cat continues. "Then, of course, there are the Twilight Lands, where both may dwell simultaneously."

The Boogeyman's cloak flares, apparently reacting to his sour mood. "It's not that complicated if you have half a brain."

"Okay, okay, I get it," I say. "Things like elves and Tinkerbell are from the Day Lands, while nasty creatures like you guys reside here in the Night Lands."

"Just because we don't fit the human ideal of what's good and beautiful doesn't mean we're 'nasty,'" the Boogeyman says, "or any less fae than the Day Lands folk. They can be just as dangerous as us, if not more so."

"He's right, Puck," Cat says. "You'd do well to remember that when it comes to fae, appearances are often deceiving. Things are rarely what they seem here in the Fae Lands." Cat grins. "But in this instance, you've more or less got it."

"Now, if you're through badgering us with questions," the Boogeyman says, "there's a bigger one here that needs answering: what to do with you?"

I swallow hard. "Can't I just go home…? Please…?"

Cat shakes her onyx-shaped head. "According to the terms of the Pact, a mortal may not venture into the Fae Lands without the consent of the crown, nor interfere with the Boogeyman's mission."

"I am well aware of the terms of the Pact," the Boogeyman fumes.

"Then you have the answer to your question," Cat says. "He must be brought before the throne. This is a matter for the King and Queen."

The Boogeyman rubs his long, curving chin in thought. "Very well."

He seizes me by the arm and begins dragging me toward the room with the hearth. I struggle to keep my feet as he pulls me along.

"You can't go before the King and Queen of all fae wearing only your pajamas," the Boogeyman says. "The last fae who tried that had his head removed from his shoulders for his insolence."

"Really?" I ask. "Who was he?"

The Boogeyman answers without pausing in stride.

"A foolish, problem-causing Day Lander named Puck."

6

I MODEL FOR A TALKING FELINE

Wow! Within the span of a couple hours, I've traversed time and space to enter the realm of Fairy, almost been swallowed alive by a shape-shifting changeling, and learned that everything I ever thought I knew about the Boogeyman is completely wrong. He isn't a monster at all. Or rather, he is, but he's a good one. Or at least his job is to capture the bad ones who come poking around the human world after dark.

Speaking of the Boogeyman, we burst into the inner sanctum of his medieval tower. It's a place of stone as dark, cold, and musty smelling as he is. The Boogeyman tosses me onto the large, broken-down chair sitting before the burning hearth. I land like a sack of potatoes, making an *Oomph!* sound as I hit. Fire ignites along the tips of several half-melted candles positioned around the room. Most of the candles stand within leering, jawless skulls of white bone, illuminating a number of high, wooden shelves full of yellowed scrolls and dusty, leather-bound books. The spines of the books bear names like "Necronomicron" and "Grimoire" and countless others in every language imaginable.

That explains the musty smell, I think. *I wonder if he has any Edgar Rice Burroughs?*

My attention is drawn away from the shelves by the sounds of fluttering and scurrying among the shadowed rafters of the high ceiling.

Cat enters the room and leaps onto my lap. She nuzzles against me, indicating her wish to be petted. Knowing she could change into a shadowy panther-monster at any moment if she so desired, I quickly oblige her.

I start as the Boogeyman lifts the end of a rotting wooden table and flings it aside, sending its contents flying in every direction. Doing so clears him a path to a large antique trunk covered in cobwebs and dust.

The trunk's lid opens by itself and the Boogeyman begins rummaging inside, tossing various black garments over his shoulder and strewing them onto the floor.

I know an emo-kid at school who would do a backflip if he got his hands on some of the laundry the Boogeyman is throwing around.

"I tell you," Cat whispers, "a messier Boogeyman I've never seen. And I've seen plenty."

I stop petting her. "You mean there's more?"

Cat's feline shoulders do something that approaches a shrug. "There have been others, though only one exists at a time. The old trains the new and then passes on the mantle."

"Really?" I say, intrigued.

Cat nods.

"The trainee is referred to as the Boogeyman's *Shadow*. I've been here at Shadow Tower since their legacy began, bearing witness as they come and go."

Cat looks up at me expectantly, and I resume petting her. As we watch the Boogeyman cover the floor in clothes, a question forms in my mind. I decide to take a chance and ask it.

"Cat?"

"Yes?"

"Is 'Cat' your real name?"

She snorts in laughter, almost passing a fur ball.

"Now, you heard what the Boogeyman said, *Puck*. Names carry power. Especially for us fae. Unlike mortals, we don't go sharing them with every stranger who comes along. So to answer your question, no. 'Cat' most definitely is not my real name."

"Will you at least tell me *what* you are?"

"That, I may certainly do. I am a boggart, Puck. A shape-shifting fae like the changeling. One assigned to keep this place safe from any and all intruders. As I said, I've been here before Night and Day were divided, and it's from me that the Boogeymen derive their title."

"Wow," I say.

"What?"

"You must be really, really old."

Cat's dark eyes narrow. "Careful, Puck. You should know better than to kid a lady about her age."

The realization that I have a monster in my lap returns, my stutter along with it. "Y-y-yes, ma'am."

"Ah!" the Boogeyman cries. "Here we are!" He straightens almost enough to take the hunch out of his back, an outfit of (you guessed it) black cloth held within his clawed hands. "Try this on for size." He pitches the clothes in my direction. Cat springs from my lap just as the garments smack me in the face.

"You may dress in there," the Boogeyman says, gesturing to the area of the room behind me. I turn around and watch with morbid amazement as hundreds of skittering black spiders drop from the rafters and spin a giant, open cocoon of thick silk webbing in seconds flat. Their job done, they scurry back up the wall to disappear among the shadows.

I walk around to the cocoon's entrance and step inside. I shed my pajamas and slip on the garments the Boogeyman has provided me. They are far too large and all but fall off of me. I waddle back outside to tell him so, trying not to trip while walking around inside them.

"They're too big."

The Boogeyman looks at me appraisingly, and then gives two quick claps of his hands. The clothes I'm dressed in immediately shrink, though now instead of being too big, they're three sizes too small and threaten to squeeze me to death.

"I—can't—breathe!" I gasp.

The Boogeyman chuckles and claps his hands once more. The clothes mercifully expand to fit. I look at the Boogeyman's amused face and wonder if he didn't shrink them too small at first on purpose.

I look down at myself. I'm now dressed in black: a capped tabard, tunic, breeches, feathered musketeer hat, and a set of down-turned leather boots with large silver buckles. I could've just come from a Goth-themed Renaissance fair.

"My, my," Cat says. "Puck cuts quite the dashing figure in your old clothes, wouldn't you say, Boogey?"

The Boogeyman grumbles in response. He waves his hand, and the silver buckles disappear from my boots.

"None but me are allowed to bear metal within the Fae Lands, and not even I within Castle Twilight," the Boogeyman says. "Most fae are allergic to direct contact with one elemental substance or another. Typically it is iron that proves toxic."

The Boogeyman crosses his spidery arms.

"Luckily, as Boogeyman, I am immune to such inconveniences. That is how I was able to bind the changeling using a mere necklace. It was forged from an iron-based alloy." His expression goes sour. "You remember the necklace, don't you, Puck? It is the one that you removed from the changeling's neck."

I feel my face go hot with embarrassment.

"Something's missing from his outfit." Cat leaps into the dusty antique trunk. She emerges seconds later bearing a black domino mask between her teeth.

"He'll need this if he's going into the Twilight Lands," she says, the mask making a mumble of her words. "Unless of course you want a riot on your hands."

The Boogeyman nods.

I take the mask from between Cat's teeth and place it on my face without bothering to wipe away her slobber or ask questions. Offending a shape-shifting panther-monster is the last thing I want to do.

"I give you Master Puck," Cat beams.

The Boogeyman shakes his head. "Come along. Time is of the essence."

"Uh, where are we going, exactly?"

"Back into the Void, then on to Castle Twilight," the Boogeyman answers, already heading for the door.

Fear sends my stomach into my chest. "The Void? You mean that dark place with the walkway and all those…*those things*?"

The Boogeyman turns. His hairless brow rises in question.

"You saw them?" He does not wait for an answer. "You must have called out. Voices attract them."

I recall having spoken aloud just before the things came at me out of the darkness. Once again, my big mouth has gotten me into trouble.

"When we go into the Void again," the Boogeyman continues, "we must move in complete silence. If we do so, we will be perfectly safe."

His eyes narrow and do the opposite of sparkle.

I guess you could say they *darkle*.

"If you do not," he continues, "well…no one escapes the Great Old Ones twice."

My eyes grow wide as I swallow hard.

"Now come." The Boogeyman exits the room with a swirl of cloak worthy of Batman. I start out after him, then pause when I notice Cat fails to follow.

"Aren't you coming with us?" I ask.

Cat shakes her head. "I'm afraid not, Puck. My place and charge are here, guarding Shadow Tower."

"You mean I'm going to have to be alone with *him*?"

Cat smiles. "He's not so bad, Puck. Remember, when it comes to fae, things are rarely what they seem."

Easy for a cat who changes into a panther-monster to say, I think.

Cat grins as though she's able to read my mind. For all I know, she can.

"Come, Puck!" the Boogeyman roars, his voice echoing down from the tower's spiraling staircase.

I bid Cat a quick goodbye and race out of the room after the Boogeyman. I reach the stairs and take them two at a time. I close the gap between the Boogeyman and myself, coming within a few feet of his trailing cloak. Suddenly, the going gets much easier. What's happening feels like what must occur when a race car pulls up to another's rear and drafts along behind it. Only this is much better. It feels like I'm gliding up the stairs rather than running up them.

A smile forms on my face. Only hours ago, the Boogeyman's presence all but pressed me into the ground. Now it's actually pulling me along, making me feel as light and as swift as the wind.

And where before I only felt trepidation, now I feel, well, alive and full of excitement.

Then the Boogeyman ruins it all by coming to a halt and being his usual sweet self.

"Wipe that stupid grin off your face, Puck. Thanks to your breaking of the Pact, more children are in serious danger."

I slouch, my excitement erased by the sound of his deep, mean voice. *And the fact he's right.* It's my fault the changeling got away.

We reach the door through which I entered Shadow Tower, and the Boogeyman flings it open. The sight of the unending walkway appears in the darkness on the other side. Looking at it causes the memory of the things that live in the Void to leap into my head, and I try unsuccessfully to repress a shiver.

"Remember," the Boogeyman warns, "we must be absolutely quiet so as not to agitate the Great Old Ones. Do you understand?"

I tear my eyes away from the Void long enough to give a quick nod.

"Good. Now, once again into the breach!"

The Boogeyman plunges through the doorway and down its adjoining walk. I start to slink away in fear, but the Boogeyman's cloak of living shadow reaches back with its inky tendrils and pulls me through after him.

Once again out of the proverbial frying pan, I scamper along behind the Boogeyman, staying as close to him as possible as my eyes repeatedly scan the dark for the horrible creatures that dwell there.

We wind along the walkway for a short time, taking one twist and turn after another. I have to remind myself not to give an audible sigh of relief when I see we're headed for a large rectangular portal hovering in the dark at our present walkway's end. The purple-orange after-hues of a sunset (or a sunrise) are visible even through the shadowy veil separating us from the portal's other side.

The Boogeyman disappears into the doorway's black membrane, and I bolt through after him. Hitting its surface is like diving headfirst into molasses. When I exit on the other side, the darkness sloughs off me like a set of wet clothes. My head spins with vertigo, though nowhere near as bad as my first trip into the Void. I guess I failed to notice the queasy sensation upon entering and leaving Shadow Tower because I was so full of adrenaline and fear.

I shake off my dizziness and see with the twilight leaking in that we are within an open, shadow-filled tomb containing a marble sarcophagus. Its lid is a carved relief of a warrior king whose fashion sense borrows from the styles of ancient Rome and Wales. Dusty runes line the carving's sides. I blink and, to my amazement, the runes form themselves into words reading,

Here lies Arcturus, Pen Draig of all Britanniae.
May he rise again should aequilibrium ere be lost.

"Come along, Puck."

I look up and see the Boogeyman gliding out the doorway at the tomb's far end. Dust motes dance in the fading sunlight, disturbed by his passage.

"Keep your big, black, scary shirt on," I mumble under my breath.

I give the sarcophagus a final glance and then move on to the tomb's exit. When I get there and step through to the world beyond, I gasp in amazement.

The Boogeyman stretches forth a spindly arm.

"Welcome to the Twilight Lands, Puck."

7

TWILIGHT ISN'T JUST FOR VAMPIRES

"Holy cow!"

Since leaving my bedroom to follow the Boogeyman into Fairy, I've seen the craziest things—cats that talk, boys who turn into monsters, and a darkness that houses unspeakable terrors. But none of them compare to what I see upon entering the Twilight Lands.

I stand on top of a grassy knoll just outside the tomb of an ancient warrior king, staring out across a green pasture ablaze with blinking fireflies and chirping with cricket song. The pasture is divided by a narrow, cobbled road. Stone houses with thatched roofs have cropped up around the road to form a tiny village. But the truly impressive sight greeting my eyes is the massive palace of quartz rising like a purple mountain from the tree grove at the village's end.

The twilight of a newly vanished sun shines from behind the crystal palace, turning its many spires and turrets into rainbow-colored prisms. The effect is especially impressive where the palace's main tower is concerned. It gleams like a pillar of fire as it stretches into heaven. Like the field surrounding it, the palace exterior is swarming with fireflies, and their flickering light adds considerably to the structure's overall magical appearance. The castle is right out of a storybook full of wizards, knights, and princesses, and it leaves me awestruck.

I take off the domino mask I'm wearing to make sure it hasn't enchanted my eyes. The view remains the same.

The Boogeyman spies what I'm doing and snaps at me. "Put that back on your face! Quickly!"

"Hello there!"

"Huh?"

I finish putting my mask back on just in time to see a tall, beautiful lady approaching us. Her milky-white skin is polka-dotted with cute red freckles. The twilight dances upon her braided auburn hair, turning it into crimson fire that's held in check only by the silver headband she wears. A large, gleaming emerald rests at the headband's center.

The woman is dressed in a forest-green robe worn beneath a breastplate of latticed gold. She carries a small, gilded harp in a hand concealed beneath a wide, draping sleeve. The jewel-encrusted hilt and guard of a thin rapier extend from a belt of white leather synched across the skirt of gilded tassels draping from her breastplate.

But the showstopper where the woman is concerned is the pair of shimmering butterfly wings extending from her back. They shine every color of the rainbow. And although seemingly made of actual sunlight, the wings flex and flitter with each step she takes toward us, every bit as brilliant as the palace, and every bit as alive as the Boogeyman's cloak.

"Hey, Boogey," she says over the noisy crickets. Her voice is a melodic Irish brogue. Her tone reminds me of the one Mom uses for Dad when he's done something especially romantic for her.

"Hello, Siren," the Boogeyman says, his own Scottish burr taking on a softness I never would've dreamed possible. "It is… good to see you."

Siren gives a smile that would rival that of the most glamorous movie starlet you've ever seen. While I can't say the Boogeyman returns the expression, his frightening eyes do seem to relax and darkle a little less as he shares her gaze.

"Who's this you've brought with you?" Siren asks. "Your Shadow?"

The Boogeyman shakes his monstrous head. "No. I've given him the title of Puck."

Siren's mouth and eyes form themselves into large O's.

"I see. Does he always go about dragging his jaw on the ground?"

I quickly snap my gaping mouth closed.

The Boogeyman shrugs his massive, cloaked shoulders. "His first time seeing Castle Twilight."

"That definitely explains it," Siren says. Her attention turns to me. "Castle Twilight was carved from pure amethyst by the finest of dwarven craftsmen, you know."

"Are—are you an angel?" I stammer.

Her voice trills with musical laughter. She leans down to look me directly in the eye, and it's all I can do not to faint.

"No, dear Puck. I am not one of the Risen." She gives me a conspiring wink. "Though I do know quite a few of them."

"Really?" I ask, flabbergasted.

She nods at the Boogeyman. "So does he."

The Boogeyman frowns. "The ones I know tend to be more of the Fallen variety. Why, I ran into a *dementia* from the sixth circle just last week."

Siren stands up straight and looks back over her shoulder as though she'd just heard someone calling her.

"Well, dawn has already come to the Mortal Lands. I'm late being about my business. I must be going."

"Must you?" the Boogeyman says, and I'm shocked to hear the sound of pleading in his gravelly voice. "Uh, that is, I mean, of course you must be going. You have your duty to fulfill, the same as I."

Siren extends her right arm as though she were reaching for the Boogeyman. "Goodbye, Boogey. I hope to see you again soon."

The Boogeyman mirrors her gesture, bringing the tips of his clawed fingers within a hair's width of touching Siren's delicate nails, but stopping just short of doing so.

"That is also my hope. As always."

After a moment, they retract their hands. Siren takes a step back and bends at the knees. Her wings spread to their full, majestic width and then she launches skyward with a series of powerful flaps to disappear among the clouds.

"Wow!" I all but shout. "Who was that?"

"The Siren," the Boogeyman answers.

"*What* is she?"

"A fae like myself. Though one from the Day Lands."

"What does she do?"

"She serves as my equivalent on the Day Lands side."

"She wrangles monsters? I thought sunlight turns you guys to stone. Other than rays of twilight, I mean."

The Boogeyman shakes his gruesome head. "No, no. I mean, aye. Sunlight does turn most night fae into stone. Just as the darkness of night likewise turns day fae into stone. But I told you before: the day fae, fae who dwell solely in sunlight, can be just as dangerous as those from the Night Lands. Especially when they trespass into the Mortal Lands. A Siren able to reside in the Mortal Land's daytime is needed to lure them back home. Usually by means more subtle than those I implore, admittedly. But then, my folk tend to be more overtly rambunctious when they go rogue. And difficult circumstances call for strong methods."

"Hmmm," I say, considering. "Wait a minute. I just realized something. It's always daytime somewhere on Earth. Nighttime, too, for that matter. And that's not even considering the Poles, where there's six months of each."

The Boogeyman cocks a single hairless brow. "So?"

"So, Siren said dawn had just come to the Mortal Lands. She said it as if all the Earth experienced daytime as a whole, implying the same occurs when night falls. But as I said, that's not really the case."

The Boogeyman crosses his dark, spindly arms. "Your point being—?"

"You guys act like you're changing shifts. As if you had just clocked out, and Siren in. But considering how day and night work in my world, the Mortal Lands as you guys call it, you both should be working nonstop."

"Well—?"

"Well, why aren't you chasing rogue fae nonstop? Other than the obvious fact you'd never get any rest, I mean."

The Boogeyman's chest rises and falls in a huff of air. "Because these are the Fae Lands. The realm of old magic, and even older mystery. Reality translates differently here."

I lift my musketeer hat and scratch my head. "I don't follow you."

"Your mistake is that you're still thinking in modern, human terms." A portion of the Boogeyman's cloak floats up before my eyes and flattens itself into a level surface. "For example, we fae still believe the Mortal Lands to be flat. And here, in the Fae Lands, despite all the human scientific discovery that has occurred since the time of the Pact, the world *is* still flat."

Now I'm the one who raises an eyebrow. "Huh? How's that possible?"

"Magic," the Boogeyman says dismissively. His answer reminds me of my old science teacher trying to answer my question about what caused the Big Bang.

"It's the same with night and day," he continues, his cloak falling away from my face. "Fae is not beholden to the laws of the Mortal Lands. Here, there are simply the Night Lands and the Day Lands, and the only place either shall ever meet is here within the Twilight Lands. This is reality when perceived through the lens of Fae—*through magic*. And when you're dealing with magic—"

"Anything is possible. I remember what Cat said."

"So you understand?"

I shake my head. "Not one bit."

The Boogeyman turns in dismissal and slinks down the green knoll at our feet, heading for the cobbled road dividing the village.

I follow. Unable to wrap my head around the Boogeyman's crazy fae logic, I decide to change the subject.

"Is she your girlfriend?"

"Who?" the Boogeyman asks.

"Siren."

The Boogeyman's dark eyes grow large with surprise as his pale cheeks redden with embarrassment. "WHAT?"

"I saw the way you looked at her," I say, emboldened by having seen the Boogeyman's softer side. "It's the same way I used to look at Michelle May. But she decided she liked Toby Cooper better, and that ended that."

"Are you daft?" the Boogeyman spits. "Didn't you hear everything I just said about division between night and day within Fairy? What you suggest is impossible. A Siren and a Boogeyman? Together? It would never work."

The Boogeyman's massive shoulders rise and then fall in time with the crickets' song.

"Granted, the King and Queen are from opposing realms and yet they remain together on a permanent basis. But that is only because fae law allows—no, *insists*—that they reside here in the Twilight Lands so that balance may be maintained. But Siren and I are not royalty. And we have our duties to fulfill. I mean, when would she and I ever see each other? Hypothetically speaking, of course. I mean, it would be hypothetically speaking if I did, in fact, like Siren. But I don't!"

I don't know whether it's seeing Castle Twilight or meeting Siren that has placed me into such a good mood, but I chuckle.

"So you're saying you're from two different worlds, huh? Michelle told me the same thing right before she dumped me. Don't sweat it, Boogey—"

The Boogeyman huffs in consternation. *"Boogey?"*

"Siren looked at you the same way you did her. She likes you, dude."

"You're being ridicu—*really?* You think so?"

I nod. "Trust me. I've been turned down by enough girls to know what to look for when they don't like you. By contrast, Siren is all eyes for you."

A grin free of any maliciousness starts to creep across the Boogeyman's ugly, crescent-moon face. But he catches me smiling back at him and quickly resumes his usual demeanor of doom and gloom.

"Enough of this childish nonsense. We're here on serious business. And don't call me 'Boogey.' *Or 'dude.'* We are nowhere near well enough acquainted for that. My title is 'Boogeyman,' and you will address me as such."

Oh well. So much for becoming fast friends.

"Sure, Boogey, er, Boogeyman, sir."

We reach the cobbled road, and I glance back over my shoulder at the tomb's exterior. Time has long covered it with earth and grass, making it part of the small hill it rests on. However, a statue of the warrior king it houses rises from the ground, green moss growing along its length and that of the stone sword it thrusts skyward.

It doesn't take long to reach the fields lying outside the tiny village. Fanged, green-skinned goblins are here, harvesting rows of wheat and barley right alongside copper-hued elves with dark, silky hair. Tiny gossamer pixies—some so dark they look like floating black holes, others so shiny they sparkle like stars—flitter around their heads.

Moments later, we enter village proper. I don't know why, but I expect to see people here, dressed in the clothing of Old World peasants, minding pens of sheep and cattle while they sell whatever foods they've managed to farm from the earth. And while this is exactly what's going on within the village, it's not being done by any people our world has ever seen.

Pointy-eared women, some young, tall, and lithe, others short, squat, and snaggle-toothed, move along the village pathways carrying buckets of water on poles borne across their shoulders. Goat-legged satyrs dance circles around them, playing flutes as they lead lines of gossamer nymphs and their own fawn children. Sprites and fireflies blink in and out of existence among them all.

We pass a gray-furred ogre with a single chipped horn sprouting from his temple. The creature walks circles around a meal stone, pushing the log serving as its lever in a feat of great strength to grind flour.

The ogre spies the Boogeyman coming and, despite the creature's size and strength, he shrinks away, deciding to take this particular moment to go on break.

"Not very popular with the night fae, are you?" I ask.

The Boogeyman growls in response.

As we continue our trek through the village, I come to realize it's a meeting place of extremes—of beauty and ugliness, youth and old age, and order and chaos. In short, of day and night fae.

"This might be a place you and Siren could be together," I start to say, but a cross look from the Boogeyman lets me know he is aware of what I am thinking and will hear none of it.

"These folk are only here for a season," he says, confirm-ing my suspicions. "When theirs is over, they will return to their respective homelands to make way for the next incoming group of day and night fae. Like the royal couple's contrasting heritages, the constant rotation of fae in and out of the Twilight Lands helps maintain peace between the Day and Night realms."

"It must be complicated to be fae."

"No more so than to be human. Trust me."

We walk the remainder of the way to Castle Twilight, the only sound between us that of the chirping crickets.

When we arrive, we're greeted by the shouts of one of the animal-headed guardsman manning the high wall surround-ing the palace. He's dressed in armor hewn from gemstone. Curving horns sprout from his head and a stringy, gray beard dangles beneath his goat's maw. He stands several stories above us at the top of the twin, jewel-encrusted doors serving as entrance into the palace's outer court.

"Who goes there?"

"'Tis I, friend gruff," the Boogeyman says, his deep voice taking on an air of formality, "the Boogeyman and my prisoner, who shall be called Puck."

"Prisoner?" I shout, flabbergasted.

"For what purpose do ye approach?"

"I seek audience with the throne. Puck is in violation of the ancient Pact, and must be tried by the crown in accordance with fae law."

My jaw lands on my chest. "Tried? I thought we were just going to seek the King and Queen's advice on what to do next—?"

"Be forewarned," the gruff calls, "the leader of the High Thirteen is at court, and has Their Majesties in a particularly foul mood. For your sake and that of your prisoner, it would be best for you to come back at a more suitable hour."

"You heard the man, um, goat," I say, frantic. "Let's come back later."

The Boogeyman ignores me. "Time is of the essence. We must have audience with the King and Queen now."

"As you wish, Lord Boogeyman. Enter Castle Twilight in peace, and leave it the same when your business here is concluded."

The massive quartz doors serving as the castle's main entrance begin to slowly swing open before us. As the Boogeyman glides in between them, I hear the gruff guardsman whisper to one of his animal-faced fellows.

"What a pity. He looks like such a young lad, after all."

The outer doors to Castle Twilight finish swinging open. The Boogeyman's cloak beckons for me to follow, and I swallow hard as I step inside the gate to face judgment for crimes I had no idea I was committing.

8

I'M SENTENCED TO DEATH

Everyone has bad days. Myself included. But up until now, a bad day for me meant having too much math homework to stream old black-and-white monster movies online.

Now I look back and realize those were the days.

My time with the legendary Boogeyman has definitely changed my definition of what constitutes a bad day. While the Boogeyman actually seems to be an okay dude, more or less, since meeting him I've almost been devoured by monsters on two separate occasions.

And here I am with him now, striding through the outer court of the amethyst palace known as Castle Twilight due to its perpetual existence on night's edge, on my way to go before the King and Queen of all Fairy and receive judgment for charges I don't begin to understand.

This is definitely a bad day.

But I don't have time to feel sorry for myself. The Boogeyman hustles me ever forward, leading me along streets of cobbled jewels and emeralds brimming with clouds of fireflies and fairies of every description. There are towering tree-people; flittering, butterfly-winged sprites; pot-bellied, gorilla-limbed orcs; shape-shifting changelings; gold-counting leprechauns; tiny, leaping gnomes; and talking, bipedal gruffs, deer, wolves, and bears.

Every one of them seemingly wants to buy, sell, or trade me something. They crowd around me, shouting and barking and smelling of strange spices and oils as they shove clothes, jewelry, and trinkets in my face. The overwhelming amount of stimulation sends my *condition* into overdrive, and I start to panic. It's too hot. I feel smothered! I tear off my black musketeer hat and reach for the domino mask encircling my eyes.

The Boogeyman's hand on my arm stops me.

"Whatever you do while here," he says, "do not remove your mask."

Then the shadows comprising his body and cloak swell to an even greater height, and he transforms into a giant, scarier version of his already large, ominous self.

"Back!" he roars, and the fairies surrounding us scatter like leaves in the wind. Even the fireflies recede before us.

The Boogeyman shrinks to his normal size and stares at the retreating fairies to make sure there aren't any stragglers.

Already beginning to feel calm again, I place my hat back on my head. "Thanks."

"You're welcome," he growls.

"You just have all kinds of tricks up your sleeve, don't you?"

He nods. "A Boogeyman's shadow cloak augments his natural shape-shifting abilities."

"You're a shape-shifter, too?" I ask, wide-eyed.

"A changeling to be precise, Puck," he says. "Much like the very one you set free back in Shadow Tower. All Boogeymen start out that way."

The Boogeyman ushers me toward a jewel-encrusted door leading deeper into the palace. It's guarded by two gemstone-armored animal-folk holding spears tipped with the biggest diamonds I've ever seen.

A fellow sure could buy a lot of bubblegum with those.

The guards lift their weapons at our approach and stand aside, word of our coming apparently already having reached them.

We enter the palace proper, and the song of the crickets outside diminishes into less than background noise. We navigate a series of crystalline hallways alight with flickering fireflies. Each passage is filled with regal stone busts and elaborate paintings, and other dazzling works of art.

At last, we reach the throne room. While Castle Twilight's

main chamber is guarded by two well-muscled gruffs, the large emerald doors meant to close it off from the hallway stand open.

An elf footman dressed in a juxtaposition of Elizabethan garb and a seventeenth-century wig of gray curls offers us a bow in greeting.

"Lord Boogeyman," he says, "the King and Queen are expecting you. They shan't be but a moment. As you can see, the Merlin and her second are still in audience."

I gaze past the footman and the two gruff guardsmen into the throne room. A lean, elderly woman with luxuriant gray hair styled up in a bun is there. She's human, and dressed in a white-leather trench coat worn over a charcoal suit. She carries a gnarled staff of ash and shakes it as she speaks heatedly to the two fairies seated before her on twin thrones of crystal.

A short human male stands beside the elderly woman. He holds a staff of woven, petrified wormwood in his left hand. He's bald, but a salt-and-pepper goatee rings his mouth to form a point at his chin. Small golden hoops pierce his ears and he sports a pair of half-moon spectacles that match the crimson trench coat he wears over his own black suit.

The male fairy sitting before them, presumably the King, wears a jeweled quartz crown and a royal-blue jacket with gold-colored trim and a ridiculously broad ruff collar. He's power-fully built. His skin is as black as night and his eyes and hair are as white as virgin snow. The female sitting beside him, who I'm guessing to be the Queen, is dressed in a jeweled quartz tiara and a silken gown with a bodice and skirt dyed differing shades of violet. The gown's ivory ruff collar is even higher and broader than that of the King's. Her eyes are the icy blue I would imag-ine for a bombardier. Her hair and skin are the color of spun gold. I'd say she's beautiful, but that would be the understate-ment of the century.

Neither she nor the King appear happy to be holding court.

"With all due respect, Your Majesty," the woman in the white trencher says, "the High Thirteen have had enough!"

Her accent places her as an American. In fact, she could be from my home town.

"Trolls running amok in New York. Boggarts overwhelming

Sri Lanka. This is beginning to look like an all-out invasion! Your Boogeyman is failing to live up to the duties assigned him in the ancient Pact made by our forefathers and mothers."

I glance at the Boogeyman from the corner of my eye.

Uh-oh. It appears I'm not the only one here on trial today.

The King leans forward on his throne, looking like an angry dog readying to pounce. "Lady Merlin, the Boogeyman is doing everything possible to stem the flow of night fae into your world."

I once watched a recorded speech of the South African President, Nelson Mandela, at school. The cadence of the Fairy King's English reminds me of his.

"He cannot be blamed if the number of rogues has increased to a level far beyond what the makers of the Pact would've dreamed possible," the King continues, "a tide his predecessors have never had to face."

"Then who are the High Thirteen to blame, Your Majesty? You?"

The King leaps to his feet. "You forget yourself, mortal!"

"And so do you, Your Grace. *And the fact that the High Thirteen still hold the Logos.*"

The Queen's penetrating gaze grows large with astonishment. "How dare you threaten the King with the Book of Names!" Her voice makes me think of some long-gone queen of Great Britain. I imagine her saying, "We are not amused," and quickly suppress a chuckle. Cracking up is the last thing I want to do in this situation.

"Please forgive me, Your Highness," the Merlin says as she bows to the Queen. "We have no quarrel with you or your people. The Siren continues to hold the day fae in check."

The Merlin raises her head, and there is a look in her eyes that could crack stone. "However, we cannot say the same for the Night Lands, the Boogeyman, or their king. The Boogeyman must remove the exponential amount of night fae who have invaded our world within three nights' time."

"And if he does not?" the King spits.

"The High Thirteen will consider failure to comply an act of open war by the Night Lands, and respond in kind using every means at our disposal. *Including that of the Logos.* I bid you good day, Your Highnesses."

Without waiting to be dismissed, the Merlin waves her staff and speaks in a language I have never heard. "Allak shak, nola rendo!"

A door-sized portal of light opens before her, rending time and space. She steps inside and vanishes. The short bald man backs into the portal behind her, bowing to the King and Queen as he exits.

"Your Excellencies." Like Cat, his voice is a drawl born of the Deep South.

Time and space mend and the portal swallows him up before vanishing all together.

The King falls back into his chair and rubs his pupilless, cue-ball eyes.

"Footman," he yells through clenched teeth, "the Queen and I would see the Boogeyman, now."

"Yes, Your Majesty."

The elf footman turns and introduces us as if we did not just hear the King's summons. "The King and Queen will see you now."

I look at the Boogeyman, scared out of my wits. His pale, crescent-moon face is impassive. You would never know that, apparently, the Night Lands stand on the brink of war because of his alleged poor job performance.

The Boogeyman glides forward into the throne room, and I follow. The room is cathedral-like in scope, and its quartz walls filter the lingering rays of the vanished sun into every color of the rainbow. We traverse a large stretch of floor lined with dangling banners and crystalline columns to reach the King and Queen. At this range, I see they're seated at the base of Castle Twilight's main tower. An especially concentrated cloud of fireflies hovers above their heads, stretching up the tower's throat to a height far beyond what my mortal eyes can register.

The sight of the throne room up close brings one word to mind.

WOW.

"Your Majesties," the Boogeyman says, bowing deeply.

I follow suit.

"Do you have ears, Lord Boogeyman?" the King asks. Tusks of ivory jut up from his dark, angular jaw.

"The sharpest in the land, Your Grace."

"Then you heard that your slacking on the job is about to draw our homeland into an all-out war with the High Thirteen Wizards of the Mortal Lands!"

I have just enough time to think, *We have real wizards on Earth?* before the echo of the King's voice causes the tower to tremble around him. I slink closer to the Boogeyman, hoping to draw strength from him as I did on our way through the Void. I think it works for the most part. At the very least, I'm not tired despite having gone without sleep all night.

The Boogeyman nods calmly. "I did indeed hear the Lady Merlin's accusations, Your Majesty, as well as your defense against them. For that, you have my boundless gratitude."

"It's not your gratitude the King desires," the Queen interjects, "but results."

The Boogeyman inhales deeply. "As I have told Your Majesties many times before, I believe trickery to be afoot. Someone or something is seeking to rend asunder the ancient Pact existing between Fae and the High Thirteen. Just this past night, I was going to interrogate a rogue changeling in regard to my suspicions."

"And where is this changeling now?" the Queen asks. "Is that him at your side? Has your Shadow gone rogue?"

I cringe at having been noticed, wishing to become as small as possible.

"Er, no, Your Highness," the Boogeyman says. "This is not my Shadow. And the truth is, the changeling I spoke of has, well, escaped."

"Great," the King says. "More failures. Pray tell how, exactly, this changeling you were to interrogate escaped your custody?"

My throat becomes tight and lizards start to leap inside my stomach.

"The youth I have brought before you released him, Your Majesties," the Boogeyman says. "Unknowingly, of course. He is but mortal."

"A mortal not of the Thirteen here within the Fae Lands?" the Queen asks, shocked.

"He followed me through the Void into Shadow Tower," the Boogeyman says.

"Yet another violation of the Pact we can mark up to your account," the King says. "Very well." The King claps his hands. "Guard!"

One of the two gruffs standing guard joins us within the throne room. "Yes, Your Majesty?"

"Off with this mortal's head," the King says. "The last thing we need right now is for the High Thirteen to catch wind of an unlawful mortal here at court."

"What?" I shout.

Oh this is bad! Soooo bad!

"Your Majesty," the Boogeyman pleads, "I beg you. You cannot do this."

"Do not presume to counsel us on what we may and may not do, Lord Boogeyman," the Queen spits. "Guard, you heard the King. Take this mortal to the headsman."

"No, Your Majesty," the Boogeyman insists. "You really may not."

The Boogeyman looks down at me. "Puck, take off your mask."

I shake my head, not understanding. "But you said—!"

I feel someone grab my arm and look up to see the gemstone-armored gruff has hold of me. A menacing smile is stretched across his goat's face.

Then a hand as cold as a tombstone seizes my other arm. It is the Boogeyman, seemingly come to my rescue again. At least for the moment.

"What is the meaning of this insolence?" the King shouts. "Do you wish to share this mortal's fate, Lord Boogeyman? Rest assured, despite your title and position, you are not above it!"

"No, Your Majesty," the Boogeyman says, his voice even. "I am not. But he is."

The Boogeyman looks down at me with his night-shine eyes.

"Puck, if you wish to live, take off your mask."

I look at the Boogeyman, frozen in indecision. "But you said—!"

He releases my arm. "Trust me."

I swallow hard and nod. I reach up and remove the domino mask encircling my eyes.

The gruff guardsman gasps in shock. He releases me and then, much to my confusion, bows before me.

"Your Grace," the gruff says, "I did not know!"

The King rises to his feet. "It cannot be!"

The Queen's hard blue eyes grow wide with surprise. She springs from her throne, takes her layered skirts in hand, and scampers down the short flight of stairs separating us, her high ruff collar bouncing with each step. She reaches me and drops to her knees to cradle my face in her hands.

To say this freaks me out is an understatement.

She looks at me, and unbridled joy fills her eyes.

"My dear prince," she says, and draws me close in a bear hug. "My beloved son."

Oh boy!

9

DOPPELGANGER IS A FUNNY WORD UNLESS YOU ARE ONE

Holy cow! My world has gone topsy-turvy in the space of a single night. I've discovered that the Boogeyman is not only real, but a good guy to boot. Furthermore, the world of Fairy also exists. If anyone knows, it's me. I'm standing with the Boogeyman before the Fairy King and Queen right now, facing imminent execution for breaking some stupid Pact between its peoples and the High Thirteen Wizards of Earth (That's right. Earth has wizards). What's next? The apocalypse? Storms of fire and brimstone? *Cats and Dogs holding paws and living together in peace?*

The Fairy Queen waves a dismissive hand in the direction of the nearby gruff guardsman. "Away with you. There is no longer any need for your presence here."

The gruff bows his horned-billy-goat head and resumes his station beyond the emerald doors of the vast quartz throne room in which we stand.

The Fairy Queen sighs, her crystal blue eyes staring deep into my dark brown ones. "My beautiful child."

Where she's gotten the idea that I'm her son I have no idea.

I gently remove her slender, delicate arms from around me and take a step back. I direct my eyes above the oversized ruff collar encircling her regal countenance to gaze at the clouds of fireflies swarming in the throne room's upper reaches, taking a moment to catch my breath.

After a few seconds pass, I lower my eyes and see the King

has joined the Queen's side, the eyes in his dark, fanged face wide with astonishment.

"Son," the King asks, "how is it you've come to be here with the Boogeyman? You're supposed to be enjoying your beauty rest."

"I, er, uh," I stammer, "I mean, uh, that is—"

"Your Majesties," the Boogeyman growls, "what this young one is trying and failing miserably to say is that he, in fact, is not your son."

"But he is!" the Queen protests. "Just look at him."

"No, Your Highness, he is not." The Boogeyman reaches a spidery, clawed hand into his cloak of writhing shadow and withdraws a crystal ball the size and shape of a pink grapefruit. "Look here."

The King and Queen lean forward to peer into the glass ball. But there is no need to draw closer. From where I stand, I'm perfectly able to see a boy who's my doppelganger—*my twin*—lying in a picturesque copse of dogwood trees. His entire body is covered in their fallen petals, save for his ghostly pale face. His resemblance to me is more than uncanny, it's picture perfect. And looking upon him like this is a little too close to seeing what I might look like dead. Especially under the present circumstances.

"As Your Majesties can see, the prince is slumbering away as peacefully as ever."

Adoration fills the Queen's face. "And what a *sleeping beauty* he is." She turns and faces the King. "You did such a good job with the slumber spell."

"Yes," the King muses, his fangs gleaming in his smile. "There, sleeping among the dogwood trees, he'll never know hurt, or fear, or heartbreak. He'll rest safely for all eternity, remaining our little boy, forever and ever."

Yikes! With parents like these, who needs enemies? A kid's safety is one thing, but keeping him or her safe by placing them in an enchanted coma for all time is simply ridiculous, not to mention cruel.

As if he could read my thoughts, the Boogeyman gestures for me to remain silent. While the King and Queen continue to gaze wistfully into the glass grapefruit, he leans down to me in that weird way of his that seems to make space conform to him rather he to it. He brings a clawed hand to the side of his face and whispers conspiringly. "The ways of Fairy are not those of the Mortal Lands. Be silent for now."

I give him a cross look.

"Trust me, Puck," he whispers, and I relent with a sigh.

The Boogeyman clears his throat, making a noise like two concrete blocks grinding against one another, drawing the Kingand Queen's attention away from the crystal ball.

"Your Highnesses," the Boogeyman says, "surely providence is at work here. It would seem a terrible crime to execute a boy, even a mortal one guilty of breaking the Pact, who is the spitting image of your son, the Prince."

"Hmmm," the King muses. He adjusts the bejeweled quartz crown resting on his furrowed brow. "I suppose you're right. Such would not set well with me. Nor the Queen, I'm sure."

The King and Queen exchange approving nods, and I exhale in deep relief. But the King's next words let me know straightaway I'm counting chickens that haven't hatched yet.

"But restitution for this boy's crimes must be made."

The Boogeyman's eyes darkle mischievously. "Surely a mutually beneficial arrangement can be reached?"

The Queen's piercing eyes come into focus as though she's seeing the Boogeyman for the first time. "I have a sneaky suspicion you have some ideas in that regard, Lord Boogeyman?"

The Boogeyman gives a wicked grin. "If I may be so bold, Your Majesties—?"

The King crosses his muscular arms. "By all means. Please proceed."

The Boogeyman presses the tips of his slender, clawed fingers together, forming his hands into a bony pyramid. He begins gliding circles around me. As he moves, the edges of his shadowy cloak brush against me like hundreds of insect antennae tasting potential prey.

"I say let the punishment fit the crime, Your Excellencies. It was this boy who allowed the changeling to escape me, so let it also be this boy who aids me in the rogue fairy's recapture. In this fashion, both justice and Fairy would be served. I think it would only be prudent."

The Boogeyman bows deeply. "Of course, I defer final say in the matter to your wise and irreproachable judgment, Your Highnesses."

"And well you should, Lord Boogeyman," the Queen says, her words dripping with venom. "Time after time, you have approached this throne with what one who did not know better would construe to be arrogance. While you are the Boogeyman, and thereby granted liberties in the course of your duties far beyond those enjoyed by most fairies, you would do well not to forget your place within the court hierarchy."

The Boogeyman deepens his bow still further. "Please forgive me, Your Highnesses, if I have ever given you reason to doubt my loyalty."

The King shrugs. "My Queen, the Boogeyman's impudence can be aggravating at times, I agree. But such must be the nature of any fairy in his position. Therefore, it is to be overlooked, if not completely forgiven.

"You must admit, as always, his thoughts on this matter would seem wise."

The Queen huffs in consternation. "Oh, my dear King. How you do love your rambunctious night fae."

The King smiles. "My love for my people is no greater or less than the affection you hold for your Day Land fairies. And what you love, so does your King. With all his heart."

The King and Queen gaze dreamingly into one another's eyes for a moment. It makes me want to barf.

"Very well," the Queen submits. "Let judgment be as the Boogeyman says. The boy called Puck shall aid in the rogue changeling's recapture."

My chest deflates in a huge exhalation of air. I'm going to remain alive. The rest is just details.

"As to the Boogeyman's wisdom and worth," the Queen continues, "the next three nights shall tell the tale. You are dismissed."

"Your Majesties," the Boogeyman says. He bows deeply once again and grasps my arm, forcing me to do the same. We back all the way out of the throne room in this position. My lower back is throbbing by the time we reach the large emerald doors leading into the crystalline hallway outside.

I place my domino mask back on as we straighten and enter the hallway. "Woo! That was a close one!"

"We're not out of the enchanted wood yet," the Boogeyman growls. "You and I still have a changeling to catch."

We exit the palace and make our way back to the tomb of the dead warrior king. From there, we re-enter the Void and traverse in silence along its walkways until we reach the portal leading to the Boogeyman's home.

We pass through and the now-familiar ancient, stony sights, and old, musty smells of Shadow Tower greet us. It's here a thought strikes me.

"Hey," I say, "tell me something. Why didn't we just conjure a portal into the throne room like the Lady Merlin did? Why did we have to walk all the way back to the tomb and then go through the Void to return here?"

"Because darkness and shadow are a Boogeyman's horse and buggy," the Boogeyman replies. "Besides, even if I had been able to open the wizards' portal, it would not have brought us home."

"Huh?" I ask. "Why not?"

"You don't understand. Neither the wizards nor I are, as you say, conjuring these portals. We are merely accessing passageways that already exist and have specific destinations."

I think about all the episodes of *Star Trek* I've seen on TV dealing with Einstein-Rosen bridges, aka wormholes, and begin to glean what the Boogeyman is getting at.

"The path we took leads between Shadow Tower and the Twilight Lands," the Boogeyman continues. "Granted, I could journey through any number of portals leading to the few shadows existing inside Castle Twilight if I wanted to, but it's best not to call on the King and Queen of all Fairy unannounced. Protocol must be adhered to whenever possible."

An image of the Boogeyman and myself emerging from a cluster of shadows within Castle Twilight forms in my head, followed by one of the Queen shouting, "Off with their heads!" and I swallow hard.

The Boogeyman leans in close, the length of his gnarled

stove-pipe hat all but curving around the back of my head.

"But as I said, the wizards' portal would not have brought us here. If I had to guess, I would probably say it leads to the Sanctum Sanctorum of the High Thirteen."

The Boogeyman turns and begins descending the spiraling stairs of his home, his cloak of living shadow fluttering behind him, leaving stray wafts of shadow in his wake.

I shake my head. "The who of the what?"

"The wizards' base of operations within the Mortal Lands."

I nod. "Oh. I see."

"Enough questions for now, Puck," the Boogeyman calls over his shoulder. "Night will soon fall in the Mortal Lands, and the changeling will be free from his stone prison and up to no good once again. Come. We have much to prepare."

I scamper down the steps after the Boogeyman, fearful of going after the monstrous changeling, but also excited at the prospect of returning home. But if I could look ahead and see what the future held, I probably would've decided spending eternity snoozing away in a serene tree grove isn't such a raw deal for a kid after all.

10

CAT KILLS MY CURIOUSITY

I've always been a fan of monster hunters. While I have posters of movie monsters plastering my walls, I also have many of the men and women who chase them: everyone from Steve Martin, the bane of Godzilla (which still confuses me sometimes because the real Steve Martin is a comedic actor who, as far as I know, has never been in a movie about giant, rampaging lizards), to the tough-as-nails Ripley, outer space's version of the Orkin Man.

But the original monster hunter is still the best. I'm speaking of course of Dracula's nemesis, Professor Abraham Van Helsing.

No matter who plays Van Helsing in the movies, the Professor is always fearless, and always in control. Whatever happens, he is cool, calm, and collected. He never has any doubts, and he always knows what to do.

By contrast, now that I'm to be a real-life monster hunter, I'm shaking in my boots. Literally! The Boogeyman gave me a leather pair during my first visit to Shadow Tower along with a mask, caped tabard, tunic, breeches, and feathered hat. All basic Boogeyman-black, of course.

But despite my ready-for-action-musketeer-garb, I feel anything but. All I can think of is my first encounter with the changeling. In my mind, I hear myself screaming as he draws me toward his impossibly large, fanged mouth.

The thought of going up against that scaly monster again sends shivers down my spine.

To take my mind off the task ahead, I begin asking the Boogeyman more questions.

"So, Boogey—"

"Boogeyman!" he roars as we descend the spiraling staircase serving as the throat of Shadow Tower. But by now, I've begun to learn he's all bark and no bite. At least in regard to me."

"Er, right. Boogeyman. I've got to ask: how is it possible that I look exactly like the Prince of all Fairy?"

A low growl emanating from deep in the back of his throat is all the answer I get.

"If you don't answer, Cat will."

"Cat will what?" Cat asks as we reach the bottom of the stairs. She sits curled in the center of the oval stone room at the base of the tower, licking a femur bone three times her size. Apparently, someone or something came calling while we were out.

Someone or something extremely unlucky.

"Cat will do no such thing," the Boogeyman barks. "It's not her place."

I place my gloved hands on my hips. "Then whose is it?"

The Boogeyman grasps one of the iron knockers adorning the wooden doors lining the walls.

"I thought I said, 'enough questions'?"

"Hey, I'm a little boy all alone in a nightmare place who just escaped death only to have to help you go after a monster that almost ate me alive the first time around. *Humor me.*"

The Boogeyman groans. "It's not a question of whose place it is to say, but *when* it is the time to do so. And the one thing I am sure about is that 'when' is not right now." He throws open the door to reveal a cavernous room piled high with gold coins, jewels, and other treasures beyond compare. They glitter so brightly it hurts my eyes to look.

The Boogeyman slams the door closed and I rub my eyes as I roll my tongue back in my mouth.

"No," he growls, "that's not right."

He grasps the sides of the door in his claws and lifts it from the wall. A blank wall of crumbling stone block stands in place of the treasure trove I just saw.

The Boogeyman walks across the room, carrying the door as if it weighed no more than a pillow, and tosses it against a blank spot of wall. To my amazement, the door hits the wall and sticks as if that's where it had been standing all along.

"Let's try that again." The Boogeyman opens the newly located door and, this time, it reveals a hurricane raging along a tropical beachfront. The storm's gale-force winds flood the oval room, stirring up dust and blowing both Cat and me back flat against the far wall of doors. I cry out, but my voice is lost in the tumultuous air.

With great effort, the Boogeyman presses the door closed.

"By the Twilight Crown!" Cat fumes. "If you would map this place like I've told you—!"

The Boogeyman takes off his crooked top hat and points at the massive curvature of forehead cresting above his furrowed brow. "I've got a map right here."

"Lot of good it does you," Cat mumbles. "It or anything else up in that backward shark fin you call a noggin."

The Boogeyman slams his top hat back onto his head. "I heard that!"

"Good," Cat shouts. "I meant for you—"

"If you won't tell me about the prince," I interrupt as I dust myself off, "at least tell me about the High Thirteen."

Cat looks at me in surprise. "You know of the High Thirteen?"

The Boogeyman nods. "The Merlin and her Second were holding court with the King and Queen when we arrived at Castle Twilight." He turns back to the doors lining the room. "Cat, I'm a little busy here. If you wouldn't mind filling in young Puck—?"

"Certainly," she says. Then in a whisper, "If for no other reason than he'd louse up the telling like he has the door situation."

I glance at the Boogeyman. If he heard Cat, he pays her remarks no mind. That's a relief as their constant bickering is beginning to get on the ends of my already frazzled nerves.

"The High Thirteen Wizards of the Mortal Lands are exactly that," Cat begins. "They serve as the governing body for all other humans with magical talent, and as their representatives to all others existing outside the natural realm."

I adjust my hat, smoothing out the long feathery plume extending from the band around its crown. "How come I've never heard of them? Heck, if they exist, how come magic is considered a myth by most people?"

Cat grins like the Cheshire Cat from the Wonderland stories. "What a smart boy you are to ask that question. You see, letting the humans think we're nothing more than, well, a *fairytale*, is all because of the ancient Pact."

The Boogeyman howls as yet another door fails to reveal what he's looking for.

I huff and cross my thin arms. "You mean the Pact that almost got me killed, I assume?"

Cat nods. "Well, yeah."

"That's also something I'd like to know a little more about. Especially if it will keep me out of another situation in which the attachment of my head to my shoulders is called into question."

Cat chuckles. "It all ties in together. Fairy. The High Thirteen. And the Pact."

"How so?"

"It's complicated, but I'll give you the nutshell version: Once upon a time, as your so-called fairy tales go, the many worlds were but a single one created from magic. So magic was in all creatures and places. Then humankind came to be. Despite there being nothing magical about them, the humans were loved above all creation, and so given dominion over it through the Book of Names."

A light bulb flashes on inside my head. "The Logos? The Merlin mentioned it when she was, uh, *voicing her complaints* against the Boogeyman."

Another exasperated yell from the Boogeyman shakes the tower around us.

Cat sighs. "Yes. The Logos—the book listing the true and secret name of every creature and object in the universe."

"Everything?" I ask, my eyes huge. "In the entire universe?"

"Well, mortals are the exception," Cat purrs. "I'm sketchy on the details. It has something to do with your kind being creatures of innate free will rather than magic, but the important thing to remember is that the Logos gives humanity dominion over creation, not vice versa."

I slap my hand to my forehead.

"Well, that's a relief. At least some would-be Lex Luthor or Dr. Doom can't come along and use the Logos to turn people into their mindless drones."

"Where is the confounded armory?" the Boogeyman roars.

Cat shakes her head and continues. "A scholarly order sprang up among the wizards serving as the Logos' most trusted keepers. That order eventually became the High Thirteen. The one among them most versed in the Logos serves as the Merlin. At least in theory."

"You mean it's not always that way?" I ask.

Cat shrugs. "There has been the rare occasion where a mortal with little or no true knowledge of the Logos has shown superior magical talent—a fluke case here and there throughout history where the Book of Names has been seemingly imprinted upon his or her heart, if you will. In such a situation, the mortal is often given the chance to serve as one of the Thirteen. Even possibly at the rank of Merlin. But such an instance hasn't arisen in countless ages."

The Boogeyman throws open yet another door to reveal a roaring Tyrannosaur. "Oh, be quiet!" the Boogeyman thunders. The Tyrannosaur turns and runs away, yelping like a frightened puppy.

I look to Cat. "That's a lot of power to have. The Logos, I mean."

"Precisely," Cat says. "So you can imagine how the Book of Names might serve to corrupt its users and make those over whom it holds sway resentful."

I shrug. "I suppose."

"Trust me," Cat says, "it did. Things got so bad that humanity and fae were left with no choice but to go their separate ways permanently. They created a set of accords outlining who stays where and does what."

"The Pact." I say.

Cat pantomimes ringing a bell. "Ding! Ding! Ding! Give

that man a prize! Right you are, boy-oh!"

Cat gets up from her bone and stretches. "In time, the human world got bigger, though those with knowledge of the Logos, innate or otherwise, became lost to antiquity. With the shrinking of the wizarding ranks and the absence of the overtly supernatural within the Mortal Lands, the Logos and all things magical became little more than long-forgotten dreams for most of your kind."

"Ah," the Boogeyman bellows from behind us, "here we go."

I turn in time to see him flip a door over onto a blank patch of wall. Instead of an open room, more crumbling stone block is left behind in the door's former resting place.

"I give you the armory."

The Boogeyman throws open the door and an underwhelming sight meets my eyes. Another stone room stands before us. Swords and chains and bags overflowing with what looks like salt rest along dusty, wooden shelves spanning the walls from floor to ceiling.

"It looks like a medieval tool shed."

"A tool shed?" the Boogeyman barks, taken aback. He oozes over so he can look me in the eye. "I'll have you know the weapons and instruments contained within this room have brought down towering giants and flesh-eating trolls."

"Whatever," I say, unimpressed. "Still looks like a tool shed to me."

The Boogeyman draws himself up straight. Well, at least as straight as he gets, anyway. "Why, I never!"

Cat enters the Boogeyman's armory, her own nose turning up at the dust and cobwebs inside. "Maybe if you cleaned the place once in a while, Boogey, visitors might be a little more impressed."

"No kidding," I laugh. "I thought my room back home was messy, but sheesh! Mom would pull her hair out if she saw this place."

"Laugh all you want," the Boogeyman growls. "But the things housed here could make the difference between you ending up home safe and sound, or simply just ending."

The Boogeyman whirls away from me with a dramatic swish of his shadow cloak and enters the armory. I stop laughing and swallow hard as I follow him into the room, the realization that I'm light years away from getting out of this mess alive and in one piece settling over me once again.

11

NOT SO PRETTY IN PINK

What a nightmare! I've been sentenced by the King and Queen of Fairy to help the Boogeyman recapture a rogue changeling—a monstrous, snakelike creature who's swallowed several kids from my hometown for safekeeping and tried its best to do the same to me. But it's a mission I must succeed in if I'm ever going to get home and see Mom and Dad.

My poor parents. They must be worried sick about me. According to the Boogeyman, I've been gone from the human world now for a full twenty-four hours. I'm sure Mom and Dad have called the police in to investigate my disappearance by now. I can just see Mom crying her eyes out in Dad's arms as the police question them—*probably harder than they should*.

I've heard on TV that, when a child goes missing, the parents are always the primary suspects. The police are probably grilling my folks right now about their whereabouts last night, asking our friends and neighbors if they ever behaved suspiciously in regard to me, and using all sorts of other horrible tactics in hopes of making them talk.

It's an unnecessary pain not only my parents are facing, but probably those of the other missing kids from town as well. It almost makes me want to charge out of here and go after the changeling all by myself.

Almost.

Whatever bravery I held in my bedroom last night has now vanished. There in my room, it was easy to believe there was some logical, rational explanation for what was happening. Even after meeting the Boogeyman and entering the Void.

But now, I've seen the changeling up close and personal. Felt the iron grip of its scaly claws. Smelled its hot, rancid breath. I can't deny it: monsters really do exist.

It's a realization that has me dying to be home with Mom and Dad, held tight within their arms as they assure me everything's all right.

But everything's not all right. In fact, everything's terrible, and it's all my fault! I was the one who set the changeling free to take still more children. So fear or no fear (and, truth be told, Fairy court sentence or no Fairy court sentence), it now falls to me to help the Boogeyman catch the rogue fairy and make things right again.

I follow the Boogeyman and Cat deeper inside the so-called armory. It contains various metallic instruments of every size and description mixed in with several large sacks of salt crystal. All but a few sit rusting or rotting on shelves lined with dust, cobwebs, and an abundance of creepy-crawlers. Only a few objects appear in good repair: a long silver rapier and its matching dagger, a length of steel chain, several collapsible semicircles of iron; and a leather satchel with iron filings spilling from its depths among them. Apparently, the Boogeyman has favorites among his tools.

He selects these—or rather, the smoky tendrils that form along the edges of his shadow cloak select them—lifting the articles from the shelves and submerging them within the cloak's greater mass where they disappear without trace.

As an afterthought, the Boogeyman reaches into his cloak with one of his true arms and pulls out the small dagger.

"Here," he says, and flicks his wrist. There's a brief disturbance in the air between us. I look down and see the dagger protruding from the floor at my feet. "It belonged to Saint George. Its name is Barb."

I cock a puzzled eyebrow. "What? Like the doll? Barbie?"

Cat laughs so hard at this she almost coughs up a furball.

"No, no!" the Boogeyman fumes in disgust. "Barb! Like on a hook. Or a wire. Its blade is a steel alloy laced with silver.

Good against any number of fae or their offshoots, including the changeling."

I smirk at the dagger I now can't help but think of as Barbie. I reach down and, with some effort, yank it from its resting place in the floor. I examine Barbie closely, noting the hypnotic way the room's dim candlelight glimmers along its edge. In my slight hands, the weapon doesn't appear quite so small any more. I thrust Barbie into the leather belt circumnavigating my waist beneath the tabard. I know I'd probably be a goner if the changeling ever got close enough for me to use the dagger. Regardless, the pressure of Barbie against my hip feels both dangerous and oddly reassuring.

The Boogeyman gathers a few final items into his cloak, including the brown sack I last saw hanging in the room imprisoning the changeling. Cat must have returned it to its proper resting place in the armory while we were gone. I guess she knew she couldn't count on the Boogeyman to clean up after himself.

The Boogeyman glares at the shelves, making sure he hasn't forgotten anything. Satisfied he hasn't, he turns and glides by me, making his exit. I follow dutifully, Cat on my heels.

Once we're back at the base of the stairs, the Boogeyman turns and eyes me warily. "Are you ready, Puck?"

"Uh, I, uh, guess—"

"There is no guessing!" the Boogeyman thunders. "Either you are, or you are not. Which is it, Puck?"

Sheesh, this guy is a jerk.

"No," I say, squaring my jaw. "I'm not ready. But I have to do this anyway, don't I?"

The Boogeyman nods. Possibly there's a hint of approval in the gesture.

Without another word, he whirls, his shadow cloak flaring out behind him like the flag of a pirate ship blowing in the wind, and races up the stairs. I run along behind him, once more drawing upon his dark energy so that I may keep pace. In no time, we're back in the Void and moving through another portal into the Mortal Lands. The vertigo I usually feel when traversing the Void is all but gone. Apparently, I'm getting used to world-hopping.

We exit the portal, coming out Earth-side through a set of deep shadows clustered beneath a weeping willow. I know the tree. It belongs to Mr. Newton. It's the crown jewel of his immaculately kept yard. He and his wife and daughter live here on Ashmore—a street in my neighborhood just a few blocks over from my own house. A jack-o'-lantern adorns his front porch as well as those of the other homes lining the block, though their lights have long been extinguished for the night. The only illumination is from the few street lamps present and the silver-dollar moon shining down like a white hole punched in the black sky. The night air has a cool snap to it, and stray dead leaves dance down the street in the October breeze.

The townsfolk don't know it, but with the Boogeyman and the changeling here, Halloween has come early.

The sight of the neighborhood and thoughts of Halloween immediately make me homesick for trick-or-treating, apple-bobbing, and most of all, Mom and Dad. I think about making a run for home, but decide against it. Any reunion I might have with my parents would be short-lived. If the Boogeyman didn't come chasing after me, I have no doubt I'd find one of the gruff guardsmen or even the headsmen of Castle Twilight himself at my door in no time. I guess, for better or worse, I've got to see this unpleasant business through to the end.

I gaze up at the Boogeyman. "So what now?"

"We lay a trap," the Boogeyman answers. "We'll wait for the changeling to show up here and try to take a child."

"How do you know the changeling will show up here?"

The Boogeyman taps the brim of his crooked black hat with the tip of his clawed index finger. "My magic hat tells me he's nearby. The hat is how I track rogue fae, or know that they've left the world of Fairy in the first place."

I realize something and frown. "Wait a minute. The changeling should have no reason to come here.

"Not that I'm doubting your, uh, magic hat, but Caroline Newton is the only kid on this block. And she's out of town on vacation with her parents. I know. Caroline's in my class. She's supposed to give a report on their trip when she returns. If the changeling is after kids from my neighborhood, this is the last block he'd be on."

The Boogeyman's eyes darkle as a grin spreads across his horrible pale face like a black zipper. "I know. That's why you'll be serving as bait tonight."

The realization of what the Boogeyman is saying causes the world to liquefy around me.

I feel the Boogeyman's steadying hand on my shoulder. "Are you all right? Can you go through with this?"

Sure! I think. *I'd like nothing better than to be the wriggling worm on the end of your hook, you nasty, horrible, no-good fairy, you!*

But once I'm stable enough, I merely nod in answer.

"Good."

The Boogeyman scoops me up into a long and deceptively powerful arm and we glide across the Newtons' yard and then scurry lizard-like up the wall of their house to the window of Caroline's room on the second floor. The shadowy tendrils of the Boogeyman's cloak crack open the window and we seep inside, our bodies flowing like black mist.

The Boogeyman lowers me onto the floor, and I pat myself down, relieved to find everything once again solid and whole.

Even under the shade of night, being inside Caroline's room is like being inside a bottle of Pepto-Bismol. Everything is pink. Pink wallpaper. Pink dresser. Pink bed. And a pink closet. It's the exact opposite of my own creature-feature room, and it makes me want to gag.

"Okay," the Boogeyman says. "Take off your hat and mask and get into the bed. We need to convince the changeling that you're the Newton child, so you've got to try and act like a little girl. Considering the way I've heard you scream, it shouldn't be that big of a stretch for you."

"Oh, hardy-har-har," I say with all the sarcasm I can muster. "You are soooo funny."

I take off my hat and mask and start to get into bed. I pause and turn around to ask the Boogeyman where he'll be. When I do, I immediately realize something is wrong. The room has changed. For a second, I can't quite place my finger on how. I'm not familiar with Caroline's room, so it takes me a moment to figure out what's different. I peer across the room past the Boogeyman and notice that the space against the far wall formerly occupied by Caroline's pink monstrosity of a dresser is now vacant. Unfortunately for the Boogeyman, this realization comes just as I see the changeling's scaly, cobra-hooded head rise above my chaperon's hunched back.

The changeling was masquerading as Caroline's dresser! He's tricked me again by transforming his shape.

I have just enough time to cry out in warning before the changeling shakes his rattlesnake tail, alerting the Boogeyman to his presence. But it's too late. As fast as the Boogeyman is, the changeling has caught him with his back turned. The monster seizes the Boogeyman in his claws and hurls him through the bedroom's window, shattering its glass, leaving me utterly alone and unprotected.

The changeling whirls to face me, moving as fast as the striking snake that he is. My eyes become twin boiled eggs in their sockets as the changeling opens his fanged maw and charges.

12

ROUND AND ROUND WE GO

I stand at the edge of Caroline Newton's pink bed, in the middle of her sickeningly sweet pink room, a shape-shifting snake-monster speeding toward me like an oncoming freight train, his twin fangs bared, the black claws at the ends of his scaly hands and feet carving up bits of wooden flooring and Pepto-Bismol-hued carpet as he charges.

My one and only would-be protector, the monstrous night fairy known as the Boogeyman, is nowhere to be seen. Like Elvis, he's left the building. Or more aptly, the snake-changeling has tossed him through it.

Either way, I'm in one heck of a fix!

Not for the first time, I mentally kick myself for ever having entered the shadowy depths leading from my closet into the Void, a nexus existing between our world and that of Fairy. Why oh why I ever thought stepping into the Void was a good idea escapes—*wait a minute!* The closet! Escape! I may have a way out of this mess yet.

Just before the changeling can bring its huge serpentine bulk crashing into me, I grab the frilly edge of Caroline's pink bedding and throw myself onto her mattress in a backward roll, pulling the sheets up after me. I release the covers in mid-roll and flop down off the side of the bed. I land on my backside just as the changeling collides with the bed. Its frame and box springs collapse under the monster's weight with a loud crunch.

Amazingly, my makeshift plan works and the raging rogue fairy entangles itself within Caroline's fluffy bedding.

The creature struggles furiously, but it only serves to further ensnare him.

That wasn't so har—!

The monster's claws find purchase and begin shredding the sheets and mattress, filling the darkened room with puffs of pink fabric and foam as he frees himself.

Not wanting to be here when he finishes, I scamper to my feet and hightail it over to Caroline's closet. I throw open the door and shove my way through an incalculable amount of pink dresses, shirts, pants, and skirts, almost falling as I stumble through virtual mounds of pink shoes.

This girl has a problem!

I reach the rear of the closet and plunge through, thanking whoever's in charge that the open portal I had hoped would be there for me actually is. If any vertigo accompanies my passage, my terror keeps me from feeling it. I hit the Void running and make for the next-closest portal, not caring where it'll take me. I just want to put as much distance between myself and the changeling as I can.

Speaking of ol' slithery, my heart skips a beat when I look over my shoulder and see the changeling galloping out of the portal leading from Caroline's room. His fanged mouth is open, but he moves in deadly silence, apparently wise to the effect voices have on the denizens that dwell in the endless dark surrounding us.

I kick my feet into high gear and all but leap into the portal in front of me. The next thing I know, I'm pushing my way through rows of hanging button-down shirts and blue jeans. I burst through the door of the closet housing them and instantly realize I'm inside Mitchell Maedel's bedroom. Pennant flags, sports trophies, and posters of baseball players line the walls. Mitchell himself is sitting straight up in his bed looking at me, his eyes wide and his mouth agape.

"What are you doing in my room?" he blurts. "And what in the world are you wearing?"

Mitchell is a grade ahead of me in school. He's one of the popular, All-American kids I was telling you about earlier. Despite this, and my contrasting low position on the totem pole that is Bradbury Middle School, he's typically friendly to me when we pass in the hall. So it's with genuine care for his person that I shout, "Run!"

"Are you crazy?" he yells back.

For a millisecond, I start to panic. Heck, who am I kidding? I am panicked! But enough of my brain is still functioning for me to realize I have to get Mitchell out of here as quickly as possible. Otherwise, we're *both* goners.

Inspiration strikes and I yank Barbie out from under my black tabard. I wave it at him like a psycho killer and repeat, "Run!"

This time Mitchell takes the hint. He springs out of bed and vanishes from the room, his feet pounding on hardwood as he makes tracks down the hallway leading to his parents' room.

And not a moment too soon, either.

The changeling appears behind me in an explosion of shredded clothes and serpentine hisses. His scaly bulk fills the entire frame of the closet door.

At that moment, I don't think. I simply act, and it keeps me out of the changeling's clutches. The monster lunges for me, and I dive for the rectangle-shaped shadow stretched out beneath Mitchell's bed. Mercifully, I slide on through it into the Void rather than crashing into hard wooden floor. Luckily for me, like the Boogeyman, I can now use *any* shadow to enter and exit the Void.

Space and time are different in the Void, and I enter on a horizontal trajectory rather than the vertical one I was on when I left Mitchell's room. I fly through the air like Superman for a moment before hitting the ground at a roll that has me on my feet and running again in one single, smooth motion. I'd be impressed with myself if I had time to stop and think about it. But time and thinking are in frighteningly short supply for me right now.

I look over my shoulder and see the changeling enter the Void in a similar fashion. However, his landing is less graceful, and he goes toppling over the edge of the walkway.

Fall! I think, having to make myself keep from screaming it. *Fall! Fall!*

But I'm not so lucky.

I curse silently as I watch one of the changeling's clawed hands snag the edge of the walkway and prevent him from plummeting into the abyss below.

He's pulling himself back up onto the walkway when I duck into another portal. When I come out the other side, the first thing I register is the sound of several young girls singing. I recognize the song. It's the latest single from that mega-popular teenager every girl in my classroom absolutely loves and I absolutely loathe. You know the one—the dude who can never seem to comb his perfectly messy mop-top out of his baby blues.

Anyway, next I realize that, this time, I've arrived under a bed rather than in a closet. I claw my way out from beneath it and haul myself to my feet. In the room's dim light, I see the girls I heard singing—a group of Asian pre-teens dressed in their pajamas. It appears they're having a sleepover. Two are stretched out on the bed I arrived under. The rest all lie on sleeping bags scattered about a bedroom adorned with pictures of the aforementioned teen sensation, including a life-sized poster that spans the length of the room's closet door.

I have enough time to think, *That portal led all the way to the Far East!* before the girls stop singing and start screaming at the sight of me.

"You have to get out of here!" I yell, trying to reason with them. This simply makes them scream louder.

I look at my right hand and realize it's still clasped around Barbie's hilt. I quickly hide the dagger behind my back.

"No!" I shout. "I mean, I'm not here to hurt you, but—!"

Before I can finish my sentence, the changeling appears. He rises straight up from the shadows on the floor, lifting the bed and the two girls lying on it high into the air above him. If the girls were screaming before, they're absolutely hysterical now.

Knowing I have to draw the monster's attention away from the girls, I stick my tongue out at him and make a spitting sound while gesticulating wildly. It may not be what a cool action-hero would've come up with, but it does the trick.

The changeling steps forward and releases the bed, allowing it to fall straight to the floor behind him. It hits and the girls atop it bounce once before coming to land safe and sound. However, this elicits still louder screams from the young Asians. The noise is enough to draw the changeling's attention back to them. He whirls to face them, his rattlesnake's tail shaking behind him.

Oh, crap!

I've got to do something, and I've got to do it fast!

I once again become aware of Barbie's weight in the palm of my hand. Having no other ideas to fall back on, I step forward and thrust the dagger toward the changeling. At the last second, I change my grip on the knife, flipping so that the flat of the blade smacks the changeling's scaly tail instead of piercing it. Maybe it's cowardly of me, but I have no desire to cause anyone or anything lasting harm. Even a monster like the changeling.

I need not have worried. Barbie's touch proves to be enough.

The changeling freezes then convulses as if in pain as the dagger makes contact with the rogue fairy's scaly hide. The monster shudders, but otherwise remains still beneath the silvery steel blade. The girls scatter out of the room, shouting and crying in what I think is Japanese. Unfortunately, the last one to leave bumps me as she rushes by and causes Barbie to slip away from the changeling.

The snake-monster's tail cracks across my gloved hand faster than Indiana Jones' whip, and I yelp in pain as Barbie clatters to the floor. Weaponless, I lunge for the closet door but duck just in time to miss the swipe of the changeling's claws. Instead of latching onto me, the creature's talons impale themselves in the closet door and tear it from its hinges.

I watch as the monster rips the door in two, poster and all. Apparently, he doesn't like the teen heartthrob's music either.

I plunge into the now-open closet through rows of prep school uniforms and re-enter the Void. As I scamper down the walkway, a plan begins to form in my mind. I briefly duck my head into one portal after another, hoping against hope I'll find what I'm looking for. Much to my astonishment, I do. Just in time, too, for the changeling bursts into the Void, its claws now free of the closet door and looking sharper than ever.

I jump into the portal before me and enter a dark janitorial closet full of shelves housing towels and cleaning supplies bearing a logo reading *Tan-apalooza*. I fling open the closet door and sprint down the dimly lit hallway outside toward yet another door at its end. I push through the door and leave it swinging behind me, not caring if the changeling sees it waving and follows me inside. In fact, that's exactly what I want him to do.

The room is long, and twin rows of freestanding tanning booths line its either side, facing inward to form an aisle leading to a junction box on the room's far wall. These booths are the latest in tanning technology and use the highest wattage VHO lamps available. The Tan-apalooza staff told me as much when I came here trying to rid myself of my sickly pale complexion once and for all.

That last, failed attempt ended miserably in blistered, red skin.

I race down the aisle to the junction box and turn off its master switch. Then I backtrack and throw open the tanning booths' doors as I flip their switches to the "on" position. With the junction box turned off, the booths remain dark. But that's okay. I expected as much. Was counting on it even.

I activate the last booth and reach the junction box just as I hear a loud clatter in the hallway outside.

I turn and face the room's entrance, my heart beating so hard and so fast I'm sure it will burst out of my chest any second.

The door to the tanning room continues swinging back and forth. The creeping snake-monster is in the hall. It draws nearer with each swipe of the door. At last, the door disappears in an explosion of wood and dust. I cringe as I throw my arm up to protect my eyes from the resulting shower of kindling.

I lower my arm and see the changeling eyeing the tanning booths warily, a confused expression on his reptilian face.

Oh no! I think. *If he figures out what I'm planning—!*

I don't allow myself to finish the thought. I place my gloved thumb and index finger in my mouth and give a loud whistle. The changeling snaps its head in my direction.

"Hey, ugly!" I shout.

The changeling's face becomes a snarl. It pops its fangs and hisses as it slithers down the aisle toward me.

"Oh, hssssss yourself!"

I reach up and throw the master switch on the side of the junction box. The tanning booths spring to life and bathe the two of us in a staggering amount of ultraviolet light.

I watch, both fascinated and horrified, as the changeling freezes in mid-lope. Ever-expanding patches of stony gray begin to form along the monster's scaly hide. Within seconds, the night fairy has become a gargoylish statue of stone.

"Gotcha!" I say, as I pump the air with my fist. "Ultraviolet light doesn't agree with you night fairies, does it?"

I must admit, capturing the changeling is the most satisfying thing I've ever done.

"Puck?" I hear the Boogeyman's gravelly voice shout from down the hall.

The door of the janitorial closet begins to open and I shout, "No! I mean, stay there. I've got him."

"You've what?" the Boogeyman calls from inside the closet, his Scottish burr full of disbelief. Regardless, he's wise enough to heed my words.

"I said, I've got him. Stay right where you are. It isn't safe for you to come out."

"You've got the changeling?" A long pause. "How?"

"You might say he couldn't take the heat."

There, I think, a smile spreading across my face. *Now that's a one-liner worthy of an action-hero. Much better than, 'Oh, hssssss yourself!'*

13

PAGING DR. DEATH

Van Helsing, eat your heart out!

Yours truly just captured the monstrous snake-changeling by zapping him with about a gazillion UVs courtesy of the Tan-apalooza tanning booths. And I did it without the Boogeyman's help to boot.

That's right. I'm now officially a bona fide, butt-kicking monster hunter. Can I get a *what-what*? Oh yeah! I'm bad! Slap me some skin! Up high! Down low!

Can you tell I'm feeling pretty psyched about what I've accomplished here?

By contrast, the Boogeyman is less than impressed. Once I bind the statue the changeling has become in the Boogeyman's metal chain and shut off the tanning booths so that ol' Tall, Dark and Scary may approach, my chaperon only grunts and says, "Being a full-grown fairy from the Night Lands, it was never a possibility for me to spring such a trap, personally. You had it easy."

Gee. So much for getting a "thank you." What a grump!

With the ultraviolent light gone, the changeling transforms from being a statue back into his usual horrible, snaky self. He struggles against his bindings and flashes us with his fangs as he hisses, but the iron in the steel alloy chain I've wrapped around him keeps him stationary.

The Boogeyman narrows his darkling gaze onto the changeling. "Now. Let's see what secrets you have to share."

The Boogeyman glides by me, and I feel the dark energy he

exudes flare in intensity. The changeling ceases his struggling at the Boogeyman's approach and cringes in fear.

The Boogeyman surges forward across the final few feet separating him from his fellow monster. He seizes the changeling's head in his bony, clawed hands and locks eyes with him. The Boogeyman's gaze becomes a storm of blackness. The changeling's serpentine pupils close to twin pinpoints. It's as though the Boogeyman is hypnotizing him.

Something invisible but palpable passes between the two fairies. I look away for fear I might also get drawn into whatever macabre exchange is taking place.

"Curses!" I hear the Boogeyman spit after a time. "It is just as before."

I look back to see him release the changeling. The snake-monster's head lulls for a moment before his senses and composure return.

"What's just as before?" I ask.

"He knows nothing."

"What do you mean he knows nothing?"

"When I used the Mesmer on the changeling to discover why he was kidnapping children from your town, I found nothing. No thoughts. No motives. No impressions. The only thing present is a compulsion for him to go to the Mortal Lands and steal children, but there is no trace of its origin. What worries me even more is that this is far from the first time I've come across such. Lately, every fairy I've captured within the Mortal Lands seems to be missing any and all memories that might explain why they've gone rogue."

I scratch my head. "How is that possible?"

The Boogeyman waves a dismissive claw. "Magic, of course. Someone or something is wiping the information I seek from their minds."

The Boogeyman produces his worn, brown sack from the inky depths of his cloak. "It is as I told the King and Queen. It is no coincidence that suddenly droves of night fairies are going rogue. Treachery is afoot. And the ones who are behind it are trying to hide themselves and their ultimate plans from me."

In a swift, flowing motion, the Boogeyman pulls the

sack down over the changeling. The sack balloons in size to accommodate the monster's bulk, then contracts again as the Boogeyman scoops both it and the creature it now holds off the floor. The Boogeyman tosses the sack over his shoulder and glides over to me.

He reaches inside his cloak with his free hand and unceremoniously dumps my musketeer hat, mask, and dagger onto the floor at my feet. "You should take better care of your possessions, Puck."

"Look who's talking!" I blurt, having had enough of the Boogeyman's sourness. "Cat's right. Your tower is a pig sty!"

The Boogeyman leans down and points a sharp claw at my face. "Now you listen here—!"

"No, you listen!" I say, bowing out my chest. "It may have been my fault the changeling escaped, but it was only because I didn't know any better. I was just trying to do what I thought was right at the time. Regardless, in the end, I made good on it. While you got yourself tossed out a window, this mere mortal caught the changeling all by his self, doing it without any of the monstrous abilities or magic you have on your side. So instead of talking to me like I'm less than the dirt on your big, spooky feet, you could show a little gratitude!"

The Boogeyman swells in size as he growls and bares his black shark's teeth, reminding me just how terrifying he can be when he wants to. I swallow hard and begin to shake with fear.

I've done it now. I've gone and put my black-booted foot in my infamous big mouth.

To my surprise and relief, after a moment, the Boogeyman shrinks back to his usual towering size.

"Thank you for capturing the changeling, Puck," he spits. Without another word, he whirls away from me and heads out into the dark hallway.

I stand watching the Boogeyman go for a moment. Not knowing what else to do, I scoop up the articles at my feet and hurry after him.

We exit through the portal in Tan-apalooza's closet in silence and continue on that way until we reach Shadow Tower.

I'm pleased to find I no longer feel any sense of vertigo traveling through the Void.

Cat greets us at the base of the tower's stony spiraling staircase. Unlike the Boogeyman, she's head over heels about my catching the changeling on my own.

"I knew you had it in you, Puck!" she beams.

"At least someone around here appreciates my help."

The Boogeyman growls at my words and retreats with the captured changeling into the room where he'd held him captive previously.

"He's proud of you, too, Puck," Cat says. "Ol' Boogey just isn't what you mortals would call a 'good communicator.'"

"Tell me something I don't know."

A few moments later, the Boogeyman rejoins us at the foot of the stairs, the now-empty brown sack in his hand.

"What now?" I ask.

"Now it's time for you to go home," the Boogeyman answers. "You've served your sentence. Your work here is finished, but mine has only just begun. I have much to do to keep Fairy and the Mortal Lands from going to war, and little time to do it."

"Will you be able to get them out of the changeling and home safe first?" I ask. "The kids from town, I mean."

The Boogeyman nods. The gesture is full of weariness. "We, uh, *you* caught the changeling in time. Your fellow mortals should be just fine."

I exhale in relief.

"There's just one more thing," the Boogeyman sighs.

"Oh, yeah?" I say. "Wha—?"

Before I can finish my question, the Boogeyman drops the sack and surges forward. He seizes my head in his skeletal hands. Panic and fear explode inside me and my heart begins to palpitate.

The storm of darkness I saw previously in the Boogeyman's eyes fills them once again, spilling out from beyond his gaze to wash over me.

I hear the Boogeyman whisper a single word from a country somewhere far, far away.

"Forget."

I sit up in my bed at home, awakened by a horrible nightmare that dances on the edge of my memory for a moment, then slips away entirely when I try to grab hold of it. I shake myself and yawn as I stretch away the last of sleep's fog.

I glance at my alarm clock on my nightstand and shut it off just before the six-forty-five alarm can sound. I get out of bed and spare a quick glance out the window. A dawning October day of crisp blue skies, autumn leaves, and orange jack-o'-lanterns waits outside.

I compulsively tap the posters on my walls featuring the Wolfman, Frankenstein, and Dracula for luck, then start for my closet, intending to grab a towel for my morning shower.

I freeze in mid-step.

My heart begins doing somersaults in my chest. Looking at my closet door fills me with inexplicable fear.

Calm down, I think, then count to ten like Dr. Stuart has taught me during our sessions together.

It helps. Some. At least enough for me to approach my closet and reach inside to grab a towel. Still, I do so and jerk back as though I was afraid there was a snake inside that might bite me.

My behavior is just plain weird. Even for me.

Once I'm showered and dressed in a long-sleeved T-shirt and jeans from my dresser (*Yet another inanimate object that frightens the stuffing out of me. What the heck is wrong with me?*), I scamper downstairs to find Mom and Dad conversing at the breakfast table in our cookie-cutter kitchen-slash-dining room as they sip coffee. Both are dressed in suits and ready for work.

The local news is on the small flat-screen resting on our granite kitchen counter. The sound is off, but I notice a crawler beneath the anchorman at the bottom of the screen reading: *Town's missing children miraculously return home.*

"Hey, Mom. Hey, Dad."

"Hey, guy," Mom says.

"'Morning, champ," Day says.

I sit down at the table and pour myself a bowl of Cheerios. Unfortunately, they aren't the sweet Honey Nut kind. Considering my *condition*, Dr. Stuart thinks I need to avoid sugar whenever possible.

"No, I can't remember, either," Dad says to Mom.

"Can't remember what?" I ask.

"What we did yesterday," Mom answers. Her normally happy face is full of confusion. "Or the night before, for that matter."

"What about you, son?" Mom asks. "Do you remember?"

I wave a dismissive hand. "Sure. I—" Much to my surprise, when I try to recall the events of the past twenty-four hours, I find I also draw a blank. The swishing tail and rolling eyes of the black cat-clock hanging on the kitchen wall catch my gaze. There's something oddly familiar about it. Something...something...but then it's gone. "I—I can't remember."

Mom looks at Dad, her confusion giving way to fear. "Maybe we should see a doctor?"

"Now everyone calm down," Dad says. "We've all been under a lot of stress lately. Me with work. You with the Charity League. And the champ here with coming off his meds. I'm sure our lapse in memory can all be chalked up to that."

Dad turns to face me directly. "But speaking of physician appointments, Dr. Stuart called while you were in the shower. His schedule has changed, and he needs you to come in this afternoon."

My eyes go immediately to the Dry Erase calendar hanging on our steel fridge. Under today's date in bright red ink, it reads: *Dr. Stuart. 1 P.M.*

"*Curses!*" I mumble under my breath, then think, *Curses? Since when do I say, 'curses'?*

The rest of the morning goes by in a nondescript blur. As usual, I go to school and either get made fun of by the cool kids or ignored by them altogether. The only thing that happens worth noting is when I wave to the normally friendly Mitchell Maedel in the hall, he screams, "Stay away from me, you freak!" He says it loud enough that the students and teachers around us all stop what they're doing and gawk at me in horrified disgust.

I make like a turtle and try to hide inside my clothes as I speed-walk down the hallway in embarrassment.

As one o'clock draws near, I sign myself out at the front office and go outside to get on my bike and make the short ride to Dr. Stuart's practice. As I remove the lock attaching my bike's frame to the steel hitching grate, I hear the sound of a shaking rattle-snake's tail behind me and yell loud enough to halt the kickball game going on in the green field across the street.

"Are you okay?" Mrs. Fuqua, the school gym teacher, calls.

I turn around to see what I thought was a shaking rattle-snake's tail was merely the school's lawn sprinklers activating.

I wave back to Mrs. Fuqua. "I'm okay."

Really, dude, I tell myself, *you need to get a grip!*

I hop on my bike and head off down the hay bale-and-jack-o'-lantern-adorned street, the cool October wind whistling in my ears and fallen autumn leaves swirling in my wake. Minutes later, I'm locking my bike up again. This time, out in front of Dr. Stuart's office—a beige, block-shaped building with poster board ghosts hanging in the slim, rectangular windows circum-venting its exterior.

Let's get this over with, I think, and head inside.

Dr. Stuart's waiting room is just like any other doctor's wait-ing room. There are less-than-comfortable chairs and a coffee table with out-of-date magazines surrounded by walls papered in unattractive shades of beige and off-white. Oddly, there's no one at the receptionist's desk. I sign myself in and take a seat. I wait for what seems like an eternity until at last my *condition* gets the better of me. Bored and impatient, I get up and knock on the oak door leading into Dr. Stuart's office.

"Dr. Stuart?" I call through the door. "Are you there? It's me."

I'm just about to turn and walk away when the door is jerked open from the other side. Dr. Stuart stands there, peering down at me through his bifocals, a glistening white smile that matches the color of his shirt and hair forming dimples in the cheeks of his fifty-something face.

He seems taller than normal. I look down to see if he's wear-ing thick-soled boots, but register it's only his usual pair of busi-ness casual Rockports at the end of his gray slacks.

"Hello!" he beams, singing the word. "I've been waiting for you!"

"There wasn't anyone at the desk," I say. "I've been out here since one."

"Yes," he sings, "Crystal is gone for the day. Had to leave town. Couldn't be helped. Her dog is sick and her mother needs to be let out."

He pauses in thought a moment and then laughs hysterically.

"Or was it the other way around?"

I've never seen Dr. Stuart act this way. Typically, he's all stone-faced and even keel. Never, well, *giddy*.

"Are you okay, Dr. Stuart?"

"Why yes," he continues in his sing-song voice. "Fit as a fiddle. Right as rain. Never felt better. Why do you ask?"

"Well, you just—"

He steps to one side. "Enough about me. Come in! Come in!"

I shrug and obey.

Dr. Stuart's office has more books than the local library. They all have titles ending in various "ologies." And, unlike what you see on TV, there's no couch, simply a twin set of leather chairs sitting across from each another. Rays from the October sun shine down on them through the vertical windows on the room's right side.

I hear a metallic click and look around to see Dr. Stuart locking his office door. He's never done that before.

He spots the concerned expression on my face. "Sorry. The new HIPAA laws. Confidentiality. Blah, blah, blah. You know how it is. Won't you sit down?"

Dr. Stuart takes a seat in the chair facing the door, his smile never wavering. I slide into the seat across from him and begin twiddling my thumbs, wishing I was anywhere else but here.

"So, how have you been sleeping?" Dr. Stuart asks as he produces a small pad and pen from his pockets.

"Not well, actually," I say. "I think I had bad dreams all last night."

He scribbles something down on the pad. "Really? What were they about?"

I shrug. "I can't remember."

"Well, now. That's just too bad." His scribbling takes on a feverish intensity that disturbs me.

"Uh," I say, my eyes glued to his manic pen and pad, "why?"

"Because a person should go into the last day of their life on a good night's sleep."

I gasp in terror as Dr. Stuart leaps out of his seat. As he does, the human disguise he's wearing evaporates like mist in the wind. It's no longer a mild-mannered doctor jumping at me while holding a pad and pen, but an armored warrior elf with a sword and shield in his hands and raging insanity in his eyes.

14

I'M SAVED BY A GIANT BUTTERFLY

You ever have one of those days? The kind where the craziest, most unbelievable thing happens to you? Well, forget it! It's nothing in comparison to the one I'm having.

"Oh no," you say? Yours is just as insane? Well then, tell me this: has your doctor ever transformed into a tall elf armored in plates of ivory? An elf wielding a sword and shield of white diamond that he is intent on using against you with extreme prejudice?

No. I didn't think so.

But that's what's happening to me right here and now. My psychologist was kindly old Dr. Stuart one second, then a berserker elf knight the next.

The elf who was Dr. Stuart yells a battle cry as he leaps at me, his silken blond hair flaring out to reveal his twin pointy ears. In his ivory plate armor, he looks like the menacing, medieval version of a stormtrooper from *Star Wars*.

I sink into myself, tears in my wide eyes, my own yell rising to meet his. This is the end and there's no escape.

At the last second, I shut my eyes, not wanting to face my death. My final thoughts are of Mom and Dad and that I'll never get to tell them goodbye.

Then I hear a sound that is somewhere between the pinging of metal and the grating of rock and open my eyes to see the elf's sword blocked by another—a thin, golden rapier.

"You!" the elf snarls.

"Me!"

I look up and see that my savior is the most beautiful lady I've ever laid eyes on. Her hair is like crimson fire and her skin is like virgin snow. She wears a breastplate of lattice gold over a forest-green gown. She carries a golden harp in her other hand. The majestic butterfly wings at her back act like twin prisms and refract the sunshine coming in through the windows so that it forms a rainbow corona around her entire body.

She looks like a valkyrie straight out of my Thor comic books.

The woman parries the elf's blade up and away, causing its wielder to stumble backward. The elf regains his footing and howls as he charges at the woman. She evades his attack, skirting to the side, carried there by a quick flutter of her opalescent butterfly wings. I remain frozen with terror in my seat.

The woman mounts her own attack, thrusting and slashing her rapier with expert form. The two of them fight from one side of the room to the other, leaving a trail of cleaved furniture and shredded books in their wake. At last, a daring swipe of the woman's blade relieves the elf of his diamond shield.

"Yield!" she commands.

"Never!"

The elf hurls himself forward, his sword raised high. He moves directly in front of my chair and something takes me over. I don't know if it's bravery or stupidity. Either way, it causes me to stick out my leg in the elf's direction. His foot entangles with my own and he trips.

His diamond-bladed sword goes clattering across the room as he lands facedown. The woman quickly sheathes her golden blade.

"Cover your ears!" she orders. I obey just as she begins playing her harp. Even with my hands blocking most of the sound, I can tell the music coming from her instrument is haunting and ethereal.

The elf climbs to his feet. An expression of serenity replaces the rage in his face. He smiles dreamily as he walks over and picks up his discarded sword and shield. I gasp with fright, but I needn't have worried. The elf sheathes his blade and hangs his shield on his ivory-armored back. Apparently he no longer has any interest in fighting the woman or killing me.

What a relief!

The woman stops playing and gestures that it's okay for me to uncover my ears. She attaches the harp to her white leather belt so that the musical instrument dangles on her hip opposite her rapier.

"Is he *cool*?" I ask, gesturing to the now-still and silent warrior elf.

"As ice crystal," she replies, her voice an Irish brogue. "How've you been, Puck? Other than this little episode, I mean."

"Puck?" I say. "My name isn't Puck, it's—"

She shushes me. "Best not to say. Even for a mortal. You never know who could be listening."

I scratch my head. "Who are you supposed to be? *Tinkerbell Warrior Princess*?"

She laughs and the sound is musical. "Resourceful *and* funny. The Boogeyman said you had talent, but he failed to mention your sense of humor."

"Boogeyman? Excuse me, uh, Ma'am—?"

"I'm the Siren. Call me Siren. We met outside the tomb of King Arcturus."

This lady may be beautiful, but she seems just as nuts as Blondie the elf.

"Er, okay, Miss, um, Siren." I start backing toward the office door. "Whatever you say. I think I'll just be leaving now." I whirl and grab the doorknob. I yank, pull, twist, and rattle it, but it refuses to turn.

Oh, that's right. It's locked.

I begin trying and failing to unlock the door when Siren says something that stops me dead in my tracks.

"Oh, you can't leave."

I slowly turn around, fear slithering up my spine like a venomous snake. "What do you mean I can't leave?"

"It isn't safe for you out there."

It can't be any worse than it is in here with you two nutjobs, I think, but merely ask, "Why not?"

"The Boogeyman asked me to keep an eye on you in case any fairy from the Day Lands showed up looking to make trouble."

Siren points to the elf. "Now that one has tried and failed, there will undoubtedly be more who come along bearing the same bad intentions."

Gulp!

I don't exactly understand what she's saying, but it doesn't sound like good news for me.

"I don't understand. Why would anyone like Blondie here wish to harm me? I'm just a kid. I couldn't bother the likes of him if I wanted to."

Siren crosses her arms over her chest. "Whoever is behind this must know the Boogeyman is on to them. The elf must have been going after you because of your recent association with the one fairy who might be able to stop them."

"The Boogeyman?" I ask, mystified. "Fairy? What are you talking about?"

"It's too hard to explain." Siren stands straight again and taps her small, freckled chin with a deceptively dainty finger. "It would be easier if I showed you instead."

"Uh, okay, I guess."

Siren raises her hands and brings them toward my face. I flinch and she smiles.

"Trust me, Puck."

I study Siren for a moment. Against my better judgment, I relent with a nod. She nods in return and places the tips of her fingers along the sides of my face. Her eyes begin to sparkle like twin jade stars.

"This may feel a little *weird*."

As Siren says these final words, I lose myself in her eyes. Literally. Her eyes become twin pools of swirling green that wash over me, bringing with them inexplicable nightmare images. There is a tall, crooked man in my bedroom. He looks somewhat like the vampire Count Orlok from the old silent horror film, *Nosferatu*. Only the man in my room has a cloak of living shadow and a black stove-pipe hat as tall and crooked as he is.

The Boogeyman! I think. *He's the Boogeyman!*

With that realization, everything else comes flooding back to me: the Void, Shadow Tower, Cat, my trip to the Twilight

Lands, my first meeting with Siren, the Fairy King and Queen, the Merlin and her second, the changeling, my capturing of him, and lastly, the Boogeyman scrambling my marbles with his Mesmer.

Siren releases my head, and I wobble on my feet for a moment as the here and now surges back into place around me.

"He did this to me! The Boogeyman made me forget. The jerk!"

"Don't be so hard on him, Puck," Siren says. "Things are not always as they appear. The Boogeyman was only trying to protect you for as long as he could."

"Protect me? He almost got me turned into shish kabob! If you hadn't showed up when you did, Siren… How did you get in here, by the way? The door was locked. I saw Dr. Stuart, uh, the elf, lock it. And then I couldn't even get it unlocked myself…?"

Siren gestures to the sunlight streaming in through the office windows. "I traveled from Fairy through the Aurora, Puck, coming out here Earth-side through a portal of sunlight."

"You did what with the who?"

Siren's melodious giggles fill the air once again.

"The Aurora is the opposing nexus to the Void, Puck. Whereas the Boogeyman travels in darkness and shadow, I make my way between worlds using brightness and light."

Siren extends her free hand. Despite the mastery with which it wielded the rapier, it's a beautifully feminine hand with nails lacquered with flecks of gold. *Real gold.*

"Come. I'll show you."

"But my parents. I can't leave them. Not again. Not without at least telling them goodbye."

Siren's expression hardens. "Every second we spend here leaves you open to another attack. You, and those you care about."

I gasp. "These day fairies would hurt my parents?"

Siren nods. "Your parents. Teachers. Schoolmates. When rogue fairies set out to go after something—or in this case, someone—they tend not to behave too kindly toward anyone who happens to get in their way."

I recall the changeling turning on the young Japanese girls

who were unlucky enough to get caught up in our chase, and begin to glean where Siren is coming from.

I point at the still-immobile elf. "What about him? Are we just going to leave him here?"

"Oh, he's coming along, too. Aren't you, my friend?"

The elf smiles, literally enchanted with Siren. "Absolutely!"

"But I'm glad you said something, Puck. First things first, after all." Siren waltzes gracefully over to the elf and takes his head in her hands. Her green eyes begin to sparkle, and I look away, already knowing what comes next.

After a moment, I hear her sigh and clap her hands together as though she was dusting them off.

"Anything?" I ask, facing her once again.

She shakes her head. "Just an imperative for him to come to the Mortal Lands and destroy you. But the reasoning behind it is absent."

I nod. "The Boogeyman said the same thing about the changeling. He said he believed someone was behind the monster's appearance in the Mortal Lands, as well as all the other rogue fairies who've apparently been popping up Earth-side of late."

A thought strikes me. "Wait a minute. You just brought back my memories. Can't you do the same for the elf?"

Siren shakes her head. "The Boogeyman simply fogged your memories. He didn't strip them away outright as was done to this unfortunate Day Lands knight. But maybe there's a clue to what's going on somewhere else—" Siren begins patting down the elf and checking the joints of his armor. When her search comes up empty, she begins sifting through the debris left in the wake of their battle.

I follow suit and begin skimming through the room's shredded books and papers. "He didn't seem too unfortunate when he was trying to kill me. The elf, I mean."

"If the Boogeyman is right," Siren says as she examines the contents of the filing cabinet in the corner of Dr. Stuart's office, "he was merely being used as a pawn by someone who knows the deepest of magic."

I toss up my hands and roll my eyes. "Great! Just great. As if

I didn't have enough problems. Now the Wicked Witch of West Fairy is trying to do me in."

Siren pauses in her search. "I would be foolish to tell you not to worry. But take heart, you are not alone."

I turn and face Dr. Stuart's bookshelf, my cheeks reddening with a complicated mixture of emotions. Standing there, my watery eyes come across something they failed to spot earlier: a black sheet of paper protruding from the top of a cognitive psychology textbook.

"Hey, what's this?"

I take the book from the shelf and remove the sheet of paper. It bears a broken wax seal featuring the Greek letter omega.

"Let me see that," Siren snaps. But the moment she snatches it from my hand, the page bursts into flames.

"Holy moly!" I shout.

Siren drops the burning page in reflex. By the time it falls to the floor, it's nothing more than a pile of smoking ash.

"What happened?" I ask.

Siren massages her hand. "I imagine the page was enchanted to self-destruct at the touch of a fae hand belonging to someone other than our friend the knight, here. But its author was not careful enough: I saw the royal seal of Castle Night before the page consumed itself."

"Royal seal? Castle Night?" The gears in my head click into place. "You don't mean—?"

Siren nods. "I'm afraid so. Whatever was on the page came from the ruling family of the Night Lands. Namely, the royal house of the King. Perhaps even the King himself."

"The King of Fairy is behind this?"

"Maybe. If he is, then this matter falls under the Boogeyman's jurisdiction." Siren shakes her head in confusion. "For a Day Lands elf to be working under the direction of the Night Lands' King... Oh, this does go deep, Puck!"

I scratch my head. "Well, what are we going to do?"

"Your protection is our first priority. I can keep you safe with me in the Day Lands until night falls. But when it does, I'll need you to go to Shadow Tower and tell the Boogeyman about what's happened. Like I said, if the King, a night fairy, is behind this, then it falls to the Boogeyman to handle it."

Siren extends her hand once more. "Are you up to it, Puck?"

I stand still for a moment, my eyes darting from Siren's face to her hand and back.

"Are you sure I can't tell my parents goodbye?"

Siren frowns in sympathy. "It's safer for them and everyone else if you don't."

I reluctantly nod and take Siren's hand in mine. As we touch, a tingle of something like electricity shoots from her hand up my arm into my chest, warming my heart and easing my fear.

Siren raises her other hand in the elf's direction. "Come along, Sir Knight. We must be going."

The elf knight obediently walks over and takes Siren's hand.

Siren's butterfly wings begin to beat—slowly at first, then accelerating to hummingbird speed. Their fanning causes a whirlwind to form in the room. The wind snatches up anything not nailed down and tosses it in every direction.

"Up, up, and away!" Siren yells. She looks down at me. "I just love mortal TV!"

The sunshine coming through the windows flares to an incredible intensity, and we vanish in an all-encompassing flash of brilliant light.

15

SUN AND FUN IN THE DAY LANDS

Before Shadow Tower, the changeling, or the Land of Fairy, there was the Void. That's where my troubles began. In a move of either great valor or enormous idiocy, I stepped through my closet into the nexus of shadow and darkness the Boogeyman uses to travel between worlds.

It was the biggest mistake of my life. One I never dreamed I'd make twice. That said, flying with Siren through the Aurora is nothing like traveling through the Void with ol' Tall, Dark, and Scary.

Where the Void is a place of deathly silence and endless dark, the Aurora is a living kaleidoscope of vibrant light and sound.

It reminds me of the videos my dad watches sometimes on VH1 classic—the ones where the bands play songs about Wonderland rabbits and men of iron as they stand in front of green screens pulsating with psychedelic paisleys and dripping, lava lamp interiors.

Except the Aurora is nothing so crude.

It's a series of branching tunnels filled with amorphous, rainbow colors that ooze along one second, then zap to and fro like bolts of lightning the next.

And the chimes!

The sound of them is everywhere, rising and falling in pitch from a low tingle to a clamorous din.

In short, the Aurora is beautiful. Maddeningly so.

I'm not exaggerating when I say that. If I were to remain

here in the Aurora too long, I have no doubt the sheer brilliance of the place would drive me crazy.

Thankfully, our stay in the Aurora proves relatively brief, and I don't have to worry about it. Siren flies the elf knight and me down a wide, radiant tunnel with a glimmering yellow light at its end. Looking at it, I can't help but think of all the stories of near-death experiences I've heard about.

I swallow hard, hoping that this trip will prove to be nothing so dire.

We reach the light and fly through. Leaving the Aurora fails to produce any of the feelings of vertigo I experienced during my early travels in and out of the Void. I guess my body has more than acclimated to traveling between dimensions by now.

We come out the other side of the Aurora above the greenest, thickest forest I've ever seen. It stretches for miles in every direction, at last greeting a cloudless sky of crystal blue at the horizon. I'm sure I would take pleasure at the sight of it if Siren wasn't flying the three of us so high off the ground.

As it is, I look over my shoulder, trying to keep my school cafeteria lunch from making a second appearance. But the sunbeams we are materializing out of prove too bright. I'm left with no choice but to face forward and close my eyes.

At last, our feet touch the ground, and I allow myself to take a peek. We stand in a clearing amid the forest. A lone redwood rises up from the clearing's center to tower over the surrounding trees. Instead of green, the leaves of the central tree are every color imaginable. They rustle soundlessly in a breeze that fails to reach the rest of the wood. What *is* sounding in the forest is the continuous rise and fall of cicada song.

Siren releases our hands and turns to face the elf. She takes his head in her hands, and her gaze begins to pulse with jade light.

"I cannot remove the knight's compulsion to attack you, Puck," she says. "The spell implanted in his mind is too strong."

I roll my eyes and chuckle. "So what's the bad news?"

"Now, now," she reprimands. "I may not be able to remove his desire for your destruction, but I can block it well enough to keep him out of your hair for at least a few centuries."

"Oh," I say, near giddy at this turn of events. "That should definitely do it. I don't think I'll be around to worry about him a few hundred years from now. As much as I might like to be."

Siren gives a knowing smile. The jade storm of her eyes strengthens in intensity for a moment, then vanishes. She releases the fairy knight, "Done," and removes the harp from her torso. She plucks a single cord on its strings, and the elf knight shakes his head as though clearing it. "And done."

The knight's eyebrows rise in question. "Siren?"

"Good day to you, Sir Knight."

His gaze finds me, and a scowl creeps over his face. I take a backward step as I try to keep from hyperventilating.

Siren's expression hardens. "I said, 'Good day.'"

The elf looks to Siren, gives me a final scowl, then turns and walks off into the forest without uttering another word.

"Are you sure he won't come after me again?" I ask.

Siren nods. "Not for a few centuries."

I wipe away the sweat that had popped out on my forehead and empty my lungs.

"Are you ready to go inside?" Siren asks.

"Inside? Inside what? We're in the middle of nowhere."

"Inside my home here in the Day Lands: *Bright Tree*."

Siren raises her arm in the direction of the central tree, and I gasp as the thousands of butterflies I had mistaken for its leaves remove themselves in a rainbow storm of flittering wings.

Now revealed in full, Bright Tree is truly a woodland giant even in comparison to its fellow redwoods. Its actual leaves are the same shimmering liquid green of the emerald riding the silver band across Siren's forehead. Bright Tree's topmost branches stretch out to brush the other redwoods along the clearing's edge before climbing above them all together.

Confronted with such a spectacle, I find a word often spoken by that wizened sage Keanu Reeves best serves to express my feelings.

"Whoa!"

Siren laughs. "Whoa, indeed. Despite having lived here at Bright Tree years beyond counting, its magic and wonder never cease to amaze me. But I'll ask again, Puck, are you ready to go in?"

Words fail me, and I simply nod in response.

Siren scoops me up, and we soar into the air once again. We fly up the length of Bright Tree, and the pleasant smell of raw wood enters my nostrils as we pass through an open knothole half-hidden among a cluster of flag-sized leaves.

Bright Tree is hollow inside, but a series of furnished landings and curving staircases carved from its inner hull span the length of its considerable trunk. The landings range in scope from minute to colossal. Mirrors have been strategically placed along Bright Tree's core to capture and reflect sunlight for all the various birds, squirrels, and other woodland creatures that have made a home here. The redwood is alive with the sound of their chirps, caws, and chattering.

Swiss Family Robinson, eat your hearts out!

We touch down inside Bright Tree upon a landing furnished with tables and chairs of woven vines and crisscrossing tree branches. They rest upon a luxurious rug of green moss. The pulpy, concave walls around us are decorated with a trellis of creeper vines polka-dotted by the blooms of roses, lilies, daffodils, and just about every other flower you can imagine.

As I stand there gawking, a mastiff hound that would dwarf most horses walks up and bows his head in greeting. "Hello, Mistress," the fawn-coated dog says. "Home early today, aren't you?" His voice is every bit as deep and gravelly as the Boogeyman's. But it also carries a weight of time far greater than even that borne by Shadow Tower's master. It makes me picture a gruff chimney sweep from Victorian England whose large sideburns curl up to meet in a thick, gray mustache beneath a large, bulbous nose full of burst capillaries.

Despite having met Cat, it's still weird for me to see a talking animal. The dog's ability to speak is yet another reminder that he isn't Toto, and I'm sure as heck not in Kansas anymore.

"Hello, Dog," Siren replies. "Something came up: we have a guest."

Siren lifts her arms and, in a scene right out of a Disney cartoon, several birds leave their nests along Bright Tree's throat to fly over and remove her weapons and armor before hanging them on pegs jutting from the redwood's interior.

I'm a bit shocked to see Siren's shimmering butterfly wings depart along with her breastplate. Apparently they were attached to her armor, rather than her back. It makes her seem a lot less fairy and a little more human. But that's all right with me.

I recall how the Boogeyman's imposing figure diminished somewhat when he removed his shadow cloak, and nod to myself.

"So I smell," Dog says in response to Siren. The enormous hound pads over, and I try my best to keep from trembling with fear as he sniffs me from head to toe. As big as Dog is, I suspect like with Cat, there's still more to him.

A lot more.

A low growl issues from Dog's throat. "The smell of the Night Lands is strong on you, boy. Could it be that you are a darkling fairy in disguise come to do my mistress harm?"

"Dog," Siren says, her voice stern, "heel! I told you, Puck is our guest."

Dog gives a reluctant groan and drops to the floor in front of me. Lying there, his tongue lolls from his mouth and he begins to pant.

"Good Dog."

"Woof!"

Siren turns her attention to me. "Would you care for something to eat?"

Despite having eaten less than an hour ago, my stomach rumbles at Siren's mention of food.

Hey, I'm a twelve-year-old boy. It's got to be written down somewhere that we are supposed to eat at least once a day for every year accrued.

I nod vigorously and before I know what's happening, a chair of unfinished tree branches is being slid under me by half-a-dozen scampering squirrels. A family of chipmunks pushes a tree-stump table into place before me so that a flock of humming birds can fly over while carrying wooden plates and bowls filled with steaming hot food.

Two chattering chipmunks slide a flagon carved from wood into my hand. I pick up the cup and take a drink. The amber liquid inside tastes like the sweetest milk and honey and warms my throat and chest. I greedily take a second sip. Then a third.

"Easy, Puck," Siren says as she takes her own seat of woven tree branches across from me. "Slow down. You know what you mortals say: too much of a good thing—"

I set the cup down and wipe my chin with the back of my hand. "What is this stuff? It's great."

"Why, it's the nectar of the gods."

"You're joking, right?"

Siren shakes her head. "Not at all."

My eyes bug out of my head. "There are gods? I mean *real* ones?"

"Of course, silly," Siren says. "There are gods and goddesses alike. If there weren't, the liquid you're drinking would have to be called the 'nectar of the gnomes' or such."

I lean back in my chair, overcome with awe.

There are gods! Actual lightning-hurling, sea-parting gods!

If I'd pondered this further, I doubt I would've remained so excited. After all, it follows logically that where there are gods, devils are also sure to dwell.

16

I TRY THE BOOGEYMAN'S HAT ON FOR SIZE

After our meal in Bright Tree, Siren armors back up and informs me she has to continue her duties in the Mortal Lands for the remainder of the day. She goes on to assure me she will return when evening falls Earth-side. She says that, in the meantime, Dog will be here to guard me just as he does Bright Tree itself.

"That's all well and good," I say, "but who will protect me from him?"

Siren laughs, and the sound is like the chimes of the Aurora. "Oh, Puck! Dog will keep you safe. Won't you boy?"

The huge mastiff huffs. "As my mistress commands."

Siren scratches Dog behind the ears, waves goodbye, then flies away, leaving Bright Tree through the knothole. I watch as her silhouette disappears into a brilliant cascade of sunbeams.

I spend the rest of my afternoon in the Day Lands taking the reverse-corkscrew staircases from landing to landing, exploring the wonders of Bright Tree. Dog follows close behind me everywhere I go, watching and sniffing more to make sure I'm not up to trouble rather than to see to my well-being.

There are things in Bright Tree beyond imagining, but every time I try to take a closer look, Dog cuts me off.

"That isn't for you!" he says as he paws closed a book that was writing itself even as I read it.

"Don't touch that!" he commands as he noses his way between me and a broadsword warbling musical notes under its own power.

"Get away from there!" he barks as I examine the swirling depths of an azure crystal ball not unlike the pink grapefruit containing my alleged twin. (Well, the Boogeyman's crystal doesn't literally contain my twin, alleged or otherwise, but you know what I mean.)

On and on it goes like that for the remainder of the afternoon. As you can imagine, my restlessness makes me Dog's worst nightmare. When at last Siren returns home, I don't know which one of us is more worn out: me from getting into everything or Dog from trying to keep me out of it.

"Thank the Fae King and Queen you're home!" he tells her, then settles down onto his great belly for a nice long nap.

"What are you doing back so early?" I ask, gesturing to the sunlight-filled mirrors that I assume give Bright Tree its name. "The sun hasn't even begun to set."

Siren starts to say something, but I raise my pale hand, halting her. "Wait a minute." I roll my eyes. "I know! I know! Day and night work different here in Fairy than in my world. The Day Lands don't have night at all. The Boogeyman told me all about it. So what happens now?"

Siren shrugs. "Like I said, considering the circumstances— namely possible treachery in the Fairy court extending all the way to the King—hooking up with the Boogeyman in the Twilight Lands is far too risky. I need you to take word of what's happened to Shadow Tower."

I think of the Void, the Boogeyman, and Shadow Tower, and give an involuntary wince. I knew this was coming, but now that I'm actually here and about to plunge back into the Night Lands in order to unravel a fairy conspiracy, anxiety starts to creep up within me.

Either the reflex or my expression gives me away.

"I know this is a difficult thing to ask of you, Puck," Siren says, "but without wasting time we can't afford, I don't see any other way around it at present."

Suddenly, the toes of my shoes become the most interesting thing within proximity.

After a moment, I feel Siren's calming hand on my arm.

"I know you are just a mortal boy, Puck, but we need you.

Me. The Boogeyman. Fairy. Even your friends and family in the Mortal Lands."

Siren gently presses her hand to my chin and raises it so that I have no choice but to look directly into her lovely, freckled face. To her credit, she doesn't do her fairy mind-trick on me. She simply lets her plea speak for itself.

"Please. Help us root out the persons behind the invasion of night fae into your homeland. Help us stop this war between worlds before it starts."

Why oh why did I ever follow the Boogeyman into the Void? I think for the gazillionth time. But I give a reluctant nod of my head. "I promise."

"Good man."

Siren extends her hand, and I take it. Her blazing butterfly wings begin to beat, and we fly down the throat of Bright Tree into the underground network of its roots. There are no mirrors here to reflect either the sunlight or my ghostly white face. Darkness and shadow, the Boogeyman's bread and butter, abound here along with the smells of earth and damp.

"From here, you should be able to enter—" Siren begins.

"The Void," I finish for her. "I know." My head swivels from left to right as I glare at the shadows surrounding us in disgust. "I can *feel* its presence here."

Siren's eyebrows rise in surprise beneath her lattice silver headband. "Can you now?"

I step up to a pocket of blackness existing at the base of one of Bright Tree's massive, gnarled roots.

"You are very brave to do this, Puck."

I turn and look back at her. "Then why do I feel so afraid?"

Siren smiles, the expression lighting up her entire face. Looking at Siren there in all her glory causes something to begin to change over inside me—something bittersweet that I won't be able to place into words for quite some time.

"Brave people always are afraid, Puck," she says, "but they don't let it stop them. That's why they're brave. But here." Siren reaches into the pockets of her skirt and then pulls out what looks like a softly glowing yellow pebble. "May this will bring you courage in the dark places you must go."

I take the pebble from Siren's hand. It feels warm and alive in my palm. It's like holding a newborn chick.

"What is it?" I ask.

"A single drop of enchanted sunlight. It's changeling in nature, and can become whatever you wish, so long as what you wish is a thing of equal mass."

"Gee, thanks."

"Choose wisely, though. It's only good for one transformation."

I pocket the pebble of light and smile. "Goodbye, Siren."

"Goodbye, Puck.

"Tell the Boogeyman I said—"

"Yes? Something other than about Castle Night?"

A long pause.

"Never mind."

I wave bye to Siren and then disappear into the shadows.

I barely notice my trek through the Void. I'm too busy thinking about everything that has happened since the Boogeyman oozed out of my bedroom closet. Within a couple days' time, I've discovered that not only are fairies and wizards real, but that they stand on the brink of war—a war that someone from the Night Lands appears to be instigating. Perhaps even the King of Fairy himself. And now here I am caught up in the middle of the Boogeyman's attempt at preventing it.

The more I think about it, the more I wish I could trade places with the fairy twin I have lying asleep somewhere in a serene grove. Peace and quiet and rest—now that's the way to go. So much better than chasing after changeling monsters or undoing devious fairy plots.

I reach the Boogeyman's tower and find Cat waiting to greet me.

"I smelled you coming," she says as we descend Shadow Tower's spiraling stairs.

"How can you smell anything over Shadow Tower's ever-present stench of damp and mildew? Anyhoo, I've had a shower today thank you very much!"

We enter the cobweb-draped, candle-lit library at the base of the stairs. The Boogeyman is there in his Elizabethan garb minus his cloak and hat, hunched over a dusty, leather-bound text the size of a small table top. Every so often, he waves his hand and the book's yellowed pages turn of their own accord.

Cat frowns. "A shower? That's more than I can say for some people."

"What people?" the Boogeyman barks. He jerks upright to his usual imposing height and sniffs the air before whirling in my direction.

"Puck! What in the Night Lands are you doing here? You're supposed to be back in the Mortal Lands with your parents."

"Yes," I say, "I am supposed to be home, living a daydream, never recalling that less than two days ago I met you, came to Fairy, or faced down a changeling."

The Boogeyman scratches his bald, pale, crescent head.

"Well, yes. But my fogging of your memory was all for your own good."

I slump my shoulders. "If only I'd been so lucky. As it is, I went home only to be attacked by a rogue elf knight."

The Boogeyman's dark eyes become twin eight balls in their sockets. "A fairy from the Day Lands?"

I nod. "Siren saved me."

"Good lass!"

I frown. "Don't get too excited. When Siren, uh, did your Mesmer-thing with him, she found the elf had no knowledge of why he had come Earth-side to attack me. It was just like with the changeling."

"And all the other rogue fairies I've encountered of late," the Boogeyman says. "The fact that both day and night fae are involved in this more than confirms my suspicions that a conspiracy is afoot."

I stare at the floor, not knowing how to phrase what I have to say next. "There's something else."

"Yes?" the Boogeyman asks, impatient. "Let's have it."

I sigh. "When the elf attacked, we found a piece of parchment bearing the seal of Castle Night, er, um, the ruling family of the Night Lands."

The Boogeyman staggers backward in shocked disbelief. "You mean—?"

"I was able to hold the parchment just fine," I continue.

"Unfortunately, when Siren touched it, it self-destructed. Apparently, it was enchanted to prevent prying fae eyes from reading its contents."

"Then...the Fae King is behind this—? Impossible!"

"Let's hope so," I add in consolation.

The Boogeyman rights himself. "There's only one way to find out for sure. But first, we must see to something else. Something as equally pressing, if not more so."

The Boogeyman gestures for me to follow him. We exit the library for the study I caught him sleeping in when I first arrived at Shadow Tower. Cat leaves to prowl for intruders, be they mice, *or men.*

The study's freestanding cloak rack in the stony room's corner bends so that the Boogeyman may easily remove his crooked top hat from its perch. The Boogeyman brushes away the dust from the hat's brim. Then, to my surprise, he hands his hat to me.

A low throb pulses from the hat into my hands and travels up my arms. It is like the beating of a heart—a terrible, black heart pumping not blood but liquid shadow.

"What do you expect me to do with this?"

Rather than answer immediately, the Boogeyman sits in the broken-down chair resting in front of the now-cool hearth.

"I expect you to put it on."

"What?"

The Boogeyman leans back in his chair. "Along with tracking rogue fae, the hat also allows me to engage in the Mesmer. You've seen the bejeweled silver band Siren wears across her brow? It is what allows her to do the same."

The Boogeyman crosses his arms and legs as he eases into full explanation mode.

"These articles are the tools and adornments of our dual station, and rarities in any realm. As a rule, only the Boogeyman and the Siren may wear and use them. But under the circumstances, an exception is called for. I need you to don my hat and use the Mesmer to look inside my mind."

"I, uh," I stammer, "er, what for? I mean, why do you want me to look inside your head?"

The Boogeyman uncrosses his limbs and leans forward, his already-dark gaze blackening.

"To make sure there are no blank spots in my memory. To make sure I am not also an unknowing pawn in whatever game is being played with my folk. If the rogue fairies' memories can be wiped, then so can mine. Will you do this, Puck?"

Everywhere I go, people are asking favors of me. Oh well, what's the big deal anyway?

"Sure. Why not?"

I start to raise the Boogeyman's hat, then pause. "You don't have head lice, do you?"

The Boogeyman growls in response.

"I'm just saying."

More growling.

I sigh and nonchalantly place the Boogeyman's hat on my head. As it slides down over my brow, fiery pain unlike any I have ever experienced sears a path into my brain.

17

AN UNEXPECTED TRIP TO THE HIGHLANDS

"Yeeeeooooow!" I shout as what feels like a thousand tiny needles impale themselves into my head. I jerk the Boogeyman's crooked top hat off my head and glare at it.

"Something's wrong," I say. "This thing is hurting me."

A tired expression covers the Boogeyman's face. "That's normal."

I look up at him in disbelief. "You mean putting the hat on always feels like that?"

The Boogeyman nods. "Each and every time. Being the Boogeyman is no easy task."

"No wonder you're always in such a grumpy mood. And, yo! You could've warned me!"

The Boogeyman shrugs his massive, hunched shoulders. "The worst of it will pass. Give it a moment."

I push the hat back at him. "Uh-uh. No way. I'm done."

The Boogeyman extends a spidery, clawed hand and gently pushes the hat back in my direction.

"Please, Puck. You know what's at stake. You must use the Mesmer and read my mind to ascertain whether or not I am yet another pawn of whoever is trying to plunge the worlds of Fairy and Earth into war. Otherwise, we cannot be sure any efforts I make going forward are pure in motive."

I look around the room, taking in the stony, tapestry-draped walls; the cold block hearth; and the worn, tattered furniture. What I don't find is a way out of my predicament.

"All right," I moan.

I slowly return the Boogeyman's black hat to its perch on my head. I bite down on my bottom lip and whimper as mingling knives of fire and ice once again dig into my brain.

Wearing the hat feels like the world's worst migraine. It hurts so bad it makes me want to vomit.

Then the searing pain passes as quickly as it came. However, a dull, throbbing headache is left in its wake. I give a shuddering breath and relax my body, only now realizing I'd gone totally rigid with the sting of putting on the Boogeyman's hat.

The Boogeyman leans forward in his seat and takes my hands in his. He positions my fingers along the sides of his pasty, crescent-moon face so that I touch his temples, cheeks, and the corners of his eyes.

"Now what do I—?" I start to ask. But then my eyes lock onto the Boogeyman's dark gaze, and I tumble forward into the pools of blackness bookending either side of his hooked nose.

When I land, I find that I'm no longer inside Shadow Tower. A rolling, green pasture now stretches out before me beneath a blanket of gray fog. Several branded cows meander about, mooing as they munch the high straw grass. I start as a bearded man and a fair-skinned boy I presume to be his son walk out of the mist, arm in arm. They're dressed in kilts draped over tunic-style shirts. The man carries a musket across his shoulders and a broadsword in a leather harness strung across his hip. The lengths of several dead rabbits swing from the end of the boy's arm, apparently the bounty from the day's hunting.

"Uh, hey!" I shout. But the two of them continue walking and talking and laughing, seemingly oblivious to my presence.

It's because they're not real, I think. *Not anymore, anyway. I'm looking at the Boogeyman's memories. And judging by them, it appears the Boogeyman was alive in Scotland centuries ago.*

"So then where is he?" I ask myself. I survey my surroundings, but ol' Tall, Dark, and Scary is nowhere to be seen.

I decide to follow the man and his son. Ultimately, we wind up at a modest house of stone and wood. We go inside. A comely, blonde woman is present in the house's sole room. She greets the two of them with kisses—the man on his bearded lips, the boy on his pale cheek.

The man's wife and the boy's mother, then.

The woman takes the rabbits from her son and begins preparing them for dinner.

A few hours later, I watch as the three of them gather around a small wooden table to eat. They discuss their day in a thick Scottish burr I can't even begin to understand. But what's clear from their conversation is the love they hold for one another in their hearts. Gazing on the three of them makes me terribly homesick for my own parents.

The Boogeyman's memories flash forward. When they begin moving in real time again, night has fallen. The man and his wife lie snoozing upon beds of thick furs, the dwindling fire of the open stone chimney lighting their slumbering bodies in a warm, soft glow.

Only the fair-skinned boy is awake.

He watches the fire's dying embers from his own bed of furs, his face a mask of fear and dread that is somehow familiar.

When the last of the embers fade, I realize why I recognize the look on the boy's face. It's the one I must have worn when the Boogeyman first appeared inside my bedroom.

I feel the Boogeyman's preceding aura, and then he comes slinking out of the shadows in the room's corner. Only, it's not the Boogeyman. At least, not *my* Boogeyman.

This Boogeyman is heavyset, and has a broad face with a protruding brow and a thick, brutish jaw. Instead of a crooked top hat, he wears a medieval skull-cap of black cloth that conforms to his bulbous head. Only the shadow cloak is the same. Its living edges swirl around him in some nonexistent wind.

The brutish Boogeyman opens his cloak to reveal another fair-skinned boy who's the exact twin of the one lying in bed. The doppelganger stands silent and motionless as though in a trance.

The Boogeyman extends a ham-sized fist and gestures for the man's son to come to him.

The boy wags his head, terrified.

The Boogeyman gestures again and says something in what sounds like Latin. The tone of his guttural voice is a mixture of aggravation and impatience.

The boy shakes his head again, and the Boogeyman continues his tirade, this time pointing at the boy's parents.

After a final moment of hesitation, the boy gets out of bed and joins the Boogeyman at his side. They both watch as the doppelganger walks like an emotionless robot over to the boy's bed and climbs inside. The twin is immediately asleep.

The boy gives his parents a final look that breaks my heart, and then he and the Boogeyman withdraw into the shadows and disappear from the room.

The rest of the present Boogeyman's memories come in superluminal flashes: years of the boy training under the brute Boogeyman with the former growing older, taller, and paler with each passing year until at last he stands—or rather, hunches—like the monstrous ghoul I know from Shadow Tower.

The revelation is almost too much for my mind to bear.

The Boogeyman was the boy. I think repeatedly. *A boy just like me.*

These memories are followed by still more of the centuries the Boogeyman has spent corralling rogue night fairies. I speed through them, not really paying attention until I reach the point where I enter into the Boogeyman's creepily long life. I relive his passage through my closet, our traveling to the Twilight Lands, his being tossed out of Caroline Newton's window by the changeling, then his scrambling through portals to catch up to us.

I see his fogging of my and my parents' memories—not to mention those of our neighbors and the local policemen—then his working of the extraction spell and subsequent returning of my hometown's missing children. It all ends in a crescendo of me putting on the Boogeyman's hat and placing my hands on the sides of his face.

I release the Boogeyman and our senses become our own once more as the present rushes in to fill the vacuum of existence.

"You were human!" I shout as I wrench the Boogeyman's hat from my head. My dull headache immediately vanishes.

The Boogeyman shakes his still clearing head. "No, Puck. You misunderstand. I have always been a fairy, *more or less.*"

"But—"

"You saw the boy who accompanied my predecessor into my highland home?"

I nod. "Yeah. So?"

"He was the human, Puck. Not me. He was the true child of the mortals I called mother and father."

"I don't understand? If he was their real son, who and what were you?"

The Boogeyman's expression becomes solemn. "I told you in the Twilight Lands, Puck. I am a changeling. One who took on the appearance of the boy you saw when we were swapped at birth."

I shake my head, still not comprehending. "But why did you trade places with him? What was the purpose in it?"

The Boogeyman huffs. "Isn't it obvious? We were swapped at birth so that I could live in the Mortal Lands and build up immunity to the elements other fairies find harmful—an immunity that now allows me to function as the Boogeyman."

I glance at the floor, searching for words. "But what about sunlight? You said it still turns you into a statue like it did with the changeling. Why didn't you build an immunity to that?"

The Boogeyman nods. "You are correct. Exposure to sunlight now turns me into stone.

"But certain fairies like me are granted a choice early on as to whether we will live and die as a mortal, or become a true fae and exist for all eternity. Before we make the choice, we may walk in both night and day."

I scratch my head. "Why would anyone make a choice where they know it ultimately means they'll die?"

The Boogeyman's gaze darkles. "Oh, there are reasons, Puck. Immortality is not all it's cracked up to be. Especially when having it means you must leave the people who have loved you most."

I recall the last, tortured look on the face of the boy who was the Boogeyman when he left his parents, and understanding begins to dawn.

"But if one chooses to become a true fairy," the Boogeyman continues, "the elemental immunity still carries over. However, the checking magic of night and day are simply too powerful for a fairy to override in any true capacity.

"At least under normal circumstances.

"But enough of this."

The Boogeyman rises from his chair to tower over me. He reaches out a clawed hand, and I give him his hat.

"Were there any holes in my memory? Any periods of time that were simply barren?"

I shake my head. "Not that I saw."

The Boogeyman leans down and looks me in the eye. "You're absolutely sure? No gaps or blank spots?"

The truth of the matter is that I skimmed over quite a lot of the things contained in the Boogeyman's mind. But when I open my mouth, I find myself saying, "Nope! Not a single one."

The Boogeyman straightens as much as his hunched shoulders will allow and breathes a deep sigh of relief.

He extends a spindly arm and his shadow cloak leaves the freestanding rack to hover over and enshroud its master. The Boogeyman slips his crooked hat down over his crescent-moon head and the terrifying monster he is stands before me once again.

"So where do we go from here?" I ask.

The Boogeyman sets the curve of his elongated jaw.

"As soon as you change clothes and don your mask, we leave for the Twilight Lands. I have a bone to pick with the Fairy King."

18

HIS MAJESTY'S SECRET SERVICE

As I change back into my emo-musketeer outfit and mask, I ponder what I discovered about the Boogeyman during my Mesmer into his mind. I'd believed him to have always been a monster, but it turns out he was once a boy exactly like me.

Well, not *exactly* like me. He was raised in the Scottish Highlands centuries before I ever existed. And, in truth, the Boogeyman was never truly human at all, but a fairy changeling swapped with a mortal child at birth. This allowed the Boogeyman to live Earth-side and build immunity to metals, minerals, and other elements he now uses to capture rogue fae.

And thank goodness for it!

We're going to need that advantage if it turns out the Fae King is behind the plot to embroil Fairy and Earth in war. And right now, all signs are pointing in that direction. That's why we're headed back to Castle Twilight. The Boogeyman's going to confront the King and see what he has to say for himself.

Freshly dressed in proper swashbuckling attire, the comforting weight of Barbie's short blade riding my hip, I climb the stone steps ringing Shadow Tower's interior and join the Boogeyman outside one of the wooden doors leading into the Void.

He taps the brim of his crooked black hat at my arrival. "My hat has tracked the Fae King to this passage leading into Castle Twilight. He should be alone."

"So we'll come out the other side within Castle Twilight then?"

"Yes."

"I thought you said we should never carry metal into the Castle, much less approach the Fairy King and Queen unannounced."

The Boogeyman gives a shrug of his monstrous, hunched shoulders. "Desperate times, desperate measures."

The Boogeyman clasps together the spidery claws he calls hands. "You know, it's not absolutely necessary for you to come with me, Puck. You could stay here safe within Shadow Tower until all this mess is over and dealt with."

I cross my black-clad arms. "Are you kidding me? For all I know, the Fae King isn't behind this, and the real culprit is outside Shadow Tower right now, waiting for you to leave so he can lay siege with only Cat left behind to guard it."

"Hey!" Cat yowls from below. "I heard that!"

"No offense, Cat," I call over the edge of the stairs. "I was just saying two monstrous fairies would be harder to fight than one."

I return my attention to the Boogeyman. "Either way, I'll take my chances with you in the Twilight Lands. At least there, I should be able to see who or whatever will undoubtedly try to kill me when they make their play."

"Well stated." The Boogeyman turns and extends a claw. The door before him opens to reveal the familiar black veil of congealed shadow separating all realities from the Void. We pass through in silence, not wishing to arouse the monsters living within the Void's inky depths.

Moments later, we've left the Void by way of a cluster of shadows gathered behind a suit of gemstone armor standing within Castle Twilight. The suit is one of many stationed along either side of the purple quartz hallway in which we have arrived.

"Where to—?" I start to ask, but the Boogeyman clamps his bony hand over my mouth, allowing me to hear the thunder of fast-approaching footsteps echoing from an adjoining corridor. The Boogeyman releases me and, in a flurry of motion, spreads his cloak like a pair of massive bat wings before furling it around us. Nausea hits the pit of my stomach as our bodies go smoky and we change form—the Boogeyman into another suit of glimmering jeweled armor, me into the diamond-tipped spear it holds.

And not a moment too soon, either. Just as we solidify into our newfound shapes, a squad of marching animal-men enters the hallway. Despite not having eyes to see with in my present state, I'm able to perceive the sharp weapons in their hands and the ferocious looks on their faces. The guardsmen stomp past us, a living train of tooth and claw and fur and hoof that shakes the corridor and parts the blinking fireflies swarming overhead.

When the, uh, *manimal* fairies are gone, my atoms swirl once again, and then I'm back in my normal human shape, my last meal coming up my newly reconstructed throat.

"I think I'm going to be sick!"

I fall forward onto my knees. The Boogeyman, now once again his usual spooky self, places a bony white hand on my shoulder, steadying me.

"Gather yourself, Puck. We have pressing business to attend to."

I nod and slowly rise to my feet.

"Does all the magic you use hurt like the blazes?"

The Boogeyman shrugs. "You get used to it."

We make our way down the crystalline hall into another with a large bejeweled door at its end. The Boogeyman takes me in an arm, and I whisper a curse as I feel the shadows of his cloak entwine themselves around us once again. We ooze beneath the door, moving as a mass of dark fog, then reconfigure on the other side.

We've entered a majestically decorated bedroom. Dark, silken drapes line the walls. Where the drapes have been drawn, they reveal tall windows and walls encrusted from floor to ceiling with diamonds, opals, and rubies. A massive, four-post bed of obsidian and ivory stands in the room's center. Sheets of black velvet and white satin serve as its bedding.

Just off to the side of the bed, a man with a high ruff collar and flowing white hair sits at a lacquered oak writing desk, his back turned to us. He's seemingly unaware of our presence.

"Your Majesty," the Boogeyman says.

That's all he has time to utter before the King of all Fairy has seized the huge broadsword of black diamond that was resting against the table and leapt at us in attack.

I cringe in reflex, but manage to still have time to think: *The King's trying to kill us! He's behind all this!*

The King roars as he brings his sword crashing toward my head.

But the black diamond blade is halted by the Boogeyman's silver-laced rapier.

"What is the meaning of this intrusion?" the King spits. "I am your King!" He spins, bringing his sword around in a wide, slashing arc.

The Boogeyman's sword once again finds the King's own, preventing it from lopping off our heads.

"Forgive me, Your Majesty." The Boogeyman throws the King off balance and "His Majesty" stumbles backward. The Boogeyman presses his attack, fighting the King across the bedroom. They leave a path of destruction in their wake.

"Normally, I love a good sparring match," the Boogeyman says. "But I'm afraid we simply don't have time for this, Your Highness."

The Boogeyman's living cloak of shadow seizes the King in its inky tendrils and then rips the diamond blade from his hand. The shadow cloak lifts the King off his feet and draws him in so that the Boogeyman may grip his face in his clawed hands.

The King goes limp in the Boogeyman's arms, and I look away as Mr. Tall, Dark, and Scary begins searching the King's mind with a Mesmer.

It's over within moments. The Boogeyman and his cloak release the King. He stumbles over to his oak writing desk and falls into the velvet-covered chair in front of it.

The King shakes his head, clearing it. "How dare you use the Mesmer on your King!"

The Boogeyman bows deeply as his cloak lays the King's sword against the desk. "I beg Your Majesty's pardon. I was only doing my duty as Boogeyman. I had to be sure."

"Sure of what?" the King spits.

"That you were not part of the conspiracy to throw Fairy into war with the Mortal Lands. I am much pleased to see you remain my ever steadfast liege and lord."

"He's innocent then?" I ask.

The Boogeyman nods.

The King gets up from his chair, anger spreading across his dark, angular face. "Still you go on about plots and intrigues? I should have your long, curved head on a platter!"

"It is true!" the Boogeyman says. The thunder in his voice is enough to make the King rock back on his heels despite his own impressive size and strength. The Boogeyman bows and adds in a whisper, "Your Majesty, each fae I have captured within the past fortnight has no knowledge of why they have gone rogue. Someone or something has been wiping their minds. And now their escalated presence in the Mortal Lands is about to plunge us into war with the High Thirteen. It can be no coincidence. Someone desires this."

The King folds his muscular arms. "What proof have you?"

"My word," the Boogeyman says. "And that of this mortal boy."

The King laughs.

"It's true," I say. "Uh, er, Your Highness. An elf from the Day Lands attacked me while I was Earth-side. Someone trying to stop the Boogeyman sent him—someone from the ruling family of the Night Lands."

The King narrows his gaze on me. "And why should I believe you, boy?"

The Boogeyman glides between us and holds out his spidery hands. "Your Majesty, if you would indulge me once more?"

After a moment of hesitation, the King nods.

The Boogeyman gently moves me into position beside the King. He touches one side of the King's face with his left hand and one side of mine with his right. Then his darkling gaze swallows us. The Boogeyman acts as conduit as the memories of Dr. Stuart's office flicker from my mind into that of the King. His mind's eye sees the attacking elf, Siren coming to my rescue, then at last our finding of the parchment bearing the seal of Castle Night.

The Boogeyman releases us and the King eases back into the velvet chair at his writing desk.

"It is true," the King mutters—more to himself than either the Boogeyman or me. "I knew he wanted my crown, but I never dreamed..."

The King's words trail off, leaving us in silence.

The Boogeyman clears his throat. The sound is like a rockslide. "Who, Your Majesty? Who desires your crown?"

The King's gaze rises to meet ours.

"My younger brother, the Duke of Night. He serves as my regent in the Night Lands while the Queen and I rule all Fairy from Castle Twilight. He has long coveted my power and position. Now I would guess he is at long last making his move to seize it."

The Boogeyman straightens as much as his hunched back will allow. "Then he is a night fae in violation of the Pact, Your Highness. It falls to me to deal with him."

The King squares his already blockish jaw. "And I give you my blessing to do so, along with vital information you will need to succeed."

The Boogeyman cocks a single, hairless brow. "Your Majesty?"

"You will of course find the Duke within our ancestral home, Castle Night. However, beware: Castle Night changes location with each moonset within the Night Lands."

"Then how will we—?" I begin, but the King cuts me off with his answer before I can finish my question.

"By knowing where Castle Night is currently stationed— something I, a member of the Night Land's ruling family, can *and will* tell you."

The Boogeyman bows. "You have our gratitude, Your Majesty."

The King eyeballs his sword where the Boogeyman's cloak placed it back against his desk. He strides over and takes it in hand, holding it like a man would a cane with its tip touching the floor.

"Castle Night now rests in the Valley of Shadow at the base of the Murky Mountains. If you leave within the hour, you should have ample time to reach it before moonset."

The Boogeyman bows. "Very good, Your Majesty."

The King hefts his sword so that it lies across his shoulder. "I shall send a detachment of gruffs along with you as reinforcements."

The Boogeyman shakes his head. "No, Your Majesty."

The King cocks a disapproving white eyebrow. "Pardon?"

"Apologies, Your Highness," the Boogeyman says, "but with both day and night fae involved, whatever conspiracy is afoot appears to reach far and deep. We don't know who all is involved."

The Boogeyman gestures to me. "I fear young Puck here is the only one I may trust to accompany me on this mission."

The King sizes me up with his gaze. "He does not appear of to be of any consequence. What talent does this young mortal possess that will be of aid to you in the Night Lands?"

The Boogeyman considers for a moment. "Puck has proven himself to be quite resourceful when put to the task, Your Highness."

"Is he even a proper knight?"

"No, Your Majesty."

"Then that is something we shall have to remedy." The King lifts the sword from his shoulder and points it at me threateningly. "Step forward, Master Puck."

I look at the Boogeyman, afraid and uncertain. He nods, and I obey the King's orders.

"Kneel," the King commands.

I knew it! I knew it! He's going to lop off my head after all!

I drop to a knee, no longer strong enough to deny my fate another single second longer.

I feel the cold, razor edge of the King's diamond sword touch my shoulder and I know my end has at last come.

Goodbye, Mom. Goodbye, Dad. I love you both with all my heart.

"By the power of the Fae Lands," the King says, and I steel myself for the worst. "In the name of the King and Queen, I dub thee knight. Be thou valiant, fearless, and loyal."

To my amazement, the King's sword taps my other shoulder and then draws away.

"Arise, Sir Puck, knight of Fairy and defender of the realm."

I stand, not believing what's just happened. I went to my

knees thinking the King was going to finish the execution he started during my first trip to Castle Twilight only to rise again as a knight of Fairy. Incredible!

What happens next, I chalk to up being caught up in the moment and overcome with emotion. The words just come pouring out of my mouth before I can stop them.

"I will go to the Night Lands, Your Highness," I say. "I will help the Boogeyman find the Duke of Night and seek to clear your name. I promise."

The Fairy King smiles and nods in approval.

"Well, *Sir Puck*," I hear the Boogeyman growl from behind me. "Shall we go?"

I'm not absolutely sure, but when I turn to face him, something approaching a look of pride appears to be in his black-hole eyes.

It is quickly replaced by his usual grim expression. "Time is wasting."

I step up to the Boogeyman and join him in a bow to the King. "Your Majesty."

The Boogeyman throws his cloak over us as though we were vampires in need of protection from the sun. Then we transform into beings of smoky darkness and flow under the King's bed to disappear into the shadows lying there.

19

WHO'S AFRAID OF THE BIG BAD WOLF? ME!

"So what was all that about?" I ask as we re-enter Shadow Tower. During our trek home through the Void, the Boogeyman and I stopped at several portals only to find them closed to us. This is the first chance I've had to ask him how that could be. I couldn't risk doing so in the Void after all. To utter even a whisper there is like ringing a dinner bell for all the terrible things living in the outer darkness.

"It's looking more and more like the King's suspicions are correct," the Boogeyman growls. "And that his brother, the Duke of Night, is the one conspiring to draw Fairy and Earth into war."

"What do you mean?"

"I mean when I tried gain entry to Castle Night by way of the Void, I found the portals leading there magically sealed."

I remove my feathered musketeer hat. "Can he do that? To you? I mean, you're the Boogeyman, dude! Darkness and shadow are your version of Route 66, right?"

The Boogeyman strokes his long, jutting chin. "I wouldn't have thought it possible, no. And yet it appears it is. Either the Duke is much more powerful than I thought, or he is in league with someone possessing magic far beyond the already immense levels of sorcery wielded by royal-blooded fairies. One thing is for sure."

"Yeah?"

The Boogeyman's already black expression darkens further. "The Duke knows we're coming. Or at least, he's made preparations for such a contingency. Puck, we're going to have to be extremely careful once we leave Shadow Tower for the open Night Lands."

The Boogeyman starts down Shadow Tower's spiraling, stone stairs. I return my hat to my head and follow, barely registering the smells of rock and mildew that permeate the Boogeyman's home. Halfway down, we pass Cat slumbering away peacefully on one of the stone steps.

We reach bottom and the Boogeyman throws open one of the many wooden doors circumnavigating the tower's base. It leads to a vast stone chamber alight with the fire of the numerous flickering torches that line its walls. The chamber's round walls, vast floor, and high ceiling are totally devoid of any doors, windows, or decorations. Standing here is like being inside the sealed tomb of some ancient ruler—a ruler whose subjects thought so little of him they didn't bother to stock the place for the afterlife before sealing it up.

I'm pretty sure this is the very room I saw the T-Rex in earlier. But neither it nor its crustaceous period environment are anywhere to be seen now.

Could the doors within Shadow Tower lead to certain places at certain times, and then to different places at others? It wouldn't surprise me. Either way, I'm thankful the king of the dinosaurs isn't here to greet us with his trademark toothy grin.

"So what now?" I ask.

"Now we leave," the Boogeyman answers.

"How?"

"We go out the front door."

The Boogeyman extends his spindly, long arm toward the chamber's far wall, and a cloud of dust bursts from between the cracks in the stones as the cacophony of hundreds of granite blocks grating against one another begins echoing throughout the chamber.

I watch in amazement as a vertical split reaching from floor to ceiling appears within the chamber's far wall. It's created as the wall's blocks retract themselves in either direction, widening the split as they go.

When at last the dust clears and the blocks finish their retreat, a tall gap wide enough to accommodate a Mack truck is left behind. Beyond it lies a land enshrouded in night brimming with black, twisted trees and high, lonely mountains partially concealed by a phosphorous green mist.

The mere sight of the landscape causes hackles to rise on the back of my neck and gooseflesh to form along my arms.

The Night Lands appear very deserving of their name.

"Behold!" the Boogeyman says, "the Night—!"

"Don't you say it," I say, unable to tear my eyes away from the spookiness before me. "Don't you dare say it."

The Boogeyman frowns as though he'd been waiting forever to give the announcement I denied him, then shrugs in acceptance.

Personality points to him.

The mist in the distance parts to reveal the bright, silvery disc of the full moon forming a corona behind the black silhouette of a castle resting in a divide between the mountains.

The Boogeyman points to the castle. "That is where we must go, Puck. And we must hurry. I wasn't counting on the portals to Castle Night being closed. Wasting time trying them has placed us behind schedule. Now the moon has almost set. If we're late and it does, Castle Night will vanish to appear in a new, unknown location."

"That castle must be several miles away," I say. "How will we—?"

I hear a sound like liquid being poured from one bucket into another and glance over to see the Boogeyman changing form. His shadow cloak becomes a wispy black mane and a long tail of hair. His lower body enlarges beneath his torso, bending like a reverse "L" as it becomes something equine in shape. This new and additional torso sprouts a pair of forelegs matching the muscular, hoofed appendages his once-spindly legs have now become.

When the transformation ends, the Boogeyman stands before me as the nightmare version of a centaur from Greek mythology. He huffs through his nose and trots in place before me, getting used to his new form. Once the Boogeyman is comfortable with his new self, he extends a clawed hand in my direction. I take it and he hefts me up onto his horse's back.

Before you can say, "Hi yo, Silver! Away!" we're racing off into the night, the icy wind blowing in my face, the beat of the Boogeyman's hooves thundering in my ears. The gnarled, barren trees cresting above the green mist fly by us at incalculable speed. I clutch the dark mane of hair running down the Boogeyman's pale, bare back like my life depended on it—because it does.

Don't fall off! Don't fall off! Don't fall off!

Unfortunately, falling off the Boogeyman's back proves the least of my problems. I begin to perceive other black shapes moving in the mist around us. Shapes that have glowing yellow eyes. Shapes that are keeping pace.

I hear the sound of whistling air and the Boogeyman's hand flies up to snatch something just before it can imbed itself in my eye.

It's an arrow. One with a crooked wooden shaft, obsidian head, and raven-feathered quill. The Boogeyman snaps it in two and increases the speed of his gallop.

"Werewolves!" he shouts.

As if on cue, the baying howls of wolves erupt around us in every direction. Whistling arrows begin to fly at us out of the mist. The Boogeyman bobs and weaves and leaps, barely dodging the incoming barrage.

I grip the Boogeyman's mane even tighter and pull myself flat against him. I look up and the mist ahead parts to reveal the moon sinking farther and farther behind Castle Night.

We're not going to make it.

Much to my relief, the onslaught of arrows abruptly ends.

I guess the Boogeyman is too evasive a target.

But the thought proves only half true, for it quickly becomes clear our attackers have simply decided to try a different tactic.

Hairy, man-shaped things come bounding out of the mist to lope along either side of us on all fours. They move with a grace and speed that seems to defy the enormous, knotted muscles working beneath their fur. Their pelts range in color from brown to black to gray and every shade in between. They're dressed in clothes and jewelry made from hide and bone. These rudimentary garments leave most of their furry bodies exposed. Quivers of gnarled wooden bows and crooked arrows ride on their backs. Sharp daggers and small throwing axes made from the teeth of some impossibly large predator dangle from leather belts strapped across their waists.

Not that these creatures would seem to have any need of them.

Their padded hands and feet end in dangerous black claws, and the sharp canines in their stumpy, wrinkled muzzles glisten in the light of the setting moon.

The werewolves begin closing in. They growl and bark as they nip at the Boogeyman's flanks. Every now and again, one of them will pause long enough to stand straight and loose an arrow. Thankfully, these warped projectiles fail to find their mark.

Somewhere in the back of my mind, I think about when—what now seems like so long ago—the Boogeyman said night fairies are the truth behind the monster legends we have Earth-side.

I always envisioned werewolves to be mindless beasts of raw power. And while that would've been bad enough, the truth behind these intelligent, aboriginal creatures is far more terrifying.

One of our pursuers makes a daring leap and lands on the Boogeyman's haunches directly behind me. I shout in fear as the roaring werewolf yanks a tooth-bladed dagger from the strap at his waist and thrusts it at me.

The Boogeyman bucks, and the werewolf flies into the air to disappear into the mist, his frightened yelps punctuating his fall.

However, the Boogeyman's maneuver allows the werewolves to gain ground and encircle us so we're forced to halt our run. The Boogeyman rears up on his hind legs, kicking several of the werewolves out of our path. Those dispatched are quickly replaced by new barking faces, the werewolf pack seemingly having numbers without end.

It takes every ounce of strength I have to hang on to the Boogeyman as he keeps the werewolves at bay with his kicks.

It's the most terrified I've ever been. At least that's what I think until two gigantic trolls with pebbly gray hides and sharp, curving tusks burst into the circle, knocking aside the werewolves under foot.

The trolls stand two stories high, every bit of it seemingly muscle and gut. They raise their massive war clubs and roar at us in challenge.

The Boogeyman shifts his shape beneath me, swelling in width and length until he becomes a monstrous black bear with glistening metal claws large enough to sever a car in two with a single swipe.

The bear that's the Boogeyman charges into the trolls, bowling them over before they can bring down their clubs. They crash to the Earth like demolished buildings, and I scream as my momentum sends me tumbling forward through the air. Thankfully, the Boogeyman snatches me in the pad of his giant paw.

"Run!" he roars, his bear-monster voice the sound of thunder. "Get to the castle! Stop the Duke!"

The Boogeyman drops me onto the ground and rolls to meet the already-rising trolls in battle. I watch dumbstruck for a moment as the three of them go at. And go at it they do! The combatants become a colossal, whirling tornado of claw, fang, sinew, and club. It's only the howls of the werewolves circling around them toward me that get my feet moving again.

I run as fast as I can in the direction of Castle Night, the baying werewolves hot on my heels. With my every other visible puff of breath, the green mist divides to show me the last of the moon's luminous round shape dropping behind the castle.

I'm not going to make it! I'm not going to—!

I slam into what feels like a rock covered in fur and slide down its length to the ground, stars circling before my eyes.

I feel a clawed hand grab the clothes at the scruff of my neck, and the ground beneath me falls away as I'm hoisted into the air to look the upright werewolf who has accosted me directly in his snarling, hairy face. His fur is black and a scar from whatever wound took his left eye runs down his face from brow to cheek. Studs of white bone and black feathers pierce his well-chewed ears and the bridge of his wrinkled muzzle.

I free Barbie from my belt only to have the werewolf slap the weapon from my hand. He flinches in pain when the back of his paw makes contact with the dagger.

"Silver," he growls. His breath is hot and smells of rotted meat.

Without another word, the werewolf heaves me over his shoulder as though I were a sack of grain. He begins striding forward in the direction from which I came. As if in mockery, the mist behind us parts to show me the last of the silvery moon sink below the horizon. As it does, the black silhouette of Castle Night vanishes from view.

According to what I've heard, the Duke's ancestral home will have now appeared at a new and secret location.

My thoughts take a bleak turn.

The castle is gone, and we have no way of finding it. We've failed. All is lost. We're done for.

Overcome with fear and despair, I close my eyes and allow darkness to swallow me.

20

CAPTURED

In my dream, I sit inside a classroom at school filled with stacks of books and pictures of Shakespeare, Edgar Allan Poe, and other historical literary figures. A storm rages outside the rectangular windows lining the room's eastern wall, spitting bolts of lightning and torrents of rain. My English teacher, Mrs. Brooks, is at the dry-erase board, oblivious to the weather as she drones on about the differences between subjects and predicates, and adjectives modifying nouns, and a million other dull, boring things I couldn't care less about.

Mitchell Maedel sits in the front row, ignoring the curly-headed Caroline Newton as she taps him incessantly on the shoulder and tries to pass a love note written on glitter-sprinkled pink paper that is sure to have "yes" and "no" boxes for him to check, depending on his feelings where she's concerned.

The note is what tells me I'm dreaming. If it were real, Caroline would have simply texted Mitchell on her sparkly pink cell-phone.

Sorry, Caroline, but judging by Mitchell's cold-shoulder treatment, I'm guessing it will be a "no."

I look down and realize that, as usual, I'm sketching a monster in my notebook rather than taking the notes I'll be in desperate need of come test time.

The monster I've drawn on the page is a particularly gruesome figure. The creature looks like a combination of that infamous Dracula knock-off, Count Orlock, and a Todd McFarlane-rendered Batman—one with a crooked top hat instead of a cowl.

The monster's black eyes seem to actually leer at me. It's as if my creation literally wants to jump off the page and attack.

Then suddenly it does!

The thing's bony claws press up out of the page and reach for my throat. I scream and leap from my desk as I brush the notebook onto the floor. Dream or no dream, I'm scared out of my wits.

"You will not disrupt my classroom!" Mrs. Brooks shouts. The eyes behind the lenses of her beaded, horn-rimmed glasses have closed to narrow, accusing slits.

My teacher's behavior is very uncharacteristic of her. Normally, Mrs. Brooks keeps discipline without having to raise her voice. She's also one of the few teachers who will go out of their way to give me the extra time and care my *condition* demands.

But this is a dream, after all.

Apparently a bad one.

"To the principal's office with you!" Thunder from the storm outside punctuates Mrs. Brooks's words.

"Freak!"

I start to walk out, and the class erupts into a chorus of laughter led by the normally good-natured Mitchell Maedel. Their hateful guffaws follow me all the way to the front office.

The principal's administrative assistant is a gorgeous African-American lady I've never seen before. She sits at a wooden desk adorned with a plaque bearing the name "Catherine" as she types away on a much-too-large antique typewriter. There is something distinctly predatory in the graceful way she strokes the keys. It makes even this mundane activity seem somehow both exciting and dangerous.

"The principal will see you now," she drawls.

"Uh, thanks, Ms. Catherine."

She winks. "Call me Cat."

I step through the front office into Principal Lawson's inner sanctum. Instead of a normal office space, I find an ominous stone chamber filled with cobweb-draped bookshelves. Burning candles are positioned intermittently along the tops of the shelves, dripping wax onto holders carved from human skulls.

The only thing here one might expect to find in a normal principal's office is the large desk standing in front of me at the room's center. An office chair is stationed on its other side, its back turned to me. When the chair whirls around, it's not Principal Lawson who I see sitting there, but the grandfatherly Dr. Stuart.

He grins wickedly and takes a single finger and pushes his eyeglasses up the bridge of his nose. "You've been a bad boy, Puck."

"Puck?" I say. "My name's not Puck. It's—"

"Silence!" he barks. And I mean literally.

Dr. Stuart rips his glasses off his face. Within seconds the five-o'clock shadow that had been growing along his jaw has become a full, bushy beard.

He abruptly stands, toppling over the chair behind him. He grimaces as if in pain and reaches up and seizes the collar of his shirt. I notice the hand gripping his shirt is no longer a hand at all, but a furry paw.

"Now look what you've done," he growls between rows of teeth that lengthen into glistening fangs before my eyes. He tears away his shirt to reveal a torso of knotted muscle covered in dense gray fur. He sucks in a huge breath of air and then gives voice to a howl that sends my hands to my ears and the rest of me retreating out the door in terror.

I burst into the front office, and my heart leaps inside my chest when I see Mom and Dad there awaiting me with open arms. I slam into them and enfold them in an embrace.

"Mom!" I cry. "Dad! Thank goodness you're here!"

"No mom or dad here," Mom says. But her voice isn't her own. It's a musical Irish brogue. I look up and see that it's not my mother and father who now hold me, but two fairies—a red-headed lady with shimmering butterfly wings and a hissing creature covered in snake scales.

"Just us freaks."

The fairies begin cackling. I try to pull free of them, but they refuse to let go. My struggles only make them laugh that much harder.

The two fairies drag me into the hallway outside the front

office, their menacing laughter adding to that of the guffaws of my classmates still echoing down the corridor.

The real-life version of the monster I drew in my notebook stands hunched over at the hallway's end, his massive bulk filling it from floor to ceiling. I realize the two fairies are pulling me toward him and I begin to kick and yell.

"No! No! No!"

As I fight, I look down and see that the T-shirt and jeans I was wearing have been replaced by a Scottish kilt and tunic.

I CONTINUE SCREAMING AS I start awake in the world of the Night Lands. Lightning streaks through the cloudy night sky, and my yell is eclipsed by the echo of thunder and the pitter-pat of softly falling rain.

"Quiet!" an inhuman voice barks.

Something to my right moves with blinding speed, and I flinch hard enough to tumble over backward. I yelp just as the clawed fist of a tawny werewolf smashes against the wooden bars of the rolling timber cage imprisoning me. The werewolf growls at me for a moment then strides on ahead, walking upright on two hind legs as he goes.

I hug myself as he leaves, shivering from the aftershock of our encounter as much as from the cold and damp surrounding me.

I look beyond the bars of my moving prison into the curtain of drizzle outside. The Boogeyman is in a similar wooden cage beside me, though his is much bigger, and what appear to be ancient runes are carved along the lengths of its bars. Amazingly, he's asleep.

Our wheeled jailhouses are pulled along on ropes by the two towering trolls the Boogeyman fought in his monster-bear form. A female werewolf covered in silvery-gray fur walks upright along behind them, cracking a leather whip at the backs of their tree-trunk-sized legs as she barks commands. While the trolls appear to be much the worse for wear, I'm guessing they came out on top in their fight with the Boogeyman as they're out there while the two of us are behind bars.

The werewolf pack that ambushed us lopes along through

the misty black forest creeping by on either side of us. Some of the pack's members move on four legs, others on two. All of them make frequent stops to shake the rain from their fur.

Despite the tawny werewolf's warning about making noise, I decide to try and get the Boogeyman's attention.

"Psssst!" I yell-whisper. "Hey! Boogey!"

"I told you to call me 'Boogeyman,' Puck." The Boogeyman doesn't bother opening his eyes. "And no need to whisper. As long as you don't have any more nightmares and decide to start screaming your head off again, I think our 'gracious hosts' will leave us alone for the time being."

"What happened?" I ask.

The Boogeyman raises his head and opens his dark eyes. A white, clawed index finger appears from beneath his furled shadow cloak like a sliver of moon emerging from a dark cloud. The Boogeyman points at the female werewolf driving the trolls. "Turns out the werewolves have a shaman priestess. While I was busy with the trolls, she conjured me into this cage. They stuck you into yours shortly thereafter."

The Boogeyman raises his spindly, long arms in a gesture of helplessness. "And so here we are."

"Can't you just change into something small enough to slip between the bars, and then something else large enough to get us out of here?" I rub my chin, considering. "Maybe a bulldozer? Or a tank? Yeah! A tank. That should do it."

The Boogeyman shakes his long, gruesome head.

"Even with my shadow cloak strengthening my natural changeling abilities, shifting into a shape of disproportionate mass requires extreme skill and concentration. The giant bear form is hard enough, but to try and become something on such a scale that's mechanical to boot…? No, I'm afraid any attempts I made at becoming something like what you suggest would not last long enough to do us any good."

The Boogeyman looks around his cage, and a thin stream of air forces its way between his ghastly pale lips. "Besides, under the current circumstances, it's a moot point. The runes carved into the bars of my cage bind me here and keep me from using my magic. And of course we no longer have any idea where

Castle Night rests, so there's little point in an escape attempt. I mean, where would we escape to?"

I stand only to be forced to snag hold of the slick, wet bars of my prison to keep from falling down again as we bump and plod along. "Then how will we complete our mission? How will we find out if the King's brother is behind the war looming between Earth and Fairy?"

The Boogeyman's massive, cloaked shoulders rise and fall in a shrug.

"So we're sunk, then?" I ask.

"Unless someone comes along and frees us."

At this moment I'm extremely glad it's raining. The cold drizzle should help to mask the hot tears that have begun to sting my eyes.

"Do not fear, Puck," the Boogeyman says, displaying an uncharacteristic moment of humane behavior. Apparently the rain isn't very good camouflage after all. "I've been in worse situations than this and come out the other side just fine."

"Really?"

"Well, no," he huffs. "Not really. But as you mortals say, look on the bright side: things surely can't get any worse."

At that moment, a roar like the explosion of an erupting volcano splits the night sky. I thrust my head between the bars of my cage. The damp wood grates against my skin and impales tiny, wet splinters into my cheeks, but I fail to register the pain.

I'm too flabbergasted by the sight of the plumes of billowing fire spraying from the long, scaly throat of the enormous winged dragon dropping out of the clouds above.

21

DRAGON RIDERS

What was that old movie with the killer shark? You know, the one with the menacing piano music and the tagline, *Just when you thought it was safe to go back in the water?*

Whatever its name, I feel like I'm in it right now. Except, the killer beast here isn't a great white torpedoing through the water after me.

It's much, much worse.

Since I ventured through my closet into the world of Fairy, I've seen shadowy Boogeymen, changeling snake-monsters, murderous elf knights, savage werewolves, and hulking trolls. But the beast of legend plummeting from the black storm clouds overhead is by far the most awesome and terrible creature I've laid eyes on yet.

I grip the wooden bars of my mobile prison as though they were the last remaining threads of my sanity and watch speechless as a great bat-winged dragon with the dark brown horns, spines, and pale underbelly of a horny toad opens its fang-filled mouth and breathes fiery death at the monsters holding the Boogeyman and me captive.

The two massive, tusked trolls at the head of our party turn stumpy vestigial tail and run, vaulting over the Boogeyman's and my cages before proceeding to knock clusters of yowling werewolves out of their path like tiny toy soldiers.

"It carries the sun in its belly!" one troll shouts.

"The day fire!" blares the other. "Run for your worthless lives!"

And run for their worthless lives they do. The trolls. The werewolves. Even their shaman priestess. In no time at all, only the Boogeyman and I remain behind to face the not-so-mythical fire-breathing dragon. But then, it's not like the Boogeyman or I have a choice in our present incarcerated state.

The ground quakes as the dragon touches down in front of our cages. I fall to the floor of my wooden prison and scramble backward on my hands and feet into a corner to cower in fear.

To his credit, the Boogeyman shows a bit more courage (to make an understatement). He glides up to the bars of his wooden cell and wraps his bony white claws around them. His fingers smoke where they touch the runes, but his face fails to betray any sign of the pain holding the bars must cause him.

Despite our growing familiarity with each other, this serves as a good reminder to me that, in the end, the Boogeyman is one rough, tough monster far removed from the Sesame Street Muppet variety.

The Boogeyman levels his darkling gaze on the dragon, and I'll be doggoned if the beast doesn't retreat a step.

"I remember you," the Boogeyman says, his voice the guttural purr of a man-eating tiger. "Didn't I bring you in once a few centuries ago? As I recall, you had quite the penchant for escaping Earth-side to devour wayward unicorns at twilight—?"

To my astonishment, the fearsome dragon bows its massive, horned head. "His shadowiness honors me with his notice. That was indeed me."

The dragon's voice is female, and echoes through the drizzling rain like thunder dipped in honey.

The dragon heaves its mountainous shoulders in a shrug.

"In my defense, unicorns *are* the most delicious of the Day Lands equines."

She begins to chuckle.

Unbelievably, the Boogeyman joins in—at least until he sees the look of mingled disgust and disbelief on my face.

He adjusts his cloak and clears his throat, regaining his composure. "My Lady, I'm afraid I must question you as to your intentions in our regard—?"

The she-dragon smiles and drool falls from her mouth to touch the rain-soaked ground and send up billowing clouds of steam.

"Oh, let me assure his shadowiness, *I am no lady.*"

Thunder cracks and lightning flashes.

With speed belying her immense size, the she-dragon raises the single, hooked talon extending like a scythe from the outward bend of her right wing and rakes it at the Boogeyman.

"No!" I shout.

But it's no good. The dragon's talon connects, severing its target completely in two.

When it's all over, the Boogeyman stands in the drizzle unharmed, his cage lying in halves on either side of him.

I breathe a deep sigh of relief only to shriek again when the dragon slashes her talon in my direction. My cage parts, and my bottom quickly finds itself soaking in a muddy puddle.

"Thanks," I huff. "I think."

I crack my arms like twin whips, slinging off the muck my gloved hands stuck themselves in when I landed.

The Boogeyman bows to the she-dragon. "We are in your debt—?"

"I am simply called Dragon by most, Your Shadowiness."

"And you may call me Boogeyman." He nods in my direction. "That mud-caked disaster over there is Puck."

I climb to my feet, brushing sludge from the seat of my pants. "Everyone's a critic."

I join the Boogeyman at his side, glad to be wearing the musketeer hat so at least the falling rain doesn't soak my head.

"While I appreciate your adherence to protocol, Dragon," the Boogeyman continues, "there's no need to carry on with such. From now on, we shall simply be three friends without rank or title among us."

Dragon bows her head. "As his shadow—as you wish, Boogeyman."

"Tell me," the Boogeyman says, "why have you freed us? Not that I am ungrateful. But not many from the Night Lands behave so favorably in regard to me—especially if they've had a chance to be in my sack."

Dragon laughs. The sound is like ominous music. Not bad music. Just *ominous*.

"When you captured me, you were in the right," Dragon says. "I knew the rules of the Pact and broke them. You were merely doing your job. I knew it was nothing personal."

The Boogeyman nods. "Quite right."

"As to why I freed you and your tasty-looking friend here—"

Gulp!

"I have no love for werewolves and even less for trolls," Dragon continues. "And any enemy of theirs is definitely a friend of mine. When I saw you, I couldn't just leave you to share the same cruel fate their clawed hands have already inflicted on so many of my kind."

Anger begins to boil in Dragon's huge, amber, serpent's eyes, and I slide as close to the Boogeyman as I can without clinging outright to the hem of his shadowy cloak.

"I will not rest until every last one of those egg-stealing thieves has met justice."

The Boogeyman reaches forth a bony, black-taloned hand and pats Dragon's scaly muzzle. "Dragon, you are one after my own heart. Thank you again for the kindness you have shown us."

The rain washes the anger from Dragon's face. "If only I could do more."

"Uh," I stammer. "P-p-perhaps you can."

Dragon smiles, exposing row upon row of jagged, yellow fangs. I've seen such teeth before. The werewolf who leaped upon the Boogeyman's centaur back tried to jab one into my heart.

"Your little Shadow has found his tongue."

"Puck is not my Shadow," the Boogeyman groans, "but if he does anything, it's find his tongue. Incessantly so."

I cross my arms and glare at the Boogeyman, momentarily forgetting my usual state of fear where he concerned. "Enough out of you. I'm trying to help us, here. You're just standing there getting wet."

Dragon chuckles. More drool. More clouds of steam hissing

up from the ground. "Please, if I may be of further service, do not hesitate to ask."

"Er," I stammer, still skittish at being face-to-face with a real live dragon, "do you, ah, happen to know where Castle Night... is...by chance? Um, right now...I mean? We, ah, kind of need to, ah, get there—?"

Dragon shakes her head. "No."

The Boogeyman and I deflate as the air leaves our lungs in twin huffs.

Thunder echoes in the distance.

"But I do know someone who would."

New ball game, folks.

"You do?" I say, my fear of Dragon and the stammer it caused vanquished by her good news. "Who? Will you take us to them?"

"Puck," the Boogeyman snaps. "Don't impose upon Dragon so. She just freed us from captivity and almost certain death. We have no right to—"

"I'd be happy to take you to her," Dragon says.

"All right, Dragon." I say. "To who?"

"To whom," the Boogeyman corrects.

"Why, the Fairy Godmother of course." Dragon says.

"Fairy Godmother?" I say. "You've got to be kidding me!"

"Not at all," Dragon replies. "She's certain to know where Castle Night appeared this moonrise. But there's good news and bad news."

I throw up my hands. "Of course. Come on. Lay it on us."

"Well," Dragon begins, "the good news is, I can take you to her, no problem."

I sigh. "And the bad news?"

"The bad news is, the Fairy Godmother tends to be one of those fairies who likes to test or bargain for her services."

"That doesn't sound so bad," I say, relieved.

"There is one other thing," Dragon says. Distant thunder punctuates her words.

"Yes?" the Boogeyman asks.

"The werewolves may have captured you to eat later as food," Dragon says, and I shiver. "Then again, they may have simply wished to collect the bounty."

The Boogeyman and I stiffen in surprise. "Bounty?" we exclaim in unison.

Dragon nods. "The Duke of Night has placed quite a price on your head." She looks directly at me, answering my unvoiced question. "Both of them. We shall have to be very careful during our journey to the Fairy Godmother."

I turn to the Boogeyman. "The King was right. The Duke *is* behind this."

The Boogeyman shushes me, but not before Dragon tilts her gigantic, horned head in question.

"Behind what?"

"I'm afraid we can't say, Dragon," the Boogeyman says. "Just know that we are here in the Night Lands on the King's official business. In aiding us, you will be aiding him. Your kind offer to continue doing so will only see you further in his good graces."

Dragon huffs, sending twin jets of black smoke from her nostrils that turn the rain in their path to steam as they go. "I'm afraid I don't have much use for anyone's good graces anymore. But I will certainly help you as I agreed."

Dragon spins around, slinging showers of rainwater from her tremendous, spiny back. Her large, brisk movements shake the earth beneath our feet. She extends her right wing to the ground, creating a makeshift ramp, and gestures for us to climb aboard.

"Hop on, gentlefairies. The Fairy Godmother awaits. We can't dally if we want to get there and still have time afterward to find Castle Night before the moon sets again."

The Boogeyman glides forward. His inky body hovers up Dragon's wing onto her back and halts among the column-length spines jutting from between the rolling hills of her shoulders. I reluctantly follow and take a place at his side.

"Hold on like your lives depended on it, my friends," Dragon calls over the sound of the wind and rain. "Because they do."

Dragon begins to flap her wings—wings that are more voluminous than the sails of the world's largest wind-powered ship. The shadowy tendrils of the Boogeyman's cloak wrap themselves around me and several giant quills within proximity, securing the two of us firmly to Dragon's back. Moments later, we're airborne and on our way to see the Fairy Godmother, death lashing out violently around us on all sides in the form of slick rain, gale-force wind, striking lightning, and uncompromising gravity.

22

THE FAIRY GODMOTHER
DRIVES A HARD BARGAIN

The storm has cleared and the Night Lands moon has risen to its zenith and begun to sink again by the time Dragon, the Boogeyman, and I descend into a valley of craggy, barren rock to approach the cliff-top remains my travel companions have informed me serve as the Fairy Godmother's home.

Although the rain stopped relatively early during our flight, the temperature of the altitudes we were traveling at proved horribly frigid. While Dragon appeared impervious and indifferent, the Boogeyman and I spent the entire miserable trip all but encased in a shell of frost. It was only the magic of the Boogeyman's shadow cloak that prevented the two of us from coming to an icy grave on Dragon's back.

We land, and the three of us shake the frost from our bodies. Thankfully, Dragon is courteous enough to wait until the Boogeyman and I are safely down before she rids herself of the ice that has accumulated on her back.

"Fr-Fr-Fr-From n-n-now on," I stutter as I shiver, "I'm t-t-t-taking the b-b-b-bus!"

While our bodies are now shed of ice, the temperature here at this high place is still near freezing. It causes our breath to issue before us in visible puffs of air. I rub my shoulders with my black-gloved hands as I survey our surroundings.

The three of us stand in an ancient, crumbling arena of gray stone. In the moonlight, the structure looks a lot like the images of the Roman Coliseum I've seen on the History Channel, only this place is in even worse shape. Fruitless black roots twist web-like over the stadium and its decrepit walls, slowly tearing them down brick by brick, century by century. There are pools of deep pitch soaked irrevocably into the already-black dust of the arena floor, and the trace smells of blood and rot are everywhere. The night sky above doesn't help matters, either. This place is graveyard eerie, and being here makes me long for home more than ever.

Why does everything in the Night Lands have to play like a bad dream?

That other annoying voice in my head answers almost immediately.

Duh! This is the Night Lands. Home of the Boogeyman. What did you expect?

"Well, well. It appears I have guests."

The three of us whirl around to see a squatty, shriveled old toad of a woman standing hunched over behind us. Everything about her is wrinkled and sagging—from her layers of chins to her huge round belly. Her nose is as pointy and hooked as the Boogeyman's. Her furrowed skin is zombie gray. Yellow cataracts stretch across her eyes, seemingly blinding her to this world. Her lips twist up into a smile revealing toothless, black gums that match the clothes draped over her squat body and the funeral veil raised above her liver-spotted forehead. She supports her substantial bulk on a cane of dark, petrified wood. Looking at her makes my creep-o-meter go off the charts. If this is the Fairy Godmother, she's definitely not the one from the storybooks. This is one dark, ugly night fae.

Her expression darkens. "I don't like guests. Especially the uninvited kind."

The Boogeyman bows deeply. The motion has the same *wrongness* characteristic of all his gestures. The ground seems to rise up to meet him rather than the other way around.

"Forgive our intrusion, Lady Godmother. We have come seeking your assistance in a most desperate matter."

"Yes. In regard to my nephew, the Duke of Night. I know."

"You know?" I exclaim. "How?" I quickly clamp my hands over my mouth, sorry to have turned the Fairy Godmother's blind eyes in my direction.

The Fairy Godmother laughs as though she was able to sense my fear. "I'm the Fairy Godmother, *Puck*. I know all—and see all—despite my physical condition."

The Boogeyman glides forward. "Then, My Lady, you know that we require the location of Castle Night. And that our need in this matter is great. Will you help us?"

A grin reappears on the Fairy Godmother's flabby, shriveled face.

"I thought you'd never ask."

She begins circling the Boogeyman and me, moving in a clumsy, tripod locomotion of petrified cane and bare, gnarled feet. The Boogeyman remains still, but I turn with her, not daring to give my back to this nasty old fairy for one second.

"In order for me to share the location of Castle Night," she says, "I require that you each pass one of three tests. One of strength. One of intellect. And one of character. If you are successful in all three, then I will give you what you ask."

"And if we are not?" Dragon asks.

The Fairy Godmother slows in her circling. "Then I shall take a year off each of your lives for my trouble."

"But we are immortal," Dragon says.

The Fairy Godmother gives a knowing smile. "Not all of you. At least, not yet. And I would be more than happy to allow the one who is not to suffer the consequences of failure for all three."

"What are you talking about?" Dragon asks.

The Fairy Godmother ignores her question. Instead, she pauses to examine the twisting talons extending from her gray, liver-spotted hand.

I guess she does have some kind of second sight. Literally.

"Three years of life," she says. "A small thing to ask, really. I mean, do you truly need to endure a few final years of frailty and sickness? Is it really all that important that you are around to see the last of your grandchildren be born?"

With speed belying her age, the Fairy Godmother whirls to face me directly.

"Do you agree?"

I gasp and retreat to the Boogeyman's side. He turns so that his broad, hunched back shields me from the Fairy Godmother.

"This is your risk, Puck," the Boogeyman whispers, "and so also your call. Dragon is right. She and I are immortal unless we come to some unnatural end. Which is entirely possible, admittedly, but highly unlikely. We fae are very hard to kill outright. Keeping us dead is harder still. You on the other hand…" the Boogeyman looks back over his shoulder to be sure neither Dragon or the Fairy Godmother can hear him. "You're mortal. By definition, your nature is to die. If we fail here, then it would mean your death would come that much sooner. And despite what the Fairy Godmother says, trust me: losing years of your life is *not* easy. Each and every moment with those you love is a treasure not to be squandered needlessly."

The agonized look on the face of the young, redheaded Scotsman as he left his parents flashes in my mind.

He wasn't just some boy, I think. *He was a younger version of the Boogeyman from centuries ago. And the pain that day held for him still pierces his heart even now.*

Suddenly, the Boogeyman's expression hardens. He steps back from me, visibly embarrassed. "I was merely stating the facts. No need to become sentimental."

He must have seen the pity in my eyes and decided he wanted no part of it.

I decide to ignore the Boogeyman's posturing and focus on our present dilemma. "If we don't find Castle Night, and Earth and Fae go to war, there'll be a lot more lost than just a few years of my life, won't there?"

The Boogeyman's head rises and falls in a slow nod.

"Then I don't really have any choice, do I? We have to go through with the Godmother's tests."

"The test of character has been passed," the Fairy Godmother proclaims in a loud voice that startles the three of us. "At least for now."

The Fairy Godmother fixes her nonexistent gaze on me. "But you and I must still have words before you leave this place, boy."

Gulp.

Dragon steps forward and the ground at our feet quakes.

"What is your test of strength, Godmother? I am ready for it."

"Indeed you are, my dear," the Fairy Godmother says. "Indeed you are."

The Fairy Godmother extends an arm of dangling black cloth and gray flab toward the arena's western wall.

"That wall has long obstructed the view of the setting moon. Remove it, and you shall have passed—"

Dragon rears up on her hind legs and roars as she spreads her wings and belches flame into the night sky. This gesture alone causes the arena to shake around us. When she comes down, she charges for the western wall, moving in a fast, herky-jerky crawl of leg and wing. Her body slams into the side of the stadium with the force of a sonic boom.

Surprisingly, the arena wall holds, anchored by the twisting black roots encasing it. But Dragon refuses to give up. She digs in with her hind legs and pushes with what must be the power of a hundred locomotives. At last, the roots holding the wall together in place pop and rip in a cacophony of sound punctuated by a rumbling avalanche of stone.

Dragon roars in victory and breathes a massive plume of fire into the sky that I'm sure is visible for miles in every direction.

When the dust clears, we are treated to a magnificent view of the fast-sinking moon.

"Well done," the Fairy Godmother says. "I can't wait to show off the new renovation to my sweetie, the Shadow Wight of Dark Hollow. He just loves a good moonset." The Fairy Godmother winks a single blind eye. "It gets him all frisky, if you know what I mean."

I try to stop my gorge from rising as I picture the Fairy Godmother making out with some other gruesome, nether-worldly thing.

The Fairy Godmother turns in the Boogeyman's direction. "Now, lastly, for you, Lord Boogeyman. A test of intellect."

"I am ready, My Lady."

The Fairy Godmother scowls. "Then riddle me this, Lord Boogeyman: a changeling hag from the Night Lands attends an evening funeral in the Mortal Lands, passing herself off to the humans as a beautiful young maid. At this funeral, she meets the most handsome of mortal men, and falls madly in love with him."

The Fairy Godmother leans over her cane and stares up into the Boogeyman' eyes.

"The following night, the hag ventures back into her lover's village and drowns a child. *Why?*"

"Hey, that's not fair," I shout. "There's no logical reason for the hag to kill a child. Much less at random."

The Boogeyman places a bony claw on my shoulder.

"Puck—"

I whirl to face the Boogeyman. "Three years of my life are at stake here, Boogeyman! She at least has to ask a riddle that's fair. One that makes sense and can actually be solved."

"Calm down, Puck," the Boogeyman bellows. "The riddle does make sense if you are fae. *Or a hunter of them.*"

The Fairy Godmother grins, exposing her rotted gums. "You have the answer to my riddle then?"

The Boogeyman nods. "I do indeed, My Lady. You see, the hag was in love with the mortal, and would've wanted to see him again."

I throw up my hands in frustration.

"Yeah? So?"

The Boogeyman sighs and shakes his gruesome head. "She met her lover at a funeral. So, in her night fae mind, the way to see him again would be to have another funeral. And in order for there to be another funeral, someone else had to die." The Boogeyman sighs. "The child was merely a casualty of the hag's twisted love."

"You mean she killed the child just because she thought her lover would attend the funeral?" I ask.

"And so that she could see him there," the Boogeyman says as if this made perfect sense.

"And you guys think that's *normal?*"

The Boogeyman nods, and I begin to feel sick.

"Ah, yes," the Fairy Godmother crones wistfully. "The things we do for love. My dear Shadow Wight had to orchestrate all sorts of destruction and pestilence before I would finally agree to go out with him. He's a hopeless romantic."

At this moment, I'm no longer feeling sick. I am sick! I bend over and the last remaining contents of my stomach heave out onto the arena floor.

"Your young companion has quite the weak stomach," the Fairy Godmother says.

"Tell me about it," Dragon says. "Thank goodness it rained on our way here. Otherwise, I would've been wearing that on my back our entire trip."

"Fairy Godmother, we have passed your tests," the Boogeyman says. "Now, we would appreciate it if you would fulfill your end of our bargain. I hate to press you, but time is of the essence. The moon sinks ever lower, and we still don't know where to find Castle Night."

The Fairy Godmother frowns. "Very well. But I shall only tell one of you and leave it to him to share the information."

From the corner of my eye, I sense the Fairy Godmother closing the distance between us.

"The boy," she says. "In private."

Without warning, masses of dark, tangled roots erupt from the ground at my feet. Moving with lightning speed, they form a cocoon that seals me off from Dragon and the Boogeyman and leaves me in utter darkness…*with the Fairy Godmother.*

23

I LEARN THE TRUTH

*A*re *you afraid of the dark?* That's the title of a show that used to be on Nickelodeon (I've caught reruns of it online). It was created by a dude who went on to write some pretty cool books. The show was about a group of kids who called themselves the "Midnight Society." Each episode, they would sit around a campfire and tell scary stories about ghosts, monsters, and just about every other nasty critter of legend. Usually, each episode had a happy ending. But sometimes...*sometimes*...the show's protagonist wouldn't make it out of danger unscathed, much less alive.

As I stand here with the toad-like Fairy Godmother—both of us enshrouded in a darkness of which I am very, *very* afraid—separated from my own spooky version of the Midnight Society by a cocoon of enchanted vines, I wonder which kind of episode this situation would qualify as: one where the hero makes it out alive or...*or the other kind.*

The Fairy Godmother's ragged voice comes to me through the dark. "Come closer, boy."

A ball of dim green light ignites before me. The light hovers in the pitch, bobbing up and down as it grows bright enough for me to make out the Fairy Godmother where she stands on the other side of it. Looking at the Godmother in the ball's dim light is like viewing her through a pair of night vision goggles—every horrendous wrinkle and hairy mole is highlighted in a ghastly shade of green.

I swallow hard and step forward.

"Who are you?" the Godmother asks.

Before I can answer, swirling green images take shape within the bobbing circle of light, only to be quickly replaced by still more. They're all of me: stuffing my face with popcorn as the light of some monster movie flickers across my face; being sent to my special, "non-stimuli" desk in Mrs. Brooks' classroom; and lastly, sitting in between Mom and Dad as the ridecar we're in begins creeping its way into an amusement park spook house. An unbridled grin of joy is plastered across the pale green image of my face.

It's at this moment that I realize the floating ball of jade light is a crystal like the Boogeyman's grapefruit—one that's streaming my memories like YouTube videos, albeit from a third-person perspective.

The Fairy Godmother clucks her disease-riddled tongue in disapproval. "That isn't you. You're not answering the question."

"Lady," I spit. Then I remember to hold my big mouth in check. "Lady Godmother," I continue, "I'm sorry. I don't have a clue as to what you're talking about."

The old hag sighs. "Haven't you ever wondered why you're so fascinated with those you incorrectly refer to as monsters? Or why you can never seem to sit still and take things at a mortal's pace? Or why you hear voices in your head?"

I shrug. "I always chalked it all up to my condition, I guess. As for monsters, well, they're just cool."

Something approaching a smile crosses the Fairy Godmother's hideous face. "Yes, I suppose we are *cool*, as you say."

Her expression darkens. "But these are superficial answers. *Mortal answers.* Now, answer the question: *who are you really?*"

My life once again starts to play within the hovering crystal ball. This time, the crystal shows us the night the Boogeyman came slinking out of my closet. Everything is the same, from Tall, Dark, and Scary's sniffing me to him coming back again with the changeling in his tattered brown sack.

Then, much to my astonishment, the ball shows the Boogeyman coming out of my closet on the previous night. The image of the Boogeyman gives my own a precursory glance before disappearing through the bedroom window.

"Hey!" I shout. "That's not right. The Boogeyman didn't... *did he?*"

I realize with some trepidation that, on that particular occasion, I slept the whole night through. The Boogeyman could've easily been in my bedroom without my knowing it.

I should've paid more attention when I was looking through the Boogeyman's memories.

The crystal continues sifting backward through my memories and my trepidation changes into outright horror. The ball plays each night of my childhood in superluminal succession. Without fail, once I'm asleep, the Boogeyman appears out of my closet each and every night. Of my entire life!

How did I miss all this before?

The crystal recedes through my memories to the years of my infancy and time inside the ball slows to a normal pace. Now on display within the green orb is my first true bedroom—the one I had in our old house. The baby-me lies sound asleep inside the wooden crib that was my bed. I can tell it's the dark of night even when viewed through the green light of the crystal.

By now, I'm not surprised when the Boogeyman comes oozing out from between the closet's folding double doors. But I gasp in shocked disbelief when the Boogeyman glides over to my crib and his shadow cloak lifts away to reveal a baby held within the crook of one of his spindly arms—a baby that is my exact twin right down to the pajamas I'm wearing.

"No!" I shout at the crystal.

The Boogeyman within the ball actually looks up as though he heard me. But my protest does not stop him from scooping up the baby from the crib and leaving the twin he brought with him in its place.

"No," I say, but this time my voice is merely a whimper. The Boogeyman retreats into the closet, the baby from the crib held within his arms, and the images within the crystal fade away.

"When you sifted through the Boogeyman's memories earlier," the Fairy Godmother says, "your mind saw what it wanted to see, and turned a blind eye to all that it did not. But now you are at last being honest with yourself."

"No," I shout. "It can't be!"

"But it is," the Fairy Godmother says.

"But all those memories and experiences," I protest. "Those are mine. I lived with Mom and Dad. I grew up in those houses. But if the real baby was taken away—?"

The Fairy Godmother's hairless, wrinkled brow rises in anticipation. "Yes—?"

"That could only mean—"

Suddenly, it takes too much effort to stand. I back against the dome of enchanted vines and slide down it onto my posterior. "That could only mean—that I'm an impostor."

It's the terrible other voice inside my head that has the strength to speak the words with my mouth. But it turns out he was me all along.

The changeling me.

With that first realization, an avalanche of others come tumbling into place.

I gaze up at the Fairy Godmother as tears begin to leak from my eyes.

"I'm a fairy, aren't I? A changeling planted in the Mortal Lands by the Boogeyman?"

The Fairy Godmother nods. "Yes."

"And the fairy prince. The sleeping son of the Fae King and Queen who looks exactly like me. He's the real me, isn't he? The mortal son my parents should've raised—the one I've unknowingly been masquerading as all these years."

The Fairy Godmother adjusts her bulk around the prop of her cane. "The Boogeyman switched the two of you at birth. Just as was done to him and all Boogeymen before him. Neither the sleeping, would-be prince nor you—nor either set of your parents, for that matter—could know until the time was right."

"Why?" I plead. "Why then? Why the prince? *Why me?*"

"Because the Boogeyman's hat told him that it must be."

"So you're saying some stupid hat—!"

"The Boogeyman's hat is no mere adornment," the Fairy Godmother growls, "stupid or otherwise. It is an ancient and sentient talisman that has aided in keeping the peace between Fairy and Earth since the Pact's origin.

"The hat is the absolute and final authority in regard all

things relating to the Boogeyman. It chose you to be his successor, his *Shadow*, and so you were placed in the Mortal Lands to develop the immunities the station requires. Even the King and Queen of Fairy would've been powerless to overrule its selection of you, their true son, had they known."

I rise to my feet, my anger at what I'm hearing giving me strength.

"Oh yeah? Well, you know what, Fairy Godmother? I've worn the Boogeyman's hat once, and I'll tell you something: it blows!"

"Why do you say such things?" the Fairy Godmother asks. "Do you not realize the gift that you have been given? You are not some deranged, hyperactive mortal. You were never meant to live by their ways or obey their rules. You're the Boogeyman's Shadow. A fae with star shine in his heart and the night wind in his veins. Even more, you are also the prince of *all* fairy. There's only been one such being before—a Shadow of royal blood. This is very special."

"I told you, I couldn't give a flip. You and the Boogeyman can take his job and shove it! I'll do what I promised. I'll help confront the Duke of Night, but then I'm out."

The Fairy Godmother huffs in amusement. "I suspect you may find things a bit more difficult than that, *Your Highness*."

"Whatever. Just tell me where we may find Castle Night so I can do what I came to do and go home."

The Fairy Godmother leans back and an even uglier scowl than the one that is her normal expression creeps across her gruesome face.

"Very well. You will find Castle Night atop Mount Despair. The Boogeyman will know where that is. With the dragon's aid, you should have no trouble getting there before moonset."

The Fairy Godmother waves her hand dismissively, and the dome of vines encapsulating us recedes into the ground, exposing us once more to the chilly night air. The floating crystal ball dims and drifts into the Fairy Godmother's hand. It disappears completely with a stage magician-like flick of her wrist.

I turn and look at the Boogeyman. His face remains a tombstone grimace, but his eyes betray him. They shift ever so slightly, letting me know that he's aware of what I've learned.

His mouth falls open. "Puck, I—"

"Castle Night is at the top of Mount Despair." I stomp past him and climb onto Dragon's massive spiny back. "Come on. Let's get this show on the road."

I turn and look the Boogeyman dead in his obsidian eyes. "My mother and father are waiting for me back in the Mortal Lands."

The Boogeyman issues something between a growl and a sigh and joins me on Dragon's back. Moments later, the three of us are soaring through the sky, heading toward Mount Despair.

24

BETRAYED

When I followed the Boogeyman through my closet into the Land of Fairy, I had no idea it would result in my finding out that my entire life has been a complete lie. But that's exactly what has happened. Earth as we know it isn't my home. The people I've called Mom and Dad for twelve years aren't my parents at all. Worse still, it turns out that I'm not even human.

I'm a fairy.

And not just any fairy, but a changeling prince. One who is not only supposed to become a Boogeyman, but who is arguably the heir to the throne of all Fae.

As exciting as all that may sound, the truth is it's not cool at all. I don't want to be a fairy. My life in the Mortal Lands may have not been the best in the world, but it was *my life*. The only one I've ever known. With the only people I've ever loved who've loved me in return.

I don't want to give them up, and I'm not about to.

I promised that I'd accompany the Boogeyman and find out if the Duke of Night is trying to frame his brother, the Fae King, and plunge Earth and Fairy into war. But once that's done, I'm going back home to Mom and Dad, their real son or not—human or not. No ifs, ands, or buts!

The Boogeyman and I fly out of a cloud bank on Dragon's spiny, winged back to see Castle Night directly ahead in the moonlight. The Duke's home rises up like a black boil from the lonely barren peak of Mount Despair.

Castle Night looks as though it was conceived by some

deranged but brilliant architect. The dark fortress is an exercise in asymmetry that pushes the laws of gravity to their limit. The castle consists of crooked, obsidian turrets that loop and cork-screw and bend and intertwine in haphazard patterns. Tattered, whipping red flags bearing the Greek letter omega hang from each.

The castle's construction reminds me of that painting of impossible staircases. You know, the one where the staircases go up, down, and sideways and yet somehow none of their climbers fall to a gruesome death?

Whether you do or not, just looking at Castle Night would bring a queasy, unnatural feeling to the pit of your stomach. Trust me.

"Take us down," the Boogeyman shouts over the whistling wind. "We need to approach in secret."

"Too late," Dragon calls back. "They've spotted us!"

At that moment, a horizontal rain of black arrows and teth-ered harpoons comes spewing out of Castle Night's upper ram-parts. The Boogeyman and I hold on for dear life as Dragon banks and rolls, making loop de loops in the night sky in order to dodge the oncoming barrage.

"I'm taking us in," Dragon calls.

"No!" the Boogeyman shouts.

"No choice," Dragon says. "I can't keep this up."

To my horror, Dragon is serious. She picks up speed and soars expertly through the sky-labyrinth created by Castle Night's well-defended spires, ultimately bringing us down in a courtyard situated at the castle's heart. The yard's crawling with green-scaled goblins and ram-horned orcs clad in ebony plate armor. They're armed with obsidian swords with serrated edges and warped, oblong shields of charred wood. The night fairies brandish their weapons and roar as Dragon tries to keep them at bay with her flapping wings and spiny, whipping tail.

The Boogeyman scoops me up into an impossibly thin arm and leaps from Dragon's shoulders onto the rocky, barren turf comprising the ground.

It's at this moment that we're undone.

The wind leaves my lungs as I'm smashed to the ground

from behind. I look across and see the same fate has befallen the Boogeyman. Just like me, he lies trapped beneath one of the massive talons extending from Dragon's immense wings. You could argue that he's luckier than me, though, as he's unconscious, and so as yet unaware of our companion's betrayal.

"Stand down!" Dragon roars. The attacking night fairies stop dead in their tracks.

"Tell the Duke I have brought him the Boogeyman and his young Shadow. I would collect the bounty he's offered."

The Duke's soldiers gaze at one another, uncertain as to how to proceed.

"Now!" Dragon bellows. A blazing pyre of flame punctuates her words.

The night fairies retreat in a frenzy of activity in their efforts to obey Dragon's command.

With the last of my strength, I look back over my shoulder into Dragon's huge, scaly face. She gives a shrug of her mountainous brown shoulders.

"What did you expect?" Dragon says. "I am a dragon. By definition, I hoard gold. And the Duke has gold to be hoarded. *A lot of it.* It's nothing personal."

In my dreams, I relive all that has happened to me since following the Boogeyman into Fairy. When at last we arrive at Castle Night and Dragon's gargantuan wing smashes me to the ground, I awake with a start.

The echo of the Boogeyman's voice sears away the last of my grogginess. "That must have been quite a nightmare you were having."

I look up and see that I'm once again in prison. I lie in a cell of dark, crumbling stone. It's cold, and the smell of damp and decay is everywhere. Ancient runes have been carved in the cell's walls, ceiling, and floor. Large spiders and even larger rats skitter from corner to corner, fighting over crumbs of rotten food. The cell's sole entrance is a door constructed from thick ebony that fills the entranceway in its entirety. The only spot on the door not covered in runes is a small keyhole. Dim light shines through it from the other side. This and the moonglow seeping in through a barred window provide the room's only sources of illumination. As things are, I almost wish that wasn't the case. At least if it was completely dark in here, I wouldn't have to match eyes with the leering skeleton propped up against the room's far wall. Its presence here doesn't exactly fill me with hope.

"Puck?" the Boogeyman's voice echoes from the door's other side. "Can you hear me? Are you awake?"

I rise to my feet, every bone in my body aching from Dragon's sneak attack, and crouch against the door so that I can peer through the keyhole. I'm able to see more than I hoped, but it's still far from enough. One of the Boogeyman's coal-black eyes looks back at me through the keyhole of an opposing cell door stationed across the gulf of a stone hallway.

"I'm awake," I call. "But my nightmare still goes on, apparently."

"You have no idea, mortal."

Blackness eclipses my view of the world beyond the keyhole. There's a blur of motion, and then I find myself looking directly into a red cat's eye. I yelp and jerk backward to scramble away on my elbows.

"Stay away from him!" the Boogeyman roars.

"Now, calm down, Lord Boogeyman," the owner of the red eye says. His voice is smooth and regal, but carries a hint of warning in it. "I mean you and your Shadow no further harm. In fact, I intend to keep you safe and sound, here within Castle Night's dungeons for all eternity."

It's the King's brother, I realize. *The Duke of Night.*

"Meanwhile," the Duke continues, "I will soon have larger responsibilities to attend to. Namely, ruling over all of Fae."

"So you admit you are behind the plot to overthrow your brother, the King, and plunge Fairy and Earth into war?" the Boogeyman shouts.

"I admit nothing of the sort," the Duke replies. "However, it is most definitely me who has been keeping you busy of late. Haven't you wondered how I've been doing it—sending all those troublesome night fae into the Mortal Lands for you to deal with—all while keeping it secret?"

"Tell me," the Boogeyman commands.

"Ah-ah-ah," the Duke chides. "Don't forget your place, Lord Boogeyman."

"I know my place, Duke," the Boogeyman spits. "It is serving the King. And I have his leave to stop all those who oppose him. Even you."

The Duke's voice is a silken chuckle. "Not doing a very good job at it, now are you? Besides, a magician never reveals his tricks."

"Magician?" The Boogeyman balks. "What are you talking about?"

"Tootle-loo!" The Duke's red eye disappears from my cell door's keyhole. "I hope you two enjoy your stay."

The Duke's retreating footsteps come to a halt.

"Well, not really." The echo of the Duke's piercing laughter hangs in the hallway long after he's gone.

I hear the Boogeyman sigh deeply behind his cell door.

"I am sorry for getting us into this mess, Puck. I should have known better than to ally us with Dragon. People and things within the Fairy Lands are seldom who and what they seem."

I fold my arms across my chest. "Is that all you have to say?"

There's a silence that seems to go on for eternity, but in truth, is probably only a few seconds.

"I am also sorry for not being honest with you," the Boogeyman says at last.

"That hardly makes up for it!"

"No," the Boogeyman says, "you are right. It does not. I know exactly how you feel, Puck. Angry. Hurt. *Betrayed.* It was the same way I felt when I had to leave my own mother and father in the highlands and become Shadow to the fairy who was the Boogeyman then. Centuries ago that was…" The Boogeyman's voice trails off. "But it still hurts as though it was yesterday."

I want to shout and rage at the Boogeyman. I want to tell him what a jerk he is for playing with my life as though it were his own personal toy. I want to scream and yell and tell him to get bent. But the hurt and regret I hear in his gruff voice keeps me from doing so.

My anger drains with a mass of air that presses itself through my lips in a huff. "I guess I should be thanking you."

"Thanking me? For what?"

"For bringing me to the Mortal Lands. My home. *For giving me my mother and father.* Without you, I would've never known them. The Fairy King and Queen may be my biological parents, but Mom and Dad are my family. And I doubt Their Majesties will be winning the awards for mother and father of the year anytime soon. I mean, locking a child away in a coma for all eternity isn't exactly what passes for good parenting back home. Poor kid."

The Boogeyman chuckles. "I don't know. I've known a mortal lad and lass or two in my time...!"

Several moments of silence pass before I pick the conversation back up.

"So what does it mean?"

"What?"

"To be your Shadow."

"A thankless existence spent in battle and strife, hated and feared by the very ones you protect."

"Gee, when you put it like that—"

"But there are also wonders untold. Dark, bleak, *terrifyingly beautiful* miracles rarely glimpsed even by fae, and beyond imagining altogether for mortal kind. Such will be your journey as my Shadow, should you choose to take up the role."

"You mean I actually have a choice?"

Beyond the keyholes, the Boogeyman's dark eye disappears and then reappears with what I assume to be a nod of his head.

"You said it yourself, Puck: there's always a choice. To be good or bad, mortal or fae, prince or apprentice. These are the decisions now before you, and ones you must soon answer."

"Or?" I ask.

"Or all choices are lost. For everyone. *Forever.*"

Gulp.

"So what do we do?"

"We need to get out of here and confront the Duke properly. If there was any doubt he is behind the impending war between Earth and Fairy, it's gone now. Agreed?"

I nod out of habit, then realize the Boogeyman can't see my gesture.

"Yeah. Sure. So how do we break out of here?"

"Good question," the Boogeyman says. "Just like the with the werewolves' cage, the runes carved into my cell bind me here and frustrate my magic. Whatever dark powers I throw at our prison will only rebound back at me. Trust me, I've tried."

Suddenly, I feel a low heat against me, that I hadn't until this moment realized had been building there.

I reach inside one of the pockets of my musketeer outfit and pull out a tiny ball of warm, pulsing light.

Siren's changeling sun drop. I'd forgotten all about it.

"You said your night fairy powers won't work," I call, "but what about magic from the Day Lands?"

"That might do the trick," the Boogeyman replies. "But it's extremely unlikely we will come across such here in the Night Lands, much less our prison here in Castle Night."

I stare at the sun drop where it lies in the palm of my right hand, concentrating on it with every mental ounce of energy I can muster. Goose-pimples race up my forearm as I experience a searing burst of pleasure in the hand holding Siren's gift. The sun drop wiggles, contracts, and expands. Seconds later, a small golden key lies in my palm where the sun drop once sat. I drop the key into my other hand. I'm shocked to see a smoking, key-shaped hole left behind in the palm of my glove.

It burned me!

I drop the key onto the floor so that I can examine my left hand. The key lands with a clatter.

"What was that?" the Boogeyman calls.

When I turn over my left hand, I breathe a sigh of relief to see it unscathed.

It must have been the sun drop's transformation that burned my glove.

I scratch my head as I engage in mental dialogue with myself.

But it felt good to change it into the key?

Yeah. So good it burned, the voice inside my head I now

know to be my suppressed fae self says. *Too much pleasure can be a kind of pain, after all.*

"Puck?" the Boogeyman calls.

I shrug and scoop the key up off the floor.

"Please let this work," I whisper.

I stick the key into the cell door. I hold my breath, and give it a turn. I needn't have worried. The lock clicks and the door swings open as though the key was custom made to cause that very thing.

"And so it was."

I peek outside the cell and look left, then right. I hold my breath, half-expecting to see the Duke of Night grinning like the cat that ate the canary as he brings an obsidian sword crashing down on my head. Luckily, all that greets my eyes is a long hallway of dark stone lined with rune-covered cell doors. The dim light I saw drifting in through the keyhole earlier is being produced by softly glowing gems embedded into the corridor wall at various intervals.

"Puck," the Boogeyman says from beyond his cell door, "how did you—?"

I hold up the golden key. "A little gift from Siren."

The Boogeyman's eye disappears from behind the keyhole. "Careful, Puck! That key must still carry traces of the Day Lands' sun within it. It hurts for me to look upon it."

"Sorry," I whisper. "It was an enchanted sun drop before it changed."

The Boogeyman huffs. "That explains it."

I tiptoe across the hall and use the key to free the Boogeyman before placing it back inside my pocket. "You'll have to take Siren out on a date to thank her for coming through for us when this is all over."

The Boogeyman flows out of his cell in a swirling mass of living shadow. "We've been through all this before. I could never—"

Before the Boogeyman can finish his sentence, a loud, horrible sound like a foghorn rips through the hallway. I look up to see a squatty, armored goblin at the corridor's end blowing into the tip of a hollow black horn. Immediately, other night fairies clad in black armor appear and shove past him to lope down the hallway toward us.

"We've been discovered!" the Boogeyman shouts.

"Gee, you think?"

My sarcasm is lost on him. The Boogeyman, or rather his shadow cloak, snatches me up and we speed down the hall in retreat only to find the other end blocked by more sword-wielding night fae.

"What do we do?" I ask.

"Nothing."

I look up at the Boogeyman, aghast. "What?"

He draws the long silver rapier out of the depths of his shadow cloak. "We are trapped, Puck. All that's left for us to do is go down fighting in service of Fairy and Earth. Are you with me?"

I try to answer, but the terrible sights and sounds of the armored monsters scurrying over one another like cockroaches as they race down the hall toward us causes my voice to catch in my throat. Despite my would-be mentor's example, going out in a blaze of glory is the last thing I want to do.

"No!" I shout at last. "I don't want to die!"

But it's too late. Hordes of night fairies crash over us like an ocean wave. The Boogeyman puts up a good fight, but there are simply too many of them. It's not long before he's enveloped by a mass of fae scale, fur, fang, and sword.

A large, gorilla-like orc with goat horns and ebony armor seizes me in the furry hams serving as his fists.

"So you don't want to die, eh?" he shouts. "Too bad!"

The orc's mouth opens, exposing canines that are more tusk than tooth, and he begins pulling my head toward his gaping maw.

25

WE'RE TOO LATE

A s the orc draws me toward the jutting teeth housed inside his gorilla-sized mouth, time slows so that I'm able to take in my surroundings with freeze-frame clarity. I see every bead of slobber on my attacker's gray, forked tongue; every cavity in his rotted, yellow fangs.

From the corner of my eye, I catch glimpses of the Boogeyman's shadowy cloak and silver rapier whipping and slashing frantically among the horde of goblins that's engulfed him.

Around us, every crack in the dark stone hallway appears to me as vast as a canyon. Every gem lighting the corridor swells into a radiant moon shining down upon our impending doom.

It can't end like this, I think. *I've got to get home to Mom and Dad. I can't die here, in Fairy, without at least having told them goodbye.*

The orc's fangs begin to close around my head and inspiration strikes. I thrust my hand into my pocket and yank out the golden key I used to free the Boogeyman and myself. I hold it out and the orc trying to eat me retreats down the corridor, shrieking the entire way.

Held high in my hand, the key twinkles like a small, odd-shaped sun. The gems imbedded within the corridor walls reflect and multiply its light. The armored monsters surrounding me yell in agony as they cringe and cover their eyes.

I press forward, and the night fae in my path retreat before me, each of them howling as the key's light touches them. I make my way toward the battling goblins clustered around the

Boogeyman. Before I can get there, the horde of night fae surrounding my mentor swells and then bursts in an explosion of
bodies that go flying in every direction. A whirring, man-sized
dervish of blackness and silver is left in their wake.

I cover the key with my hands. "Boogeyman!"

The Boogeyman stops spinning long enough to sheathe his
rapier and scoop me up into a spindly arm. He begins whirling
again, moving so fast that the world around us becomes a blur.

To my astonishment, we lift off the floor and plunge into
the ceiling above like a drill bit rotating at high speed. We pass
upward through floor after floor of black stone and terrified
night fae, ultimately coming to a stop within Castle Night's cavernous throne room.

The dust clouds produced by our entrance clear, and I see
that the main chamber of Castle Night is a far cry from the
cheery spectacle that is Castle Twilight's throne room. The
moon's silver light shines in through open, asymmetrical windows, illuminating the stalactites and stalagmites of obsidian
flanking the chamber's rough stone walls like twin rows of
giant, black teeth.

Tattered red flags bearing black omegas hang from the
throne room's cave-like upper reaches, scattered among rows of
dangling, bat-winged vampires.

The throne itself is constructed from hundreds of yellow
skulls piled atop one another into the shape of a ridiculously
large chair.

The Duke of Night sits atop them, an androgynous, rail-
thin version of his brother, the Fairy King. His hide is coal-black
and his white hair is cut short in the style of an ancient Roman
emperor. He wears an outfit of red leather and black ruff that
perfectly matches his eyes and skin.

*He could be one of the rock stars pictured on granddad's old record
album covers—the ones who liked to wear strange makeup and put on
elaborate stage shows filled with dark pageantry. Those drew me in
almost as much as any poster of Bela Lugosi ever did.*

To the Duke's credit, he doesn't so much as flinch at the sight
of the Boogeyman and me here, free, and storming his inner
sanctum.

I guess that's because he has backup.

A number of hulking, pale-skinned ghouls clad in cloaks and armor soaked dark red with blood appear from behind the throne to surround the Duke. They point long spears tipped with black diamond heads in our direction.

They must be the Duke's personal guard...or his backup singers. I think, and almost chuckle in spite of my desperate circumstances.

The Boogeyman's shadow cloak reaches into itself to produce what appears to me to be several silvery boomerangs. Fast as lightning, the cloak's tendrils send the metal boomerangs flying toward the ghouls. Each projectile strikes home and attaches itself to its target, effectively freezing each ghoul in place.

The Duke rises to his feet and unsheathes the black diamond rapier that had been hanging from one of the many leather belts encircling his waist.

"I'm not afraid of you!" he shouts.

The Boogeyman surges forward, his torso once again going smoky in the process. His upper half reaches the Duke within the blink of an eye and knocks his weapon from his hand. My mentor's lower half catches up to him nanoseconds later, just as he's seizing the sides of the Duke's dark face within his bony claws.

The Boogeyman smiles, exposing twin rows of fangs.

"You will be afraid. *Very afraid.*"

The Boogeyman's eyes begin to darkle as he takes the Duke into a deep Mesmer. However, when the Boogeyman is done, it's he who appears frightened.

The Boogeyman releases the Duke and the King's brother slumps to the floor in a daze. "Impossible."

"What's imposs—?" Before I can finish my question, squad after squad of gruffs, werewolves, and other manimals clad in the bejeweled armor of the Twilight Guard burst through the gargantuan ebony doors serving as the throne room's entrance and surround us.

"Hey! How did they—?" Two manimal guardsmen, a snarling ram hybrid and a squawking, raven-headed Taheenie, stride into the room, the toad-like Fairy Godmother held captive between them, minus her funeral veil and cane.

Well, that explains how they found Castle Night.

My under-mind has time enough to realize the soldiers of Castle Twilight must possess the capacity to travel within both the Day and Night Lands. Maybe it has to do with them being manimals rather than straight goblins or elves? Or maybe there's some powerful jurisdiction spell that grants the Twilight Guard access to all of Fairy?

Before I can ponder the question in depth, my would-be executioner from Castle Twilight steps his goat hooves forward. "Surrender in the name of the Fairy Queen!"

"We are here on the King's authority," the Boogeyman says. "Our mission is of import equal to your own. I must be allowed to return to His Majesty."

The gruff shakes his head. "The King no longer holds the throne. *He has no authority.*"

"What?" the Boogeyman and I ask in unison, both of us shocked by the gruff's news.

"The High Thirteen have taken the King prisoner—*due to your inability to do your job as Boogeyman, I might add.* Sole rule now belongs to Her Majesty. Her main forces lead an assault upon the Mortal Lands in retaliation for the King's capture as we speak."

The Duke's smooth, mocking laugh echoes from behind us, and I whirl around to see him rise to his feet and dust himself off. "You're too late, Lord Boogeyman."

From the corner of my eye, I see the gruff gesture for two manimal guardsmen to approach the Duke.

"The war between Fairy and Earth has begun," the Duke continues. "All that has happened has done so according to plan. Now I will ascend to the throne of Fairy in my brother's stead and…*What is the meaning of this?*"

The two manimals seize the Duke in their furry paws and begin escorting him out of the throne room.

"What are you doing?" the Duke screams as he's taken away. "I'm supposed to join the Queen in Castle Twilight! I'm supposed to take over as King! I'm supposed to—!"

The Duke and his escort exit the chamber. The Twilight

Guardsmen standing by the throne room's ebony doors slam them shut, effectively sealing us off from the sound of the Duke's cries.

The Boogeyman draws his rapier from his cloak and stares the gruff captain down.

"I could fight you."

Scores of night fae clad in ebony armor scurry into the throne room from entrances hidden in the walls to join the ranks of the Twilight Guard. The vampire bat-men leave their perches on the throne room's ceiling to shriek and circle threateningly above our heads.

Now that the King has been captured, they're all directly under the Queen's rule, I think. Day and night fae alike. Even the Boogeyman can't stand against that many.

"You would lose," the gruff says with finality.

The Boogeyman smiles and sheathes his rapier within the depths of his cloak.

"You surrender," the gruff says. "Wise choice."

The Boogeyman shrugs. "Discretion is the better part of valor."

"Take them away," the gruff says, and several manimals armed with diamond-tipped spears encircle the Boogeyman and me. Others come forward to search our persons with paws sheathed in some kind of opalescent material that's obviously enchanted. They find the key within seconds, and place it in a bag made of the same iridescent substance as their gloves. When they're done with me, I look over to see them attempting to remove Boogeyman's shadow cloak and hat. They are rewarded for their efforts with several smacks from the Boogeyman's cloak that send them tumbling over backwards.

The gruff rolls his eyes, bored. "Guards."

A number of diamond-headed spears come to touch my person in several ways that would prove lethal if followed through.

The gruff folds his furry, muscular arms across his chest. "Now, Lord Boogeyman—your cloak and hat, if you please. Or my men ventilate your young Shadow, here."

If I were brave, this is where I'd shout to the Boogeyman to save himself and not worry about what happens to me. But as things are, I keep quiet and watch in terrified suspense to see if the Boogeyman will do as ordered.

Coward or not, I exhale in deep relief as he begrudgingly removes the raiment of his station and hands it over to the gloved manimals. The Boogeyman's hat goes peacefully enough, but the guardsmen have to struggle to stuff his rebellious cloak into one of their shimmering bags.

Shed of the garments that are the staples of his title, the Boogeyman once again loses much of his menacing presence. Despite all the times we've been captured, the Twilight Guardsmen are the first wise enough to relieve the Boogeyman of his greatest weapons. Needless to say, I'm none too happy with this turn of events.

The Boogeyman nods as though he could read my thoughts. "Never fear, Puck. Enchanted weapons or not, we've been in similar situations before and yet still lived to fight another day."

The gruff captain laughs. "I fear your luck has run out at last, Lord Boogeyman. We have orders to escort you back to Castle Twilight."

I ignore the smirking gruff's comments. "You're right, Boogeyman. We've been in prison before. We'll escape again."

Every fairy in the room laughs, and an icy snake of dread slithers up my spine.

"What's so funny?"

"Dear boy," the gruff captain says, "we aren't taking the two of you to prison."

I swallow hard. My spit is filled with the acrid taste of fear. "You mean—?"

The gruff nods. "That's right. I'm going to finish what I began in Castle Twilight. You and the Boogeyman are to be executed immediately upon arrival."

26

THE FAIRY GODMOTHER SWEEPS ME OFF MY FEET

Our return trip to Castle Twilight among the manimal legions proves an especially long and despairing one. We march for days—or, uh, ahem, rather *nights*—uphill and down through the bleak and abysmal Night Lands countryside before at last coming to a series of dark caves leading to a vast lake housed deep underground. The light of the fireflies held captive in the guardsmen's honeycombed lanterns reflects off the lake's glassy surface, illuminating the rocky firmament above our heads.

But don't let me give you the wrong idea. For the most part, darkness and shadow reign supreme here. And cold and damp are second in command.

The Boogeyman steps up beside me. Seeing his bald, crescent-moon head and spindly frame without his top hat and shadow cloak is sign enough that we've failed in our mission to keep Earth and Fairy from falling into war. But the sight of his bony wrists bound together with rune-inscribed rope really drives our defeat home.

"This is it, Puck," he says. His voice is grave even for him. "This is where we cross over into the Twilight Lands."

I look around, mystified. "What? The lake?"

He nods.

"But I can't swim!"

At that moment, the gruff captain's goat hoof strikes my backside, and I go tumbling into the lake's murky depths.

I open my mouth to scream and succeed only in swallowing what seems like a million gallons of frigid water. The brackish liquid floods my lungs and pain and terror engulf me. I panic, and begin flailing and kicking as much as my own bonds will allow.

In this eternity-long moment, I don't think of our mission's failure, or all highlights and horrors I've experienced here in Fairy. I don't even think of Mom and Dad. In fact, I don't think at all. Because right now, thought is beyond my capacity. Here, struggling in these dark, icy waters, I'm a creature of a capable of only a single, primal urge—that of surviving.

Just as the black snow heralding unconsciousness begins to fall before my eyes, I'm yanked out of the lake. My lungs burn and hot tears sting my eyes as I retch water and inhale the painful joy of crisp, clean air.

Just as I catch my breath, I'm dumped soaking wet onto the ground. The first thing I notice is the change in temperature. It's no longer cold, but merely cool. The earth beneath me is covered in soft grass rather than hard rock. Instead of the stench of decay that seems to permeate the Night Lands, my nose registers the ripe scents of flora and fauna. Most telling of all that I'm no longer in some underground cave is the sound of the crickets chirping all around me.

I rise up on my knees and see that I'm back within the Twilight Lands. Castle Twilight gleams before me amid a tree grove alight with dancing fireflies.

I look behind me and see that I'm on a shore of a vast, lily-pad-covered pond stretching forth from the castle's rear. My manimal captors emerge from the pond by the drove. They shake the water from their fur as they shove the dripping-wet Boogeyman and Fairy Godmother toward me.

As the Boogeyman approaches, I start to ask him how we got here, but stop myself. I've traveled from one realm of Fairy to another now by Void, tomb, Aurora, and tree root. The idea that a pond could also serve as a magical gateway between the realms isn't so farfetched at this point.

A wingless hawk-man with spotted brown feathers shoves my water-soaked musketeer hat back onto my masked head (I'd lost it in the lake) and lifts me unceremoniously to my feet.

"March," he shrieks. Having little choice, I obey.

From here, it isn't long before we're all marching over the jewel cobbles of Castle Twilight's outer court. We press through the masses of anxious fairies who've gathered to watch our impending executions.

The Twilight Guardsmen lead the three of us onto a platform rising from the center of the courtyard. The headsman stands atop it, an enormous diamond-edged axe held in his beefy hands. When I'm close enough to see the horned rhinoceros snout sticking out from beneath his black hood, I turn and run in terror only to trip over the foot of a large, tusked elephant-man. My face smacks the jewel cobbles, and the coppery taste of blood fills my mouth.

I begin to cry.

The elephant-man and his fellow Guardsmen rush in to teach me the error of my ways. Before they can, the Boogeyman places himself between us. Despite my mentor being bound and cloakless, they back off. I can only imagine what look in his obsidian eyes caused them to do so.

The Boogeyman turns and lifts me to my feet. "Are you all right, Puck?" The touch of his bony hands on my shoulders and the deep bass in his voice is oddly comforting. His words and actions are the kind of things Dad does and says when I trip over my own two feet, which happens often.

But Dad is light years and eons away.

Before I can answer, several Guardsmen take the Boogeyman from behind and wrestle him to the ground. Other manimals lift me off my feet and begin tossing me from hand to hand. Before I realize what's happening, I'm on my knees before the headsman, my neck stretched out across a block of purple quartz. The gruff captain and a select squad of his manimals stand guard around us.

The headsman knocks off my hat and plucks a single dark hair from my head. I crane my neck and see him grin as his axe splits my strand of hair in two with ease.

The Boogeyman and the Fairy Godmother come to rest beside me on quartz blocks of their own. The headsman lifts his axe into the air like a rock star brandishing his guitar before an arena of thousands. The result applies in either case. The crowd of fairies goes nuts.

"Off with their heads!"

"Off with their heads!"

The Boogeyman begins shouting over the crowd. "You can't do this. He's the prince of all Fairy. Just take off his mask. You'll see. He's the—!"

The Boogeyman's words become unintelligible as the gruff captain gags him with a strip of soiled cloth. "That's enough out of you. At least try to meet your end with some dignity."

Amazingly, I hear the Fairy Godmother cackling like a mad woman on the other side of him. "Well, it appears I'm about to lose ten pounds of ugly fat."

I close my crying eyes. I may not be able to drown out the sound of the crowd, but I don't have to face them as they cheer me on to my death.

All the things I'll never get to do begin scrolling in my mind. Go to high school. Drive a car. Kiss a girl. Have a family.

And thoughts of family bring to mind memories of Mom and Dad. As sorry as I am for myself, I'm almost as sorry for them, and the agony their love for me will cause them when I fail to return home. They'll never know what happened to me. That'll be the worst. They'll never have closure.

I'm so lost in my despair that it takes me a moment to realize the roars of the crowd have gone silent. In their place is the soft, melodious sound of someone strumming of a harp.

Hope and calm swell within me, and I open my eyes.

Siren is walking directly toward me. The silent, smiling crowd parts before her like the Red Sea before Moses as she plays her golden harp. The fading sun's twilight catches her iridescent butterfly wings and turns them into shimmering twin prisms.

"Hey," the headsman roars. "Stop playing that—!"

The music of Siren's harp is joined by that of a flute. The jaunty, carefree song it plays bounces across the courtyard. I turn my head left and see the new musician. He's a dancing satyr right out of the Narnia stories. His bare torso is pale, but fit. Small, curving horns jut from his luxurious mop of dark, curly hair. His dimpled, angular jaw is lined with five-o'clock shadow. He looks like that British comedian—the one who stayed married to that famous pop diva for all of three weeks. He would be quite handsome if not for the shaggy goat legs extending from the maroon loincloth at his hips. As he approaches, the fairies in his vicinity smile and join him in his jig, seemingly helpless to resist his flute's lively tune.

I look up and see the headsmen swaying in time with music, a grin beneath his horned snout, his axe forgotten at his feet.

The gruff captain leaps onto the platform and seizes the headsman by his mountainous shoulders. "Cover your ears! Cover your—!"

The notes of a third instrument fill the air, joining with the others to create a complex three-part harmony. I look right and see a creature resembling a female centaur trotting through the crowd toward us. She plays a crude violin with a bow better suited for shooting arrows.

Her lower extremities are more like those of a deer than a horse, and two long, backward-sloping horns extend from her forehead. Her skin and fur are the color of dark chocolate, and every muscle, both human and cervine, ripples with lean, chiseled perfection as she moves. She's clad in sparse leather armor constructed with speed of movement in mind as much as protection. It matches the quiver of arrows draped across her human back.

Looking at her, one word comes to mind: *dangerous*.

But the weird thing is, I couldn't care less about any of this.

All I want to do is get up and dance to the music. That in and of itself is weird enough. This is *me* I'm talking about after all, and I don't dance. If not for the bonds tethering me to the block of quartz beneath my torso, I'd be on my feet moving and grooving with the others in the dance party that has broken out across the yard.

Hundreds of elves, goblins, orcs, and sprites cavort and frolic before my eyes, twirling from one partner to the next with complete abandon. Even the gruff captain is at it. He and the headsman hold each other arm in arm as they waltz across the platform.

I'm terribly jealous.

Siren reaches us and flutters onto the platform. She sets her harp down, standing it on its edge. Amazingly, it continues playing of its own accord. Siren unsheathes her golden rapier and slices through the ropes binding me to the block of quartz. I leap to my feet and begin doing a clumsy, manic version of the Running Man.

Siren sheathes her blade. "Puck! Are you in pain?"

"It's the only dance I know," I say between elbow pumps. "I know it's lame. But I can't help myself."

Siren reaches into the white leather satchel hung across her torso and produces two tiny acorns. "Stick these into your ears."

"Why would I want to do that?" I grab the back of my neck with my left hand and my right ankle with the other and repeatedly hunch my body in the middle, performing a crude hip-hop dance.

Siren's harp continues playing on automatic. "By the Green Knight's beard! You're convulsing!"

Everyone's a critic.

Siren places a steady hand on my shoulder and then shoves an acorn into my left ear. The sound of the music playing throughout the courtyard diminishes, my urge to dance along with it. When Siren places an acorn into my other ear, my need to dance vanishes altogether.

Thank goodness.

"Can you hear me?" Siren asks.

Amazingly, I can. "Loud and clear. But I don't hear the music anymore."

"That's the idea."

Siren takes out her rapier once more and slices the Boogeyman's bonds. The Boogeyman jerks off his gag and springs to his feet. Siren yelps in happy surprise as he scoops her up and twirls her around and around. She laughs and then, reluctantly, places acorns into his ears. The Boogeyman shakes his head to clear it and then lets her down.

"You dance divinely, Lord Boogeyman," Siren says.

The Boogeyman stares at her, a proverbial deer in headlights. "Yes, er, well, um..." His embarrassment depriving

him of words, the Boogeyman turns his attention to the Fairy
Godmother's bonds. She bobs her head in time to music I can no
longer hear, singing the unwords, "La! La-la! La-la!"

The second she's free she leaps up and lunges toward me,
the support of her cane apparently no longer necessary.

"Oh no!"

I turn to run, but I'm too late. The Fairy Godmother snags
me, whirls me around, sticks her gnarled hand in mine, and
presses a fat, warty cheek to the side of my face.

We begin tangoing across the platform and I scream.

"Help!"

After laughing at my expense for several minutes, Siren
catches up to us and places a pair of her magic acorns into the
Fairy Godmother's ears.

She comes to her senses and gives me a big blind wink.
"I thought I sensed you making eyes at me back in the Night
Lands, Puck."

"Whoa! You think that—? Heck, no!"

"Thank you for rescuing us, Siren," the Boogeyman says. "I
am in your debt once again."

"I couldn't have done it without Satyr—" Siren says. Now at
the platform, the handsome, goat-legged fairy gives a wink and
a nod as he continues playing his reed flute.

"And Gazelluride," Siren continues. The half-woman, half-
gazelle warrior is now also at the platform, strumming her
archaic violin as she trots in place.

"But we'll call in your marker later," Siren says. "Right now
we have bigger things to worry about. The Fairy Queen has
taken control of the Mortal Lands. She has set up a palace there,
among the clouds, from which to rule both Fairy and Earth."

"She's been behind this all along," the Boogeyman says.
"The Duke of Night was merely her cat's paw. I saw as much in
his mind, though he was too arrogant to realize he was being
played."

Siren nods her head. "We figured that was the case when
the Queen left the King under the spell of the High Thirteen
despite having taken them all prisoner."

"Imprisoned the High Thirteen?" the Boogeyman growls.

"Then she has duped any pawn she may have had within their ranks as well."

"If this is the Queen's grab for ultimate power, it's unlikely she will ever set the King free."

"Agreed. Our only option is to go Earth-side and try to stop her."

"Ideas?"

"I'll need my—!"

One of the guardsman's opalescent bags comes hurling toward the Boogeyman. He snatches it from the air.

"Forgive me, Your Shadowiness," Satyr says, his flute momentarily away from his lips. "I went a little too high on that last note. Made the gruff a bit too eager to return your clothes, I'm afraid."

The Boogeyman nods and opens the sparkling bag. His top hat and shadow cloak come swirling out like a violent, black tornado to take their rightful place on his person.

He's once again a monster to be reckoned with.

Looking at him standing there in all his dark glory, I begin to think we may just have a chance at getting out of this mess yet.

"What now, Lord Boogeyman?" the Fairy Godmother asks.

"The Queen will have an army of fae guarding her new palace. In order to infiltrate it, we'll need powerful magic. The kind we'll find in the High Thirteen's Sanctum Sanctorum."

Gazelluride huffs. "And just how are we supposed to get inside the home base of the High Thirteen? Legend has it that it's guarded by literally hundreds of spells—every one of them deadly to faekind."

"There's a passage leading directly there from Castle Twilight's throne room," I blurt.

The Boogeyman nods. "Right you are, Puck. If we can open it, we should be able to get inside the High Thirteen's lair unscathed."

The Fairy Godmother folds her arms across her extremely gravity-challenged chest. "That just leaves us with what to do about the Twilight Guard here in the Castle."

"The majority of Fairies, guardsman and civilian alike,

are out here," Siren says. "Gazelluride and I will leave our enchanted instruments behind to keep them occupied.

"Satyr and his flute can take care of any stragglers we may find inside."

"Let's get to it then." The Boogeyman whirls with a dramatic swish of his cloak and heads toward the bejeweled set of doors leading inside Castle Twilight proper. The rest of us follow him, each of us knowing this may be the last time we ever see Fairy.

27

A NARROW ESCAPE

When I agreed to help the Boogeyman find the culprit behind the plot to plunge Fairy and Earth into war, my plan was to go home as soon as we accomplished our goal.

Ha! So much for that.

Little did I know then there wouldn't be a home to go back to. At least, not the home I know and love.

It turns out we weren't fast enough to keep the conspirator, aka the Queen of all Fairy, from following through with her schemes. The war has already been fought and lost, despite the Mortal Lands having the power of the High Thirteen Wizards protecting it.

The Queen of Fairy now has a castle in the clouds Earth-side from which she rules both realms (*I have to believe that Mom and Dad are okay. To consider anything else right now won't do anyone any good*).

In other words, we blew it. Big time!

But we're trying to fix our mistake. If we're going to overthrow the Queen at this late date, we're going to need some strong magic to back our play. That's why the Boogeyman, Siren, the Fairy Godmother, Satyr, Gazelluride, and I are standing in the throne room of the Queen's old hangout, Castle Twilight, trying to open a portal into the High Thirteen's Sanctum Sanctorum. Because when it comes to strong magic, you want what the keepers of the Book of Names have to offer. That's right folks, *Logos Co.* is your brand. Accept no substitutions. Operators are standing by!

"Go ahead, Boogey," Siren says. "Give it try."

The Boogeyman nods and stands in the same spot where we saw the Lady Merlin and her Second exit the vast quartz throne room days before. His cloak spreads out on either side of him of its own accord to whip in a nonexistent wind like a giant, tattered pirate flag. He raises a bony claw and bellows, "Allak shak, nola rendo!"

While I'm impressed with the Boogeyman's powers of mental recall, his words fail to open any magical portals or anything else.

He tries again, this time thrusting both his arms forward as though he were a *Star Wars* Sith Lord trying to shoot lightning from his hands. "Allak shak, nola rendo!"

The result is the same.

Siren shrugs. "Maybe if all of us try together?"

Seconds later, the fairies have gathered beside the Boogeyman, their arms homed onto the same spot of empty space.

"Allak shak, nola rendo!" they shout. Again, nothing happens.

Siren shakes her head. "This is not good."

"Who goes there?"

A squad of manimals enters the throne room and Satyr begins playing his reed flute. The guardsmen's angry looks disappear from their faces to be replaced by dreamy smiles.

"What's to be done?" the Fairy Godmother asks as she scratches the few gray, scraggly hairs actually growing from her liver-spotted head.

"You're the Fairy Godmother," Gazelluride says. "Shouldn't you know?"

Several other manimal guardsmen drift into the throne room to join the squad already listening to Satyr's flute. These are soon accompanied by several elven servants. And several goblin housekeepers. And then still more guardsmen.

"Whatever it is, you chaps best do it quick!" Satyr says in a rush, then resumes playing his flute.

My chest gets tight as I begin to see looks of awareness dawn on the faces making up Satyr's audience. It's as though the hypnotic effect of his flute is being diluted by each new fairy who joins the crowd.

"If all of you combined can't allak shak nola rendo us out of here," I say, "then what chance to do we—?"

The empty air in front of the Boogeyman and the others quivers as if distorted by heat.

"Puck!" the Boogeyman shouts, his demeanor the closest to elation I've ever seen. "Of course. Why didn't I think of it?" The Boogeyman pounds the meat of his palm at the space between his obsidian eyes. "Stupid! Stupid! Stupid!"

"What?" I ask, not following him.

"You're mortal, Puck," the Boogeyman says.

"He's what?" Gazelluride asks in bewilderment.

"Puck is a mortal boy," Siren adds.

The Fairy Godmother gives me a malicious wink. "For now."

"It goes to figure the spells of the High Thirteen would need to be spoken by a mortal tongue." The Boogeyman gestures toward the wavering space in the air. "Try again, but concentrate this time. Put everything you've got into it!"

More fairies meanderer in to join those already assembled before Satyr.

"More fairies!" Satyr calls, then blows his flute like Louie Armstrong times a hundred.

"Uh, okay." I say, and close the distance to the wavering space in throne room's center. I stretch out my hands and call. "Allak shak, nola rendo!"

Time and space wobble before me, but hold.

Dang it!

A lupus manimal among the crowd shakes his bunny's head, clearing it. "What are they doing back there?" His question is repeated several times over by those gathered.

"That's it, mates," Satyr says as he drops his flute. "She's outta juice."

The Boogeyman's rapier rings as he draws it from his cloak. I take a backward step, my eyes wide with horror.

"I'm doing the best I can!"

The Boogeyman shakes his head. "No! No! You need a talisman like the Merlin's staff—something to give the magic of your words focus."

The Boogeyman flips the rapier around so that its hilt is toward me, and I take it in my hand. The weight of it is cold and heavy, but it also feels powerful—like it could really do some damage in the proper hands. Unfortunately, the only hands available are mine.

I stab the rapier in the direction of the temporal distortion and shout. "Allak shak, nola rendo!"

A door-sized rectangle of light opens before us, and not a moment too soon! Satyr is the first one through. He comes rushing by me in a frantic mass of skin and fur. I turn and see why.

The crowd of fairies has become a mob—one that appears to be of the lynching variety.

The Boogeyman seizes his rapier and throws me into the portal of light before I have a chance to protest. Not that I would. Right now, I want to be as far away from the charging mass of angry fairies as possible.

I fall through the door and shriek when I see that I'm just going to keep on falling. Forever!

Only, I don't.

I land on my hands and knees on what must be an invisible floor. It has to be invisible, or at least transparent, because all I can see beneath me is a sparkling cosmos that stretches into eternity. I feel warmth on my back and look up to see a blazing, beach-ball-sized sun rotating above me in the emptiness of outer space, several teeny planets with heavenly satellites of their own orbiting it. The entire setup looks exactly like our own solar system.

I climb to my feet, having to duck to miss Saturn as it comes whizzing by my head, and gaze at the small-scale galaxy serving as my surroundings. It seems to be giving off a faint, machinery-like hum—one that reverberates through my entire body. It's as if every star, planet, and moon were *singing* just a decibel or two below hearing range.

Satyr is already here, leaning on one of three wooden doors positioned around the tiny solar system like vast gateways for gigantic gods.

My jaw finally lifts off my chest. "This is the coolest planetarium I've ever seen."

"Welcome to the meeting room of the High Thirteen, my prince." The Fairy Godmother comes waddling in behind me through the portal of light leading from Fairy, followed by Gazelluride, Siren, and the Boogeyman. Her reminder that I'm not human in the truest sense unnerves me all over again. I decide to ignore both it and her in favor of miniature star-gazing.

"Thankfully their model of the solar system is only that," the Fairy Godmother continues, "and so poses no threat to any fae, day or night."

Once they're all in, a fourth and final door I hadn't noticed closes on the rectangle of light, eclipsing the angry shouts echoing in from Castle Twilight's throne room.

"We made it!" Siren says. Whether she's elated or shocked, I can't tell for sure.

The Boogeyman points a single claw at the miniature Earth circling around the room. "We should have ample time to arm ourselves for an attack on the Queen's Castle. I can tell from this mock-up that the pre-dawn twilight in which we all may travel is still hours away."

"I thought you said the mortal rules of night and day didn't apply to you and Siren?" I ask.

"We are both here, now, Puck," Siren answers. "And together, we cancel much of the effect we have on the Mortal Lands."

I open my mouth, but Siren holds up a halting finger.

"In regard to your next question, the Sanctum Sanctorum is enchanted. Its protective spells will keep Satyr, Gazelluride, and me safe from any ill effects that nighttime has on our kind. The fact that I'm talking to you here and now and not a block of stone is proof enough of that."

Gazelluride prods a single hoof at the nonexistent ground in wonder. "So where do we start?"

"I've heard rumor the High Thirteen maintain a repository of magical relics," the Boogeyman says. "There should be a number of artifacts there we can use against the Queen and her armies."

"Why not go straight for the granddaddy of them all," I ask. "The Logos?"

The Fairy Godmother shakes her head. "The Logos was created for mortals. It would be useless to us. Even yourself, though mortal you still may be, as you are not of wizarding kind."

"But I—?" I start, but the Fairy Godmother shushes me before I can get the question out of my mouth.

It's getting to be an annoying habit fairies seem to have in regard to me.

"Opening a fixed gateway in a land already brimming with magic is one thing," the Fairy Godmother says, "but wielding the Logos' immense and highly volatile power is like handling dynamite that some stupid human has left sitting around for years. One mistake, and boom! The Logos is only of use when in the hands of a master wizard."

"Well," Satyr huffs, "I'm glad we've got it all sorted. Now, if you don't mind, I'd like to get the heck out of here and get started looking for that repository. Watching the universe swirl up close and personal makes my lunch want to come back up my throat."

Gazelluride crosses her arms. "Well, if you would stop acting like a goat and eating everything in sight."

Satyr gives her a wink. "You know you like watching me eat, Love. *You like watching me, period.*"

"Ha!" Gazelluride scoffs. "Don't flatter yourself."

The Fairy Godmother cackles and claps her hands, causing the drooping, gray flesh of her arms to quiver. "Lovers' quarrel! Lovers' quarrel!"

Gazelluride's brown cheeks flush bright red. "Quiet, you old bat!"

A beaming grin crosses Satyr's whiskered face. "Struck a nerve, I see? The truth will find you out, Gazelluride."

I hear a whistling in the air and then gasp as the wobbling, wooden shaft of an arrow appears as if by magic in the door behind Satyr.

Satyr's eyes become twin boiled eggs beneath his nubby goat horns. "Eek!"

He throws open the arrow-impaled door and escapes deeper inside the High Thirteen's Sanctum Sanctorum. Once Gazelluride has put away her bow, and our laughter quieted, we remove the magic acorns from our ears and follow.

28

I GET MY BUTT KICKED BY A GIRL

We exit the High Thirteen's planetarium-on-steroids meeting room and enter a world of cold, white sterility. That's not an exaggeration. Frosty air blasts of out multiple vents located along the room's spotless white walls, floor, and ceiling. I'm sure the AC overkill is to keep all the computers housed here running at top capacity. This place looks like the bridge of the starship *Enterprise* as brought to you by Apple Inc.

Only, it's not.

Instead of life form readings and planetary schematics, the screens of the computer monitors are filled with algebraic equations featuring ankhs, pentacles, and other occult symbols rather than numbers and letters.

Gazelluride prances cautiously through the rows of machinery, an arrow knocked in her bow. She's obviously *waaaay* out of her comfort zone. "Where are all the shelves of dusty scrolls?"

"And the wax candles and bubbling cauldrons?" Satyr echoes.

"These are computers," the Boogeyman growls. "I've seen many such clockworks in my travels. These appear to be running hundreds of spells simultaneously. All at incalculable speed."

Siren nods in agreement. "This is the Mortal Lands. Magic has been streamlined and modernized right along with everything else."

Hmmmph, I think, *i-magic*.

"A shame," the Fairy Godmother says. "Factory magic is no

substitute for the real thing. Perhaps that is why the Queen was able to defeat the High Thirteen with such ease. In their efforts to cut corners and save time, they've lost something infinitely more valuable."

We follow the Boogeyman into a second room, one seemingly devoted to alchemy. But it's hard to tell for sure as the place is a lot closer in appearance to a *CSI* crime lab than a Hogwarts classroom. I reach up to touch a beaker of boiling blue liquid only to be quickly reprimanded by the Boogeyman.

"Puck!"

"Sorry."

The six of us move on, passing from room to room, covering a lot of ground, but getting nowhere. While most of the scenery is humdrum, certain undeniably magical things are occurring around us.

For instance, right now we're walking down a long hallway of mirrors. Sounds like a bad carnival attraction, I know. However, some of the mirrors appear to be windows to the outside world, and reveal scenes of day and night simultaneously. (Neither seems to have any negative effect on my fairy traveling companions. Points to the protective spells of the Sanctum Sanctorum.) I head farther down the hall, moving out ahead of everyone else to take in panoramic vistas of Earth, Fairy, and other strange and weird places I can't even begin to describe.

I am standing at a mirror showcasing a gushing orange waterfall when the imminent and undeniable urge to pee strikes me.

I bite my bottom lip and look back at the Boogeyman.

"Boogeyman, I've got to—"

"In a moment, Puck."

He waves a hand to shush me as he gazes longingly into a mirror displaying the mist-enshrouded highlands of his childhood. The other fairies are behind him, each equally enthralled in their own mirror-show.

Against my better judgment, I strike out ahead to find a bathroom. Unfortunately, my search comes up null and void, and I'm forced to, *ahem*, "water" a potted plant standing in the corner of what looks to be some sort of administrative office.

While the act embarrasses me, it also gives me a kind of guilty pleasure—the type you might enjoy from getting away with faking sick to stay home from school. I don't know what that says about me, and frankly, at the moment, I couldn't care less. The physical relief my body feels drives out any further thoughts I have on the matter.

I sort myself, cleaning my hands with some sanitary wipes I find on a shelf, and exit the office to realize I'm totally and utterly lost.

"Way to go, moron."

I try to backtrack, but wind up only getting myself further disoriented. The Sanctum Sanctorum is a deceptively massive place, with room after room intersecting seemingly without end.

And we haven't even been to the other floors.

That's the most magical thing about the High Thirteen's lair—it's an impossible amount of indoor space confined within a single building.

I start opening doors and calling for the fairies.

"Boogeyman? Siren? Satyr? Anyone...?"

Eerie silence is my only reply. The Sanctum Sanctorum seems to even swallow the echoes of my voice. I begin to get that creepy feeling that comes from being by yourself too long—*the feeling that you're not really by yourself at all*—and the hackles rise on the back of my neck.

"Will someone answer me, please?"

More silence.

More hushed whispers not heard.

More watching eyes unseen.

As large as the Sanctum Sanctorum seemed before, it feels small now. Tight. Cramped. And closed in.

Like a trap.

"Okay, stop it," I say under my breath. "You're freaking yourself out."

Unwilling to heed my own advice, I begin running from room to room and throwing open doors. More computer labs greet my eyes, along with staff break rooms and janitorial closets.

"Where are you?" I shout, and fling open a final door. I gasp at what I see on its other side.

I gaze out over a warehouse-sized chamber filled to the capacity with black iron cages housing strange animals of all shapes, sizes, and descriptions. The air here is hot and thick with their growls, caws, and musky aromas. Halogen lights hang from the chamber's rafters, spotlighting the cages while leaving their peripheries in shadow.

Taking caution, I step inside and make my way between rows of bipedal, bat-winged horses and gigantic, furry ape-men who leer at me in silence as they grip the bars of their cells.

What the heck are these things?

I'm just about to enter a new section of cages when one of the horse-bats sneezes, blanketing my black musketeer hat with slobber and snot. I take off my hat and curl my upper lip in disgust as I examine the damage.

"*Eeeeeew.*"

I clean my hat on the floor the best I'm able before placing it back onto my head and continuing on. I come to a number of cells containing scaly lizard men with sharp claws and long tusks—and surprisingly, bandages. Each of them has one limb or another splinted or in a sling. Despite their apparently injured limbs, they scamper from cage bar to ceiling and back again as easily as I walk across the floor. Their appearance and manner are too close to that of the monstrous changeling for comfort, and I double-time it around a corner to the next section of cages.

I'm moving so fast that I have to slide to the floor in order to keep from hitting the growling, saber-toothed wolf crouched on the other side.

More surprising is the girl riding on this Ice Age monster's shoulders. She's Hispanic, and probably only a year or two older than me, though a full head taller.

She's also very, very cute.

She has a platinum-blonde streak in her otherwise dark hair that I'm sure was meant to be très emo, but makes her look more like she's wearing a skunk for a hat. She's dressed in a screen-printed T-shirt, skinny jeans, and Chuck Taylors, though most probably wouldn't notice with the glowing shepherd's staff she's holding obstructing the view of her.

As for the saber-toothed wolf...well, he's gray. And big.

Very, very big.

And he's looking at me like he hasn't eaten in weeks.

"Which cryptid were you planning to steal from infirmary, thief?" the girl shouts.

"Thief?" I remember the black domino mask encircling my eyes like an infinity symbol. "Oh, I'm not a—!"

The wolf begins barking, and I scramble backward on my elbows in fear.

"What's his problem?" I shout. "I wasn't doing anything!"

The girl's face darkens.

"He's caught the scent of a Fairy."

The girl thrusts her staff forward, and I roll just in time to miss the bolt of golden lightning that comes snaking out of its end. It strikes the space I'd occupied nanoseconds before and leaves a smoking black scorch mark.

"Hey," I shout, "take it—!"

I duck as another bolt of lightning arcs through the air above my head, passing close enough to set ablaze the long feather jutting from my black musketeer hat. I yelp and knock away my roasting headgear with a gloved hand. Then I'm on my feet and running, the girl and her wolf literally dogging my tracks.

Streaks of lightning zap through the air all around me, creating sparks and puffs of smoke where they strike the cages. The saber-toothed wolf's barks reverberate throughout the chamber, upsetting the strange animals surroundings us, sending them into fits of flailing and howling. The imprisoned—(What did the girl call them?)—*cryptids* stick their limbs out between the bars of their cages and swipe at me. Thankfully, the only thing they snatch is air.

"I don't want to die! I don't want to—!"

I round a cage and this time I do crash into the monstrous being standing on its other side. The Boogeyman's cloak furls around me just in time to deflect a bolt of magic lightning from the girl's staff. The living cloak releases me as the Boogeyman leaps into the air and lands directly in front of my attackers, his shape changed into a larger, scarier, saber-toothed animal—a white tiger with glowing red eyes and black stripes. He roars and the caged cryptids are shocked into silence. The girl's wolf tucks its bushy tail and runs away, yelping as it goes. It's then that I realize, as big as the saber-toothed wolf is, he's only a puppy.

The frantic movements of the wolf's retreat unsettle its rider. The girl goes tumbling from the creature's muscular shoulders, her shepherd's staff going one way and she the other. The Boogeyman goes smoky, transforming back into his usual ominous self as he scoops the girl off the floor with a single hand and eyes her with disdain.

"Go ahead, Fairy," the girl shouts as she kicks her feet helplessly above the floor. "Take me just like your stupid, fae friends took my mother!"

This girl may very well be either the bravest or the stupidest person I've ever met.

A growl leftover from the Boogeyman's tiger-form rumbles out of his throat.

"Boogey!"

I look up and see Siren descending from between the chamber's hanging lights, their shine captured, refracted, and magnified through the prisms of her flapping butterfly wings. Gazelluride and Satyr come bounding up seconds later, followed by a waddling, breathless Fairy Godmother.

"Don't hurt her," Siren says. "She's just a child."

"I'm not just a child!" the girl barks. "I'm a Santera. Like my mother."

"There. You see? She's a sorceress," the Boogeyman scoffs. "One who almost roasted young Puck here alive."

"Give me back the staff," the girl says, "and I'll take on all you fairies. The whole stinking bunch of you!"

The Boogeyman shakes his head and turns his grim attention to me. "And why in the Night Lands did you go wandering off by yourself anyway, Puck? You could've gotten yourself, well, *this.*"

I shrug. "Sorry. Nature called."

"Put me down," the girl demands.

"That doesn't change the fact that she's just a young girl," Siren says.

Gazelluride lowers her bow and shrugs. "I made my first kill at age seven."

It earns her a gaze from Siren that could crack glaciers in two. "Gazelluride, hello! Not helping here."

"Little girl," Siren says, then pauses. "What's your name?"

"Ha! I know better than that, Fairy. Not that it matters if you knew my name. I'm mortal after all, and so it wouldn't give you any power over me. But one can never be too careful."

Siren shakes her head. "No, what I mean is...here, look." Siren removes her golden breastplate and its attached wings.

Satyr gives a wolf whistle which earns him a shoulder slap from the Fairy Godmother.

Without the trappings of her station, Siren's fae glory seems to diminish somewhat. However, even without her armor, she's still very striking. But now she appears kind and approachable, with a heart as red and warm as the freckles on her pale skin.

"We're not here to hurt you," she says. "In fact, we're here to help out the Mortal Lands."

"That's a little hard to believe with Mr. Gruesome here dangling me above the floor."

Siren gestures for the Boogeyman to set the girl down. He reluctantly obeys. The girl stands, eyeing Siren and the rest of us suspiciously. I can almost see the wheels in her head turning as she tries to figure out what game we're playing.

"Satyr," Siren says, "please fetch the girl's staff for her."

"*What?*"

"We have nothing to fear from her, just as she has nothing to fear from us." Siren moves her gaze over the rest of us. "Agreed?"

We reluctantly nod in unison.

"Blimey!" Satyr grumbles several unintelligible curses under his breath as he walks over and scoops up the girl's staff. "Here." Satyr tosses the girl her staff. "Be mindful you don't hurt yourself—*or anyone else*—with it."

"You see," Siren sing-songs, "you can trust us."

The girl thrusts the staff at Siren. "You're just trying lull me into a false sense of security. Just like your Queen did the High Thirteen. She invited them to her palace in the sky under the pretense of negotiating her King's release. But it was a double-cross. She ambushed them to clear the way for her Fairy army to take over Earth. That's all you fairies are good for—lies and tricks!"

Before I know what's happening, my feet and mouth are moving of their own accord. I take a step forward.

"Uh, I'm not."

The girl shakes her staff at me. "Back, Fairy!"

I take another step forward. Believe me, I'm as surprised as anyone else. "See, that's where you and your pet wolf are wrong. I'm not a fairy."

At least not yet, I think, very aware of the Fairy Godmother's cold blind eyes boring into my back.

I take off my mask. "I'm just a kid, like you. And based on what you said earlier, I'm guessing also like me, this mess has you scared for your parents' safety—?"

The girl nods and tears begin to swell in her eyes. "My mom. The fairies took her. I was the only one left to guard the Sanctum Sanctorum." She chuckles even as tears begin to roll down her cheeks. "Can you believe it? As a 'mere' Santera, Mama was beneath the High Thirteen's notice. *She was just one of the maids, here.* But her name was on the wizarding rolls, so when the Fairy siege began, she was taken."

The girl gives me a teary-eyed smile. "The Thirteen didn't even consider me important enough to be on the rolls. I guess I should be thanking them. Their dismissal of me is ultimately what…what…"

The girl lowers her staff and begins sobbing into her free hand. When I approach to comfort her, she goes back on the defensive.

"Whoa! Whoa!" I say. "*Easy.* You can trust me." I gesture to the fairies behind me. "Heck, you can trust them, too."

"Prove it."

"Okay. I'll tell you my real name, if you'll tell me yours."

"You first."

"Sure."

"Not out loud for everyone to hear, Puck," the Boogeyman booms. "Corrupt ears may be listening in."

"But it doesn't matter—"

The Boogeyman's smooth, hairless brow wrinkles beneath the brim of his crooked black hat. "Maybe it does where you are concerned, and maybe it doesn't? Best to be safe."

I look at the girl and shrug. "I better whisper it into your ear."

A look of uncertainty crosses her face. It makes her look vulnerable and lovelier than ever. "Okay."

I cup my hand to the girl's ear, having to step up on tiptoes to do so. She smells of the cryptids—animals she must be caring for in the absence of the Sanctum Sanctorum's staff. But the mingling, frilly scents of soap and lotion lie beneath. Being this close to her makes me feel warm and dizzy.

I take a deep breath and whisper, "My name is—"

29

I ACCIDENTALLY BECOME KING OF ALL BRITIAN

Once we've dispensed with introductions, the girl, *Eliana*, takes us to a staff break room where we help ourselves to potato chips and canned soda. We gather beneath the blue-white glow of fluorescent lights at tables of Formica surrounded by tall, boxy vending machines. I take a seat next to Eliana, trying to be as nonchalant about it as possible. Her cuteness aside, it's just nice to be in the company of another mortal for a change. For Eliana's part, she doesn't so much as look in my direction.

The last eligible boy on Earth—*figuratively speaking*—and I still don't merit a second glance from the last eligible girl. Only me!

Gazelluride prods a foil-covered pack of Doritos with the end of her bow. "This is what passes for food with you mortals?"

"What are you on about?" Satyr asks as he munches on an empty Coke can. "This stuff is delicious."

The Fairy Godmother slurps down an empty cellophane wrapper. "Especially once you scoop all the mush out of the middle."

Gazelluride turns up her nose. "If it didn't once grow in the sun's light, I want no part of it."

"Fine. More for me." Satyr snatches Gazelluride's bag of Doritos and crams it down his throat without bothering to tear it open.

"How does he manage to stay so slim?" Eliana whispers to me.

I shrug. "Goat's legs. Goat's metabolism, I guess."

Eliana giggles and it dawns on me with great pride that, for once in my life, I've somehow managed not to feel awkward when speaking to a girl. Even better, I've actually made one laugh without being the butt of the joke. Points to me.

"She likes him," Eliana says, her voice still low.

I match her conspiring tone. "Gazelluride? No way. From the way I've seen her act, she'd like to stomp him beneath her hooves. *All four of them.*"

Eliana smiles, and it lights up her entire face. "That's how you can tell. Take your Mr. Gruesome for instance." Eliana gestures to the Boogeyman. "Look at him, sitting there with that scowl on his face as he studies everything in the room *but* your redheaded friend. Have you ever seen someone work so hard *not* to make eye contact with the person sitting next to them?"

"Uh, no," I say, my eyes glued to the floor. "Never."

"Meanwhile, Siren sits patiently, pretending she doesn't notice, waiting for him to summon the courage to ask the question they both want him to say."

My eyebrows rise in question. "What are you doing after the rebellion?"

My face goes hot as Eliana's own eyebrows arch on her forehead.

"No, wait. I didn't—of course I didn't—I was just—"

Eliana leaves me wriggling on my self-imposed hook. The look on her face tells me she's enjoying every second of it. Whether it's out of fun or meanness, I can't tell.

"Young Miss," Siren says, mercifully drawing Eliana's attention away from me, "if you are done eating, I would like to ask another favor of you."

Eliana nods.

"We need to know exactly how the Queen came to power here in the Mortal Lands."

"I told you," Eliana says, "the Fairy Queen tricked the High Thirteen, then took them prisoner."

Siren nods. "Yes. But we need specifics. Even the slightest detail of what you know might prove vital. I realize with everything that has happened to you, a rigorous questioning

by the Boogeyman and I wouldn't be the most enjoyable course
of action for any of us. Therefore, if you would permit me to—"

"You're talking about a Mind Mesmer, aren't you?" Eliana
interrupts. "One that will throw my thoughts and feelings up
in the air like splatters of paint for all to see?"

"Well," Siren says, "actually yes. Indeed I am."

"S'okay. I've had experience with them before. I don't see
how one from a fairy could be that different."

Eliana stands and places hands on her hips, cinching in the
length of the T-shirt dangling over her skin-tight blue jeans.
Siren rises and crosses the floor to stand in front of her. She
places her delicate, freckled hands on Eliana's bronze face,
touching her at the temples, cheekbones, and chin. The emerald embedded in Siren's silver headband begins to glow and
Eliana's eyes roll back into her head.

I watch, breathless, as the fluorescent lights dim and new,
rainbow-hued drops of light form in the air to dance above
Eliana's head. These lights swirl and flitter like sprites from the
Twilight Lands before at last coalescing into a single, vibrant
mass of colors. The colors take on shape and definition, at last
crystallizing into actual images. They picture a crowded street
packed to overflowing with people whose faces are painted in
black and white so they resemble the skulls beneath their skin.
These same people are dressed in elaborate, brightly colored
costumes. Fresh flowers, smoking firecrackers, and candy skulls
are everywhere. A small girl with a platinum-blonde streak in
her hair (it's natural, after all) stands in the center of everything,
clinging to the hem of a lovely young woman's dress. They're
unmistakably Eliana and her mother.

Viewing Siren's Mesmer broadcast of Eliana's memories isn't
anywhere as near as intense as my experience sifting through
the Boogeyman's memories. In fact, this is more like watching a
movie. But it's still pretty amazing to say the least.

Siren's face tightens with concentration, and the images
above Eliana's head blur and swirl once again. When they
come back into focus, they reveal Eliana, now at her current
age, in what appears to be a basement. The walls and floors
surrounding her are concrete. Boxes of every size and color

are stacked haphazardly in every possible nook and cranny. A rusted water heater, antique sewing machine, and an armless, headless mannequin wearing Eliana's current T-shirt complete the setting. Eliana reads aloud what must be the garbled nonsense written on the old, dusty scroll holding her attention as she continually rotates the two glass balls held within the palm of her left hand.

Suddenly, a light appears at the top of the basement stairs as though someone had just opened a door.

"Who's down there?" a shrill voice calls.

Eliana jerks upright, surprised. She drops her left hand, but the glass balls continue rotating in mid-air. Moving with frantic speed, Eliana begins rolling up the scroll. As to what happens next, I can't say, because the images above Eliana's head blur once more.

But when they come back into focus, all I want them to do is fade away again.

The Mesmer broadcast now shows Eliana crying as she chases after a massive Cyclops dressed in tattered Renaissance-era clothing. The one-eyed giant pays her no mind as he lumbers away with a number of wailing humans stuffed into the crook of his arm. Among them is Eliana's mother. She pleads with her daughter to hide in the one place the Fairies can't infiltrate—the Sanctum Sanctorum.

Abruptly, the Cyclops pauses and lifts his load to the sky just in time for the humans to be scooped up by the talons of a passing dragon whose flapping, golden wings glisten in the sun.

The dragon flies toward the clouds, going where Eliana can't follow. Having no choice, she turns and runs for the lair of the High Thirteen, having to zigzag through squads of ivory-armored elves who are thankfully more interested in ransacking the skyscrapers lining the street.

The jewel at Siren's forehead dims, and the Mesmer broadcast vanishes. Siren releases Eliana, and the girl shakes her head, clearing it.

"This is baaaaad," Satyr bleats. For once, he isn't trying to be funny. What we saw simply upset him enough to cause him to lose control of his voice.

"But it hardly sheds any new light on what happened here," Gazelluride adds.

"I already told you," Eliana says, her senses now regained, "the High Thirteen were lured to the Fairy Queen's palace in the sky where they were taken prisoner."

"But did you see it?" the Fairy Godmother asks. "Were you actually there when it happened?"

Eliana's gaze drops to the floor. "Well, no. But that's what Mama told me before she was taken, and she wouldn't lie. Especially not to me."

Siren turns to the Boogeyman. "Thoughts?"

If it's possible, the permanent scowl plastered across the Boogeyman's face becomes even more pronounced. "I don't like it. There are still too many unanswered questions here."

"Like what?" Satyr asks.

"For one, the Queen simply isn't powerful enough to defeat the High Thirteen all on her own. Especially with the power of the Logos backing them."

The Boogeyman turns to face Eliana. "The High Thirteen *did* take the Logos with them, didn't they?"

Eliana shrugs. "I guess so. It's no longer in its vault in the library."

The Boogeyman nods and folds his spindly arms across his dark torso.

"Another thing that bothers me is the question as to why the Queen would establish her reign in the clouds? Sure, it would be a grand thing during the day. But at night, a castle in the sky would leave the Queen, a Day Lands fae, all the more vulnerable to darkness.

"It just doesn't add up."

"All the more reason to charge in there packing!" Gazelluride pops the string of the bow she carries for emphasis.

Siren nods. "We have to find the High Thirteen's repository of magical artifacts."

"The repository?" Eliana asks. "I can take you there, no problem."

"Well, for darkness's sake," the Fairy Godmother says, "you are a credit to your race, child. Lead on."

Minutes later, the seven of us are in a large, ornate chamber within the Sanctum Sanctorum, picking our way through a virtual museum of magical instruments, baubles, and—even more importantly—*weapons*.

These objects of power are kept behind glass cases and velvet ropes, their history stamped into metal plaques serving as part of their displays. Most are either the wand or staff of some famous wizard I've never heard of. (Heck, I didn't even know we had real wizards until this mess started.) But there are also amulets, swords, and shields aplenty, not to mention common household items from the modern era.

"What's this here do?" Satyr asks as he plucks a seemingly harmless hairdryer from an ivory pedestal cordoned off by purple rope.

"No! Wait—!" Eliana shouts, but she's too late. Satyr thumbs the "on" switch and a plume of fire like the exhaust of a fighter jet shoots out from hairdryer's nozzle. A smoking black scorch mark the size of a highway is seared into the wall and ceiling by the time he manages to shut off the magically enhanced appliance.

"I'll take that." Gazelluride plucks the hairdryer from Satyr's shaking hands. She marvels at the contraption like a child who's just received the best Christmas present ever.

"And this?" Satyr reaches out a tentative hand and takes a small velvet bag from a shelf.

"Pixie dust," Eliana says.

"So you can fly with it?"

Eliana scrunches her mouth, considering. Did I mention how adorable she is?

"Not literally. But it sure makes people happy."

Satyr slips the bag into the band of the loincloth at his hip and gives a wink. "Definitely more my speed. I'm a lover, not a fighter.

"What's that you've got there, Siren? It's very you."

We turn to see Siren holding an umbrella. Even closed, it's easy to see that each triangular section of fabric is dyed a different shade of the rainbow.

"Gazelluride's clockwork dragon's breath will make for a

good offense," Siren says, "but we're going to need defense, too."

"Defense from what?" I ask. "A good downpour?"

Siren smiles and shakes her head. "Come pre-dawn, there will be legions of elves and goblins on patrol in the twilight, not to mention giants and dragons."

"And you plan to use that umbrella to shoo them away like a flock of birds?"

Siren laughs. "No, no. You see, this belonged to the doctor."

"The doctor? What doctor?"

"Not what. *Who.*"

I throw up my hands in confusion and Siren laughs harder still. "Trust me, Puck. You'll see."

Then the smile fades from her face. "Unfortunately."

Eliana taps her staff on the floor. "I think I'll just stick with my staff. It served the prince of Egypt well enough. It should do the same for me."

A grunt from the Boogeyman draws our attention. I turn to see him struggling to open an ancient wooden trunk decorated with Arabic script. Despite his size and power, the trunk is getting the better of him. The rest of us crowd in around him to assist.

"What's inside?" I ask as I tug on the trunk's lid.

"Our ride," the Boogeyman groans, "to the, *uh*, Queen's, *uh*, castle."

We all yank and pull to no avail.

"We need something to pry it open," Gazelluride huffs.

I look around the room and spot a sword corroded with rust sticking out of a large, moss-covered boulder. The boulder itself is balanced on top of a small pedestal.

"That should do it." I run over and, without thinking, yank the sword from the stone. It pulls free with an unexpected metallic ringing that causes me to freeze in place.

A woman's voice echoes from both everywhere and nowhere. "All hail the King of Britanniae!"

At the moment, the rust falls away from the sword, leaving it as bright and shiny as the day it came out of the forge.

"Oops!"

The Boogeyman shakes his head and gestures for me to

return. "Never mind that right now, Puck."

I rejoin him and plunge the sword into the slight crack between the trunk and its lid. I work the blade back and forth, using it like a crowbar to pry open the lid as the others continue to tug. Just when I think there'll be no budging it, the lid flies open with an audible pop. We stumble backward with the lack of resistance as a flowing Persian rug with tasseled edges spills out of the trunk. But the carpet cascades in reverse, moving into the air rather than onto the floor. Once completely free, the rug spreads out to hover unaided above our heads.

"A flying carpet," I say. "Cool!"

Eliana crosses her thin arms so she holds the staff across her chest at a diagonal. "So that's where it's been hiding."

"You can fly that thing?" Satyr asks.

Eliana smiles. "I don't exactly have a license, but yeah. I can fly it."

"Good," the Boogeyman growls. He rolls up the carpet and plunges it into the deep shadows of his cloak where it disappears. "Because that's how you, Puck, Satyr, Gazelluride, and... *has anyone seen the Fairy Godmother?*"

Each of us look around, realizing we haven't seen *her ugliness* in the last few moments.

Siren shrugs. "She came in here with us. But after that—?"

The Boogeyman shakes his head. "I'm sure she's fine. She's rumored to have such ways about her. Regardless, come pre-dawn, we leave. With, or without her. And on that note, I suggest we all get some much-needed rest while we still can. I would guess it is only an hour or so before pre-dawn. We're going to need our strength, to say the least."

The group mumbles in agreement before splitting up. Each of us retires to some quiet corner of the Sanctum Sanctorum.

I find a nice comfy couch to stretch out on in a room with antique clocks and fleur-de-lis wallpaper. When Eliana's silhouette appears in the doorway minutes later, I don't say anything. I simply scoot over. She lies down beside me and we snuggle together like family as we wait for what may very well be our last day on Earth.

30

CHARGE OF THE TWILIGHT BRIGADE

An hour later, Eliana wakes me from a sweet dream of being at home, eating popcorn with Mom and Dad as we watch movies. It leaves me all the more cold and empty inside when the present hopelessness of waking reality comes surging back.

"Come on," Eliana says, "it's time. Everyone's ready."

She leaves the room, and I yawn as I rub the sleep from my eyes. I fumble around in the semi-darkness with my hand until it finds the sword I drew from the stone back in the magical artifact repository. The blade is too long to stick in my belt, so I simply carry it in hand as I exit the room. I make my way down a long corridor and enter a large but sparsely decorated foyer. Everyone but the Fairy Godmother is already there. Eliana, Satyr, and Gazelluride sit on the magic carpet where it hovers inches above the floor. The Boogeyman and Siren stand beside them. A look of resolve adorns each of their faces.

Being in such brave company bolsters my own faltering spirit. I move with a spring in my step and butterflies in my stomach that have nothing to do with Eliana as I take my place beside her on the carpet.

"Still no sign of the Fairy Godmother?" I ask.

Eliana shakes her head. "She may very well be the smartest one in the bunch. You and me included."

Eliana and I smile at one another in spite of our grim circumstances.

"Here." Siren extends her hand to us. Two tiny acorns lie within her palm. "Eat these."

Eliana plucks an acorn from Siren's hand and swallows it. "What are they?"

"You'll need them since you won't be flying directly under fairy wing," Siren says. "They'll allow you to breathe and keep you warm once we're high, and the air becomes cold and thin."

I scoop up the remaining acorn and plop it into my mouth. "We sure could've used some of these when we were flying around, looking for Castle Night."

The Boogeyman whirls to address us, his shadow cloak fluttering menacingly with the gesture. But his usual fearsome demeanor is actually comforting. I know what it means for his enemies when he turns his grim face upon them.

"We've all been through much together in a very short amount of time. However, we must fortify ourselves, for worse still is yet to come."

The Boogeyman places his hands behind his cloaked back, taking on the air of the lecturing general he is.

"We're charging the Queen's sky castle in the pre-dawn twilight so that we may all attack simultaneously. But that also means we won't have much time, and that we will be facing the full force of the Queen's army. I don't have to tell you their numbers are far greater than our own. Therefore, in order to succeed, we must be quick, cunning, and merciless." The Boogeyman punches the palm of his hand three times to emphasize each adjective. "Surprise is on our side, so let's make the most of it. We have the fate of both Earth and Fairy depending on us. Now, are you with me?"

"Yes," the group replies in unison.

"Then say it like you mean it!" the Boogeyman roars.

"Yes!" we shout.

"Louder!"

"YES!"

The Boogeyman draws his rapier from his cloak and points it skyward. "Then, charge!"

Eliana shouts a single word in some ancient language and I have to snag the front edge of the carpet with my free hand to keep from tumbling off as it shoots forward like a bullet from a gun. I glance over my shoulder and see Siren's fluttering butterfly wings lift her into the air as the Boogeyman changes shape into a dark, horned owl and flies after us.

We bank left and enter a twisting, curving stairwell. We race up its throat at what feels like Mach speed until we reach a set of steel doors aptly marked as the rooftop exit.

Instead of slowing down, Eliana increases speed and raises her staff.

"Infligo!"

A bolt of golden lighting leaps from the staff's wooden head to zap the door. The latter disappears completely, leaving a rectangle of purple twilight in its wake.

"Here we go!"

We soar out into the pre-dawn. "Hold on!" Eliana screams. I obey, and not a moment too soon. We take a nosedive just in time to miss being swatted from the sky by a large tree—or, at least what's left of one. The towering giant who wields the tree like a club has shaved off most of its branches, but there are still plenty of sharpened nubs along its sides that could easily impale a mortal—or fairy, as the case may be.

"So much for the element of surprise."

The giant's follow-through is brought to a crashing halt seemingly by thin air. The sky ripples outward from the weapon's point of impact as though it were made of liquid rather than gas, but holds fast. I'm confused until I see Siren and the Boogeyman-owl come flying out from behind the tree-club, unscathed.

The spells of the High Thirteen don't just protect the Sanctum Sanctorum, they cloak it so that you can't see the building's exterior.

Eliana flies us through a scissor-roll, dodging two more tree-clubs wielded by twin gray trolls who look like the very ones the Boogeyman fought in his giant bear form. Their weapons collide with the skyscrapers surrounding us, and we scream along with the steel girders bending with the force of their blows as showers of broken glass rain down on us.

"I think I'm going to be sick," I shout. Thankfully, last night's chips and soda stay in their proper place.

"Take us higher," Gazelluride shouts over the whistling wind. "We've got to fly beyond their reach."

Eliana takes us above the towering buildings lining the street, and immediately I know we're in big trouble.

Stretching across the indigo skyline as far as the eye can see are legions of elves, goblins, and orcs sitting astride winged mounts of all descriptions. Intermixed with these riders of pegasi, griffins, and chimera are harpies, bat-winged vampires, giant eagles, and other flying terrors.

Two dragons bring up the rear of the fairy air force. One is the golden scaled monstrosity we saw from Eliana's memories. The other is my brown fair-weather friend from the Night Lands.

"Don't worry!" Satyr shouts over the wind. He takes the pouch of pixie dust from his loin cloth and begins unraveling the cord at its neck. "I've got this—!"

The pouch's cord comes free and the wind scoops up every last spec of pixie dust and deposits it directly into Satyr's eyes, nose, and mouth. He coughs and spits for a few painful moments. Then the biggest, dumbest grin I've ever seen spreads across his face.

He places a steadying hand on Eliana and me and chuckles. "Great news, guys: we're all going to die!"

This sends him into a fit of laughter that would be comical under different circumstances. But as things are, it isn't funny at all.

"What's that?" Eliana asks.

Black, horizontal rain zooms through the sky directly toward us.

"Siren!" Gazelluride screams. "Incoming!"

Siren zooms out in front of us and throws open the rainbow-hued umbrella she's carrying. A multicolored wave of energy surges from its rainbow top just in time to catch the barrage of arrows the Queen's flyers sent hurtling our way.

"A force field," I shout. "Now I get it."

Satyr begins clapping his hands. "De-fense! De-fense! Rah-rah-rah! De-fense! De-fense! Sis-boom-bah!"

The goat-man grabs his sides as he doubles over with laughter. His guffaws are eclipsed by an ear-piercing shriek. A shadow drops over us. I look skyward and see a several tall figures in hooded black robes riding on the backs of horrific birds that are part vulture and part pterodactyl.

"Shriekers!"

As quick as Eliana names them, they dive-bomb us.

"Back, you fell beasts!" Gazelluride shouts. "Back, you abominations of men!" She points the hairdryer in the shriekers' direction and lets loose a massive torrent of flame. The pyre does the trick, and the shriekers scatter. One of them fails to get out of the way fast enough. The flames catch his robe and the wings of his mount. The two of them go spiraling Earthward like a smoking, bullet-riddled fighter jet, both of them shrieking all the way down.

"London bridge is falling down!" Satyr sings between guffaws. "Falling down! Falling down!"

"Will someone please shut him up," Eliana shouts. "I'm trying to concentrate here!"

"My fair La—!"

"Here, take this." I hand Satyr my sword so that I may clamp my hand over his mouth and silence him.

We travel ever higher and burst through the airborne mass of fairies and their mounts. Eliana actually has the skill to pave the way before us with bolts from her staff while navigating the flying carpet. Gazelluride keeps our flanks free and clear with the flame-spouting hairdryer. Siren uses the umbrella's force field to shield us from any return fire. Meanwhile, I'm relegated to keeping Satyr under control. But considering his current state and our extreme speed and altitude, it's more than enough job for me.

We breach the cloud cover, and my jaw drops at what I see looming over this second, cottony horizon.

When I heard that the Queen of Fairy had set up her seat of government in the clouds of Earth, I expected her palace would be some grand, Elizabethan structure like Castle Twilight. But that's not what greets my eyes at all. Instead of a castle or tower, a ridiculously tall skyscraper with a penthouse apartment at its apex stretches into Earth's upper atmosphere.

The others share my surprise.

"It's..." Gazelluride stammers, "it's like something a mortal would build."

Before we can discuss the matter further, more fairies on winged mounts come pouring out of the building to attack us.

Suddenly, something wallops us from below, and the carpet flips in midair. Luckily, everyone aboard has the presence of mind to hang on.

Everyone but me, that is!

I fall from the carpet and the clouds we breached earlier rush up to engulf me. I hit them and continue to drop, my screams swallowed by the whistling wind. Then I'm snatched from the air by what, at first, appears to be an enormous, living shadow. It's only after I've had a moment to regain my breath and focus that I realize I'm held tight within the talons of a dragon. At first, I think it's one of the Fairy Queen's flying beasts, and believe myself a goner. But then I notice the dragon holding me is neither gold nor brown, but pitch-black.

"Boogeyman!"

The Boogeyman turns the white, horned head at the end of his long, gray neck in my direction. These portions of his dragon's anatomy are the only ones not covered in scales of pure darkness.

"Climb up, Puck," he roars. "I have need of my talons."

"Climb up? Are you serious?"

"Now!" the Boogeyman thunders, and I scuttle up the black scales covering his giant, muscled leg to cling to the larger ones protecting his immense back, more terrified of my mentor at this moment than of gravity's pull. It's a good thing I do, too. The Boogeyman doesn't waste any time in attacking the golden, people-snatching dragon in the Queen's employ.

The Boogeyman strikes from above and hits the dragon unawares. He sinks his talons into his opponent's back and latches onto his neck and shoulder with enormous, razor-sharp fangs.

When the Boogeyman said "merciless," he wasn't kidding. They may call themselves fairies, but I know the truth: I'm in the company of monsters.

The golden dragon shrieks and tries to buck the Boogeyman from his back. Then, abruptly, he stops struggling and actually levels off to fly through the sky at an almost lazy pace. Luckily for us, the Boogeyman realizes what is happening seconds before I do. He rolls, turning up the golden dragon's belly just in time for it to catch the green fire cascading from the brown dragon's throat. The fireworks end, and the Boogeyman releases the glittering beast so that it can beat a smoke-trailing retreat through the sky.

The two remaining dragons circle one another in mid-air, waiting for the other to slip up and provide an opening for attack.

"Surrender now, Dragon," the Boogeyman bellows, "and I will have mercy on you."

Dragon laughs. It's a sound that will give me nightmares for years to come. "It must be murder holding such a form as one of my kind for so long, Boogeyman. Especially after all the energy I'm sure you expended attacking my brother. If you think me so foolish as to surrender to you now, then you have another thing coming, *My Lord*." Dragon spits the title in mockery.

"I was hoping you would say that."

The Boogeyman streaks toward Dragon. She opens her fanged mouth and time slows to a crawl. My eyes go wide at the sight of the green fire I see building in her gullet.

Rather than counter Dragon's flame with one of his own, the Boogeyman changes shape, shrinking back into his humanoid form. I give a startled yell as I grope frantically for the lifeline of his billowing shadow cloak. I snag hold of the cloak just as the Boogeyman pulls out what looks like a pack of bubblegum from its shadowy depths.

Each passing second continues to stretch into hours as our forward momentum heralds us through the sky toward Dragon's open maw.

A time like this and all the Boogeyman can think to do is chew gum?

The fire building in Dragon's throat begins leaking into her mouth, threatening to surge out at us at any moment.

I'm too frightened to even close my eyes, so I see the Boogeyman sling the pack of gum through the air. It seems to move at a snail's pace as it crosses the final gap of sky separating us from Dragon's mouth. As the pack of gum approaches, the heat from the coalescing flames causes it to swell like a balloon—*a sizzling, boiling balloon, that is.*

At the last eternity-long second, the swollen pack of gum reaches Dragon's mouth and explodes, filling her gargantuan jaws to capacity with a mass of stretchy pink goo.

For a fearful moment, the gum bubbles outward under the onslaught of flame trying to escape from Dragon's throat.

But to my amazement, the sticky pink candy holds.

Having nowhere to go, the fire turns on its master. Now it is Dragon who swells like a balloon.

Time leaps forward once again and, in a flash, the Boogeyman transforms into a black-winged griffin with the white head of a bald eagle. I cling to his feathered neck as the Boogeyman flaps his wings for all he's worth in an effort to get us out of there.

I don't see the explosion that removes Dragon from reality, but I certainly feel it. My eardrums pop with the resulting boom, and a shockwave accompanied by a rush of hot air pushes the Boogeyman and me upward with such force that we speed through the clouds and actually pass our companions on the flying carpet.

"What the heck kind of bubblegum was that?" I shout over the wind.

"Just a little something I picked up in the High Thirteen's repository. Worked out quite well, don't you think?"

"You can say that again!"

"No time to celebrate," the Boogeyman shouts. "We must hurry. Dawn is almost here."

I look back over my shoulder, past our companions and the hordes of mounted fairies chasing us, and see the Boogeyman is right. The horizon along the cloud line has lightened to a coppery-orange hue.

Siren and the carpet riders close the distance between the Boogeyman and me, and we quicken the pace of our flight as a group. Seconds later, the roof of the penthouse apartment atop the skyscraper is directly beneath us. I gulp to see the beautiful Queen of Fairy sitting motionless on a throne among immaculate Grecian pillars supporting open sky. It's as if the Queen doesn't consider us to be any sort of threat whatsoever. And that makes me worry, big time.

The Boogeyman and I fly across the sparkling blue water of a concrete swimming pool flanked by more white pillars and well-manicured shrubs in order to reach the Queen. She doesn't so much as shift in her royal, Elizabethan garments at our approach, and that worries me more than ever.

We touch down directly before her, and I leap off the Boogeyman's back so he can transform into his normal ominous self. Eliana lands the carpet behind us. She and the others are up and moving in seconds flat.

"You are in violation of the ancient Pact between fae and mortalkind, Your Majesty," the Boogeyman thunders as his gallop becomes a two-legged stride. "Therefore, your authority is no longer recognized. You will—"

"That will be quite enough out of you, *Ian MacGregor.*"

To our shock and surprise, the Merlin's Second steps out from behind one of the Grecian pillars. He holds a large, leather-bound book open in his hand. The book is so old and dusty that it appears ancient beyond imagining. It contrasts heavily against the Second's modern red trencher and black suit. He grins, the gesture widening his salt-and-pepper goatee and lifting his pierced ears. However, I'm unable to tell if his smile reaches the eyes hidden beneath his crimson, half-moon shades.

"You be still, now, you hear?" he drawls.

I gasp as the Boogeyman freezes unmoving in mid-stride. The rest of our band looks on in shocked horror.

Siren throws down the umbrella so she may draw her golden rapier and point it at the Second. "What did you do?"

The Second looks at her from above his sunglasses, his expression that of an irritated librarian. He scratches his bald head, then licks the end of a ringed finger he uses to turn a page of the book he's holding.

"That goes for you too, *Sarah McKenzie.* Be still. And you, *Pan.* And you, *Ghazal.*"

One by one, Siren, Satyr, and Gazelluride all become as still and silent as the Boogeyman.

"How could you do this?" Eliana shouts. "Infligo!"

Lightning leaps from the end of her staff. The Second raises his book, using it to deflect the sizzling bolt Eliana sent hurtling in his direction.

"Foolish, child." The Second points a finger and shouts something incoherent. Eliana's staff leaps from her hand into his as if yanked there by an invisible cord. "I always said you had promise, sugar. Too bad it's all for naught."

I turn and run for the only means of attack I have left—my sword.

"Uh-uh-uh!" I hear the Second's silky, Southern voice reprimand from behind me. "Remove yourself, *Excalibur*."

I dive to the ground just in time to miss having the sword cut off my head as it slices through the air, drawn on its own invisible tether. The sword impales itself almost to the hilt in one of the Grecian pillars lining the swimming pool, burying my last faint hope of winning the day along with it.

Eliana and I try to run as shriekers, orcs, and elves drop out of the sky. But our attempt at escape proves futile. They capture us easily.

"Well, well, well." The Merlin's Second waltzes up to the Boogeyman. He reaches up and places a hand on my mentor's shoulder like they were old friends. "I hear tell you is some fine kind of monster hunter, Your Shadowiness," the Second says, but with his accent, it comes out sounding like, 'I hear tell youz is some fine kine ah monsta hunta, yo shahdowiness.'" The Second smiles and looks out over the top of his shades. I was right. The grin doesn't make it to his eyes. "Too bad it wasn't a monster you need've been a-huntin'."

"Why isn't the Boogeyman fighting back?" I ask as I struggle within the black-gloved hands of a shrieker. "Why aren't any of them? What did he do to them?"

Before Eliana can answer, the Second whirls to face me. "I'll tell you why, young sir." He waves the ancient book he's carrying at me like a naughty child taunting a sibling with a stolen toy. "The Book of Names. I've used its power to make your friends here stop and sniff the daisies, so to speak. This little volume has proved oh so handy in my conquering of Earth and Fairy."

I look to Eliana. "The book he has is the Logos?"

Eliana sags in defeat within the grip of her fairy captors. It's all the answer I need.

The Second stuffs the Logos inside his trencher for safe-keeping. "Too bad I can't use it to do the same for you, my two fellow children of Eden. But then, that's what dungeons are for, now ain't they?"

"No!" Eliana screams as she struggles in vain to free herself.

"Now don't you worry, sugar," the Second says. "You'll get to see the show before I let them take y'all away."

"Show?" I ask. "What—?"

The shriekers and goblins holding us captive flee, leaving us solely in the hands of tall, handsome elves and massive, furry manimals. The night fae vanish into the building just as dawn breaks. It comes in the form of golden sun rays that crest the parapet of the penthouse roof to bathe everything in their path—including the Boogeyman.

I watch helpless as his clothes and skin gray and then harden into stone. Only the dilation of his pupils gives away the pain and terror he must be feeling. Then they, too, marble over, leaving the Boogeyman a lifeless statue of his former monstrous self.

"I've been meaning to put a sculpture garden up here," the Second laughs. "Looks like I'm off to one heck of a start."

The Second waves his hand in dismissal, and his remaining fairy minions spirit us down a stairwell into the skyscraper's interior. Our captor's mocking, good ol' boy laughter echoes in our ears long after we've left his presence.

31

MOM AND DAD DANCE THE MACARONI

The war between Earth and Fairy is over, and the good guys lost.

Again.

That's all I can think as I stare out into the shadows of the pitch-black room serving as my prison. The elves and their manimal buddies tossed me in here what feels like hours ago before dragging Eliana off to who knows where.

Sitting here alone in the darkness, I've had a lot of time to think about what went wrong. It all boils down to one simple fact: we were outsmarted.

"We were played for chumps," I say, my voice bouncing back at me from faraway walls. "It was the Merlin's Second. Not the Queen. She was only his cat's paw, held under his sway by the power of the Logos."

We were chasing after the wrong baddie all along, despite the fact that the clues leading to the true culprit were starring us in the face the entire time. And now we're all paying for our ignorance. Even the Boogeyman.

The poor, poor Boogeyman.

The fear and pain I saw in his eyes as his body turned into stone plays over and over in my head like an MP3 set to repeat. Even he was powerless to stop the inevitable in the end.

In his defense, like the rest of us, he never had the final piece of the puzzle to put it all together until we arrived here at the floating high-rise of the Merlin's Second. It was seeing the wizard with the Logos that brought all the other clues tumbling into place.

"Things are seldom what they seem."

I shake my head. *What a clever guy the Second is,* I think, then say aloud, "What a massive butt-head."

The ego on that guy! To pull off what he did, to maneuver such powerful people and fairies like they mere pawns on a chessboard. I'd almost admire him if he wasn't such a self-serving tool.

A spotlight flicks on with an audible *thunk* several yards away out in what must be the room's center, and I'm forced to shield my eyes. When my vision adjusts, I see a man and woman standing side by side within the visible circle created by the light. I focus my gaze. The dark-headed man is tall and skinny. The woman is an attractive, short blonde. I realize with a gasp that I know them better than anyone else on Earth.

"Mom! Dad!"

I bolt across the room into the circle of light and throw my arms around my parents. When they fail to return my hug, I look up at them with dawning fear.

"Mom! Dad!" I shout. "Don't let the emo-musketeer garb fool you. It's me. Your son!"

My parents don't move. Even their faces remain still, both of them frozen in unending smiles. Only their eyes and the tears draining from them reveal their true state of terror.

"Oh, no," I say, tears now swelling in my own eyes. I step forward to hug them again but jerk back when Spanish dance music begins blaring throughout the shadow-darkened room.

Mom and Dad come alive. They straighten, then begin swaying to the music. Moving in unison, they extended their right arms, then their left. They fold one arm over the other, then move their hands to their hips as they swing their torsos around in a big circle just as the dance mix hits a crescendo where the recorded voices singing over the track shout something that sounds like, "Hey, macaroni!"

Then, to my horror, it all begins again. And again. *And again.*

"What have they done to you?" I cry loud enough to be heard over the dance music.

"Not they. Him!"

I whirl around and fear seizes me when I see a dark

silhouette standing within a vertical rectangle of light created by an open doorway.

"Eliana?"

The person behind the silhouette enters the room, and I see that I'm right. It's Eliana. She's dressed in her screen-printed T-shirt, jeans, and canvas tennis shoes. Like me, she's on the verge of panic, but otherwise in good shape.

I breathe a sigh of relief when at last she reaches me and takes both my hands in hers. But the din of electronic music and the flickers of dancing I catch from the corner of my eye remind me things are far from okay.

"How did you—?"

The Fairy Godmother appears out of nowhere directly before me, and I give a startled yelp as I scramble backward several steps.

"I thought you'd left us."

The Fairy Godmother cackles, impressed with herself to no end. "And so I had, young Master Puck. Out of sight, and so out of mind. I came along on the Boogeyman's foolhardy charge of the Second's fortress, but stayed as invisible as the air you breathe. And a good thing I was invisible, too, or else the sunlight would have had me as stiff and stony as your shadowy guardian. Appears now it was best for all concerned, wouldn't you say?"

"But, how?"

The Fairy Godmother lifts a gnarled, liver-spotted hand to show me the small, wooden hoop she's holding between her claw-like thumb and forefinger. "A ring of power from the High Thirteen's repository. Usually they're nasty, corruptive little buggers." The Fairy Godmother grins wickedly, exposing twin rows of gray gum and yellow, rotting teeth. "Good for us that I'm already corrupt."

The Fairy Godmother cackles. "Regardless, I'm safe enough here within the Second's fortress. He's thrown up more protective spells around this place than there are guarding the Sanctum Sanctorum. I guess the fae serving him here in the Mortal Lands need sanctuary from both sun and moon, respectively. Still, I haven't seen any of my kind loping about inside today. They're probably cowering down in the building's cellar, being overly cautious to make sure no sunlight touches them."

Instead of my usual response of eye-rolling where the Fairy Godmother's concerned, I actually smile.

"What a deceitful, black-hearted, and wonderfully conniving old bat you are, Fairy Godmother."

The Fairy Godmother places a crooked hand to her sagging bosom. "Why, Puck. What a wonderful compliment. I'm touched beyond words."

"We need to get moving," Eliana says. "Wizard Bottom's Day Fairy guards could be here any second."

"Wizard Bottom?" I ask.

"That's his name. Nick Bottom is Second in the order of the High Thirteen Wizards. He's outranked only by the Lady Merlin. But, as you saw, it appears he's broken his oath of service and gone warlock, using the Logos for selfish means."

The Fairy Godmother nods. "He's the cause of all this trouble. It began with the Second, and so it will end. That's why we have to stop him."

Eliana shakes her head. "Is that possible? Wizard Bottom's extremely powerful even by the standards of the High Thirteen. With the Book of Names in his possession…well, we've seen what he's capable of now."

My gaze finds Mom and Dad. Their arms extend, fold, and go to their hips over and over again as the music repeats without end.

"It has to be us," I say. "Both Earth and Fairy hang in the balance." I turn back to Eliana and the Fairy Godmother and shrug. "Besides, we're the only ones left to get the job done."

The Fairy Godmother gives a slight bow. "Spoken like a true prince of Fairy, *Your Highness.*"

I step up to the Fairy Godmother, my anger toward her returning. "Listen," I whisper so that Eliana can't hear, "I don't care what you say. I'm no changeling, and I'm no prince. Just a kid from the States. Okay?"

The Fairy Godmother's triple chins wag as she chuckles. "We shall see, Master Puck. We shall see indeed."

I whirl away from her, fuming.

"What's she talking about?" Eliana asks.

"Nothing," I say as I stalk by Eliana. "Give me one more second, then we're out of here."

I approach Mom and Dad, my sorrow for them eclipsing my anger toward the Fairy Godmother. I slow then stop as I reach them, a chorus of what sounds like "Hey, macaroni!" echoing repeatedly in my ears.

"I'll be back for you," I say, tears swelling in my eyes once again. "I promise. I love you both."

Locked in their enchanted dance, they're unable to respond, of course. But the look in their eyes tells me they hear me. Even more, it tells me they believe me—*believe in me*—and it's all I need to keep going.

Without another word, I turn and march up to Eliana and the Fairy Godmother.

"Who're they?" Eliana asks.

"My parents," I reply flatly.

"Your—? Oh, Puck."

"Let's hope your own mom is in better shape. But anyway, the one way we can help them all is to bring the Second down." "Now you're talking!" The Fairy Godmother slips the ring from the High Thirteen's repository onto her finger. As it slides over her knuckles, she disappears from sight.

"Take my hands," her voice echoes out of nothingness.

Through the fabric of my glove, I feel a cold and very invisible hand grope its way into mine. When my fingers close around it, my body vanishes.

I'm still here. I can still feel my clothes against my body and the force of gravity holding my feet to the floor. I simply can no longer see these things. Eliana vanishes, and I realize no one else can, either.

I feel the Fairy Godmother tug my hand, and I join her and Eliana in their walk toward the room's open door. I give Mom and Dad a final, parting glance as we exit the room and enter a long hallway lined with ornate wooden paneling and expensive works of art.

"So what's the plan?" I whisper.

"We must seize the Logos," the Fairy Godmother says under

her rancid breath. "If we can steal the Book of Names, then we can use it to defeat the Second and set things right again."

"How're we supposed to do that?" I ask. "Judging by what we saw, Bottom keeps the Logos on his person."

I can't see it, but I imagine the Fairy Godmother shaking her head. "Not at the moment. Right now, the Logos is in his personal study."

"How do you know?" Eliana asks.

"Silly little mortal. I'm invisible. I sneaked inside and saw it there."

"Well why didn't you take it and use it then?" I ask.

"I couldn't," the Fairy Godmother says. "I told Puck before, the Logos was created for wizards of the Mortal Lands and may only be used by such."

"Well that doesn't help us," I blurt. "I'm not a wizard."

"I am," Eliana says, and, even through the haze of invisibility, I can almost see the grin spreading across her lovely butterscotch cheeks.

32

WE PLAY HIDE AND SEEK

The Fairy Godmother, Eliana, and I creep through the plush hallways of the Second's high-rise in the clouds, flattening ourselves against walls or ducking inside doorways to avoid passing squads of Day Lands fairies despite the added protection of our invisibility. But then, you can never be too careful, especially when the fate of two worlds hangs in the balance.

The three of us are hiding in an art gallery just off the beaten path when I hear the sound of muffled music playing in an adjoining room. The beat's familiar.

Sickeningly so.

I give the Fairy Godmother's hand a tug. Eliana and I have to hold on to her in order to share in the powers of invisibility the ugly old bat's ring grants her.

"Come on," I whisper. "This way."

"No," the Fairy Godmother says. "The Second's study is in the opposite direction, just down the hall from which we came. That's where we'll find the Book of Names."

"I want to see something," I reply. "It might be important."

The Fairy Godmother huffs, and I'm glad I'm unable to see the cross expression that must be stretched across her gruesome face. "Very well."

Holding hands, we cross the room and approach a door leading out of the gallery. The source of the music is coming from its other side. From here, I have no problem making out the all-too-familiar chant of "Hey, macaroni!"

I crack open the door and loud techno music comes pouring

into the gallery. The three of us lean in to peek into the other room. I immediately wish we hadn't.

Inside is row after row of people, both fairy and mortal, all of them dancing beneath a spinning disco ball, doing the same simple moves as Mom and Dad. Among them are the King of Fairy, the Lady Merlin, and the rest of the High Thirteen taken captive by the wizard Nick Bottom. The Merlin is dressed in her familiar white trencher, but the coats of her subordinates span the colors of the rainbow. His Majesty is dressed in his usual Kingly regalia, but his dress goes to only further emphasize the indignity he's being forced to suffer.

"It's the same enchantment as before," the Fairy Godmother says. "It's horrible!"

"Hey, macaroni," I mumble under my breath. "You can say that again."

Suddenly, Eliana gasps. "Mama!"

She's there, three rows deep among the dancing crowd—the attractive, middle-aged Latina who is Eliana's mother. She's no better off than my parents after all.

Eliana appears out of thin air as she releases the Fairy Godmother's hand. I let go and also become visible once again.

I place my black-gloved hand on Eliana's arm. "We can't do her any good here. But we're going to save her. *We're going to save them all.*"

Eliana nods and wipes away the tears that have begun to leak from her eyes. We take the Fairy Godmother's hands back in our own and withdraw back into the gallery, knowing the enchanted dancers will be best served by our seizing the Logos.

From the gallery, it's a short trek down the hall to Bottom's study. However, the only problem is that a tall, fearsome-looking elf armored in plates of ivory stands guard at the door. We backtrack down the hall just out of earshot.

"Curses," the Fairy Godmother spits. "He wasn't there before."

"So now what?" Eliana says. "We may be invisible, but we aren't ghosts. We can't just phase through the wall into Wizard Bottom's study. We have to get past the guard and through that door."

I scratch my invisible head, having no idea of what to do or how to answer.

"There's only one thing for it," the Fairy Godmother whispers. "Take this. Mind you don't wear it too long. Doing so will most certainly prove detrimental to your health."

I gasp as I feel the Fairy Godmother's hand leave mine. Immediately, the three of us become visible once again. The elf guard jerks upright, frozen in surprise at the sight of us. It buys the Fairy Godmother enough time to shove something into my gloved hand. I open my palm to see her ring of power lying there.

"Who are you?" the elf thunders as he regains his composure. "What are you doing here?"

"Are you daft?" the Fairy Godmother yells. "Hurry! Put it on!"

Without wasting any more time, I slip the ring onto a gloved finger. The world around me grows cold and I vanish from sight. I feel a mixture of negative emotions boil up within me. My sorrow for my parents. My despair at the direness of our situation. And most of all, my hatred of the Second for causing all this trouble. I shake my head and seize Eliana's hand. It helps a little. Enough to allow me to think somewhat rationally again, anyway.

Eliana disappears from sight just as the elf reaches us. The two of us stand by the Fairy Godmother, not daring to move for fear of detection.

"Where did they go?" the large elf demands.

"Why whoever do you mean?" the Fairy Godmother asks, batting nonexistent eyelashes at the guard.

"The two who were with you. The boy and the girl."

"I'm afraid I haven't the slightest idea what you're talking about, my dear."

"They were just here!" the elf shouts, now enraged.

"Who?"

"THE TWO WHO WERE WITH YOU, I SAID!"

"Oh my!" The Fairy Godmother places a twisted hand on the elf's forehead, catching him by surprise. "Are you running a fever, dear?"

The guard seizes the Fairy Godmother's wrist. "Get your claws off me, Night Lands trash!"

"Oooo," she coos, giving the guard a wink of her blind eye. "Aren't you fresh? I like that."

"That's it! You're coming with me."

"Now you're talking, handsome."

I watch as the elf leads the Fairy Godmother down the hall and out of sight.

"She may look like death warmed over," Eliana whispers, "but she's one sharp old lady."

I nod reluctantly, forgetting for a moment that Eliana can't see the gesture. "Yeah. I guess so. But anyway, come on. Let's get that book."

We trot up to the ornately carved wooden door the elf was guarding. I grab hold of its golden knob and twist as I push on the door. Nothing happens.

"The knob turns, but the door won't open."

"The lock must be enchanted," Eliana whispers. "Let go of me for a moment. I may need both hands for this."

I reluctantly release Eliana's hand and take off the Fairy Godmother's ring. Immediately, we reappear within the hallway. Our being visible is a big risk, but with a little luck, we'll be inside the study and away from any potential prying eyes within a matter of seconds.

I move aside to allow Eliana access to the door. Instead of hocus-pocusing the door's lock, Eliana kneels down and pulls something out of her sneaker. She holds it up for me to see that it's a tiny, beaked skull of a chicken joined to a small drumstick bone.

"Gross."

Eliana frowns. "It's a skeleton key. One of my mother's. A true Santera never leaves home without one."

She sticks the drumstick end of the key into the lock and twists. The lock gives with an audible click.

"I figured as much," Eliana says. "Every member of the High Thirteen could've stood here blasting spells away at this door, and it probably wouldn't have budged. Sometimes, the simplest solutions are the best."

She pushes the door open, and we step inside the Second's study, locking the door behind us. Thick carpet as red as the Second's trencher covers the floor. A sleek, modern desk adorned with a laptop and Eliana's staff rests before walls of vertical windows showcasing the clear blue sky outside. The only book in the room is the dusty, leather-bound Logos. It rests on a thin podium of dark metal stationed at the room's center. All in all, the room looks more like the office of some eccentric corporate executive rather than the sanctuary of a practicing wizard.

"My staff," Eliana says. She snatches the gnarled wooden stick from the desk and examines it from end to end as though it like a long-lost old friend—which I suppose it is.

Eliana and I turn our gaze to the Logos, then each other.

I shrug. "Go ahead, I guess."

She takes a step forward, and I place a halting hand on her shoulder. "But be careful."

She nods and starts for the Logos again only for my hand to fall back on her shoulder. "You're doing great," I say.

"Thanks."

She moves toward the Logos again only for me to stop her a third time. "Maybe you should—?"

"Puck!"

"Okay! Okay! Pardon me for being concerned."

Eliana and I hold our collective breath as she reaches for the Logos. At the last second, she pulls back. "You know what? You're right. Better safe than sorry."

She stretches out her staff and touches it to the Book of Names. The second she does, there's an explosion of light and sound that knocks us both down and sends her staff flying across the room to bounce off the windows and roll behind the desk.

We rise onto our elbows and shake our heads, clearing them. "Did you get the license plate of the truck that hit us?" I groan.

"Mellon!" a familiar Southern voice cries from beyond the study door. I've just enough time to slip on the Fairy Godmother's ring and snag Eliana's hand so we may become invisible before the Second and his entourage of elf knights burst into the study.

My stomach goes into my throat as Nick Bottom strides toward the Logos, his red leather trencher flaring out behind him like a devil cape. The muscular elf who led away the Fairy Godmother trails at his heels.

"What do you mean, 'she got away'?" the Second asks, visibly miffed.

"Forgive me, Your Imperialness," the elf pleads. "I looked away but for one second and then, poof! She was gone."

Good for her, I think, surprising even myself to be on the Fairy Godmother's side for once.

The Second slows then stops as he reaches the podium bearing the Logos. He stands only inches away from Eliana and me. I try to breathe as quietly as possible as I will my heart to beat in silence.

It doesn't work. My traitorous ticker pounds like a jackhammer inside my chest.

"Claudo," Bottom whispers. He speaks so softly you'd have to have been nearly on top of him to have heard what he said. But as that's the case with Eliana and me, more or less, we have no problem making out the word.

A film of light fizzles over the Logos then disappears. The Second reaches down and takes the Book of Names off the pedestal so that he can thumb through its tattered, yellow pages. Satisfied, he slams the Logos closed and returns it to its resting place.

"Claudere," he whispers, and the film of light flashes to reseal the Logos.

Bottom exhales and turns to face the guard.

"Poof, you say?"

The elf shrugs. "Yes, my emperor. Poof!"

Lightning leaps from the wizard's hand. It strikes the guard, and I throw my hand over my mouth to hold back a scream when the elf explodes into bits of confetti that rain silently onto the blood-red carpet.

"How's that for a poof?"

The Second turns his attention to the now-cowering elves.

He stabs a finger in their direction, and the fairy knights all but drop to their knees in fright.

"You, archer!" the Second says, pronouncing the word like, *ahchah*.

"Y-y-y-yes, Your Imperiousness?" a knight armed with a bow stutters.

"You've just been promoted. You'll guard that door with your life. You hear?"

"Yes, my emperor! With my life!"

The Second spins, his eyes darting about the room as he circles. "Let that be a lesson to all of you. I will not tolerate such—!"

Bottom's eyes fall on the empty space on his desk formerly occupied by Eliana's staff, and my heart sinks.

He rushes to the desk and scans the floor around it. It only takes the wizard a moment to find the staff. He snatches it from the ground and whirls to peer about the room.

"They've been here," he growls.

Bottom snatches the half-moon sunglasses from his face to reveal a pair of dark, beady eyes bookending either side of his nose. To my surprise, the wizard's eyes flare to become twin searchlights. He turns his head to and fro, allowing their beams to wash over the room.

Eliana and I cling to each other in a frightened hug. I don't know about her, but I send up frantic prayers that whatever magic the Second's using, it won't be enough to penetrate the power of the Fairy Godmother's ring.

The beams from Bottom's eyes shine down on us, blinding us with their light, and I swear I feel my heart stop dead inside my chest. It kicks back up again a second later when the searchlights streaming from the Second's head move on to continue their sweep of the room.

Moments later, his eye lights blink out.

"We must find them."

"Who, Your Imperialness?" one of the braver elves asks.

"Those meddlesome brats. Eliana and her little boyfriend. I should've had them dancing with their parents to begin with."

"That would have been wise, My Emp—"

The unusually brave elf is confetti before he can finish his sentence.

"Find them!" the Second bellows.

The elf knights gaze at one another, fear and confusion battling for supremacy on their faces.

"NOW!"

A few choice bolts of lightning from Bottom's hand get the elves scrambling out the door. The Second strides out after them. Once outside the door, he abruptly halts and turns to the newly appointed guard.

"I'll be up on the roof where I can think. Spread the word to your fellow knights as they pass: I'm to be informed the moment the Godmother and those bratty kids are found."

The Second gives a magical wave of his hand, and the study door slams shut before the elf can respond.

33

HIGH NOON

After being threatened, chased, attacked, kidnapped, imprisoned, shot at, lied to, and nearly killed on more occasions than I've had birthdays, we've finally caught a lucky break.

The Merlin's Second himself has unknowingly given Eliana and me the magical password needed to access the Logos. With the Book of Names in our hands, we should be able to undo all the havoc the Wizard Bottom has visited on Earth and Fairy.

I release Eliana's hand, and she appears before me in the Second's ultra-modern study wearing her homemade T-shirt and trendy jeans. I remove the Fairy Godmother's ring from my gloved hand, and I snap into focus myself, black musketeer garb and all.

"He took my staff," Eliana moans.

"Let him have it," I say. "I know how to get to the Logos."

"Yeah, I overheard him say the password, too."

Eliana turns to the sleek, metal podium bearing the Book of Names. "Claudo."

A thin glow envelops the Logos, then vanishes.

Eliana reaches out a tentative hand and, after a moment of hesitation, takes hold of the book.

Nothing happens, and we both exhale in deep relief.

Eliana lifts the Logos and begins flipping through its ancient yellowed pages. "Since he's mortal, we won't be able to use the Logos directly against the Second. But...here," she says, "the Queen of Fairy's true name."

I give her a quizzical look.

"The Fairy Queen is a creature of pure magic. One at least as powerful as the Merlin. And she'll be on the roof with Bottom. I'll say her name and free her from the Second's Logos-augmented spell. If anyone can put Wizard Bottom in his place, it's the Queen."

Eliana opens the Logos wide enough for me to read the text. "The Queen of all Fairy's name is Gertrude Picklesimer Sparklebottom?"

Eliana shrugs. "There's no accounting for fairy taste, I guess."

I scratch my head, actually missing my feathered musketeer hat. "Will we be able to use the Logos if we're invisible?"

"Hmmmm," Eliana says, the wheels in her head working, "I hadn't considered that. Technically, it shouldn't be a problem. But then again, sometimes simultaneous spells of great power can interfere with each other, or even cancel each other out—" Eliana hangs her head. "Especially if the wizard casting them is a novice like me."

I squeeze her bicep. "Better not to take the chance, then," I say. "We may only have one shot at this. We'll remain invisible until the last second. But I'll take off the ring when you're ready to use the Book of Names."

"You could just let go of my hand," Eliana says.

"And leave you alone out there, hanging in the wind? No way, Eliana. We're in this together, for good or bad."

Eliana takes my hand in hers and smiles. "My brave, little Sir Puck."

I pull my hand away and look at the floor, my cheeks going hot as I fill with pride, embarrassment, and frustration all at the same time.

I'd be lying if I said I hadn't imagined what it would be like for Eliana to be my girlfriend. She's one smokin' hot teen Latina, after all.

But she's also a couple of years older than me, and while I'm thankful for her compliment, I realize it's the kind of thing you'd say to a little kid, rather than a potential boyfriend.

Always the buddy, never the guy who gets the girl. Story of my life.

I mentally shake myself. If anyone's ever going to have time to feel sorry for his or her self again, I've got to focus on the job at hand.

"Are you ready for this?"

I look Eliana directly in the eye. I hope that my own gaze reflects the look of resolve I find there.

"Let's go kick some warlock butt!"

We clasp hands like teammates going out to play in the Super Bowl, only the stakes of our game are much, much greater. I extend a single finger and slip on the Fairy Godmother's ring of invisibility, and we fade from sight.

We jog hand in hand to the door leading from the study, and I pound on it with my free arm.

"Mellon!" shouts the elf standing guard outside.

Eliana and I scramble aside just in time to miss being flattened by the door when the elf knight comes barging in.

"Who's in here?" the archer bellows.

Instead of answering, Eliana and I run out of the study, slamming the door closed behind us.

"Claudere!" Eliana shouts, sealing the study shut with the very same magic word the Second uttered to seal the Logos. A film of light momentarily engulfs the door, signaling the spell's effect. The glow dissipates just as the trapped archer beings beating on the door's other side.

"Let me out of here! When I get my hands on you—!"

Eliana and I take off for the stairwell the elves used to bring us deep inside the floating high-rise earlier today, leaving the archer alone with his threats. We arrive there, and I kick open the steel door leading out onto the landing, only to fling Eliana and myself back against the wall as a horde of ferocious manimals armed to the fangs comes flooding out of the stairwell and into the hall.

Once they pass, the two of us duck inside. We head for the roof, taking the steps two at a time. We pass several more bands of roving fairies along the way. Bottom's command that his forces find us has thrown the building into a terrible uproar. Every floor is being scoured by countless elves, manimals, sprites, and nymphs.

Too bad for them, they're all looking in the wrong place. But then, who would ever think we'd be crazy enough to take the fight directly to the Second?

I hardly believe it myself.

We reach the topmost landing just as a final troupe of elf knights bursts into the stairwell from the roof. Thanks to our invisibility, they march on by, down the stairs. Once they're gone, Eliana and I take a moment to catch a much-needed breath.

I release Eliana's hand and remove the Fairy Godmother's ring, causing us to reappear. Then I press my face to the small, wire-reinforced window of the steel door leading out onto the roof.

My gaze finds the white pillars and manicured greenery lining the sides of the concrete swimming pool resting before the Fairy Queen and her mock throne. The Queen sits as motionless as ever.

Siren, Satyr, and Gazelluride also stand still and silent right where we left them.

So does the Boogeyman.

I frown to see the noon sun at his back, forming a corona of light around the stone gargoyle it's made of him.

The only one I don't see on the roof is the Second.

Eliana peeks over my shoulder. "Do you see him? Where is he?"

A cloud of despair begins to expand inside me. "It's really going to stink if we came all this way and—wait. There he is."

Nick Bottom appears from behind one of the Grecian pillars at the opposite end of the pool. He meanders up to the Boogeyman and uses my mentor's pointy, stone nose to crack open a walnut before tossing its meat into his mouth. Eliana's staff is nowhere to be seen.

"This is it."

Eliana doesn't answer. Fear and indecision are etched into her normally smooth, attractive face.

And I don't blame her.

As the one wizarding person left who can use the Logos against Bottom, Eliana has a heck of a lot riding on her shoulders. The fate of two worlds, in fact.

If I was in her situation, I'd be shaking in my shoes even more than I already am.

But I know that's far from what she needs to hear right now, so I take her hand in mine.

"It's okay to be scared. Heck, I'm terrified right now, too. But just remember, we've got the Logos—the book that has the true and secret name of everything in the entire universe. All you have to do is say the word, literally, and almost everything and everyone is yours command. On his own, the Merlin's Second doesn't even begin to approach that kind of power."

Eliana nods tentatively. "You're right." Then, once my words have a moment to sink in, "You *are* right."

"That a girl."

Eliana opens the Logos to the page containing the Fairy Queen's true name and double-checks the text. "All right. Let's do this."

"On three," I say. "One. Two." I bring up my leg and kick open the steel door separating us from the high-rise roof.

"Three!"

We leap through the door. Across the pool, Bottom whirls to face us.

"Gertrude Picklesimer Sparklebottom," Eliana reads from the Logos. "Rise and subdue the Merlin's Second. I command you!"

Bottom gasps and flattens himself against the statue of the Boogeyman, bracing himself for the onslaught to come.

But the joke's on us, and Bottom begins to guffaw when the Queen fails to move.

"Say it again," I shout.

Eliana repeats the Queen's name, then the command, shouting even louder this time. Nothing happens, and the bottom of the world falls away beneath my feet.

"But we have the Logos—?"

"Do you, now?" the Second laughs. "Haven't you learned by now that things are seldom what they appear to be?"

Eliana and I look down to see it's no longer the Logos she holds, but the biography of the teen pop sensation whose image was plastered on that closet door back in Japan.

"Do you think me so stupid as to leave the Logos lying about so pitifully guarded?" Bottom withdraws the real Book of Names from his crimson trencher and waves it at us tauntingly. "No, my dears. The Book of Names never leaves my possession. Otherwise my control over my Fairy minions could be overridden.

"What I left behind for ya'll was a trap. One meant to see the two of you right here at this very moment should you have tried to escape and thwart my plans. My thanks to the both of ya'll for complying so readily."

Eliana yells in rage and hurls the biography at Bottom. But we all know it's an empty gesture. The wizard proves as much a second later when he magicks the biography off the roof.

Bottom sighs. "Pan, Sarah, Ghazal. Take 'em."

At the Second's Logos-reinforced words, our day fae friends spring to life and swarm us. Siren and Satyr seize Eliana by her arms. I almost have the Fairy Godmother's ring on my finger when Gazelluride bowls me over and knocks the magical artifact from my hand. The ring rolls across the roof and disappears down a metal grate.

I try to scramble to my feet, but Gazelluride pins me beneath her forelegs. I struggle in vain to free myself for a moment, then collapse.

"Mom, Dad," I moan. "I've failed you."

I think of all the other moms and dads of Fairy and Earth. I think of all their children and grandchildren. Their faces pass before my mind's eye locked in a grotesque smile as their bodies dance without rest for all eternity.

"I've failed them all."

Everyone on the roof flinches in surprise as a geyser of water surges from the pool to splash out onto the concrete and leave a half-submerged Fairy Godmother in its wake. She points a gnarled claw in my direction and locks her blind eyes onto mine, ignoring everyone else.

"Your true test is at hand," the Fairy Godmother crows even as she begins to ossify beneath the sun's rays. "Time to decide: will you be prince or pauper? Mortal or fairy? Boy or *changeling*?"

That's all the Fairy Godmother has time to say before the sun reduces her to a grotesquely sculpted water fountain. But her last word continues to echo in my ears.

Changeling. Changeling. Changeling.

"Senile old witch," Bottom spits. "At least she saved me the trouble of having to deal with her." The Second grins and folds his arms over his chest. "Now I've got time for more important things like tormenting the lot of you forever and ever, eh?"

My enchanted friends stare unblinking at Bottom.

"That's funny," the Second scolds. "Y'all better laugh, now."

The wizard smiles, pleased with himself to no end as Siren, Satyr, and Gazelluride all break into fits of hysterical cackling. The sound is horrifying, and representative of everything that has gone wrong thanks to one small man's lust for power.

It's in this moment that I realize what I must do in order to stop the Second, and the huge sacrifice it will force me to make.

But the truth is, I don't have a choice. Not one that would allow me to ever look at myself in the mirror again, anyway.

If I've learned one thing through all that I've experienced since the Boogeyman came out of my closet, it's that life is unfair, but we must press on anyway.

So I press on.

An image forms inside my head. I try to ignore the sound of my friends' cackling and focus on the mental picture with all of my being. Doing so is like trying to push a huge boulder over a mountain peak. There's nothing, nothing, nothing. And then, all of a sudden, it crests and begins to roll, picking up speed as it goes.

With that initial push, the floodgates inside me open. I scream with the worst pain I've ever known as my body transforms itself into the black-feathered raven I've pictured inside my mind. My yell becomes a caw as I cross the line from mortal to changeling and fly out from under Gazelluride with a flap of my shadowy wings. I zoom over the pool so fast even Bottom doesn't have time to react. He stares at me, a stupid, shocked look on his face.

I decide I need to change his expression into one of fright.

I remember how scared I was when Eliana's wolf came

bounding after me, and I go with that shape, willing my wings into forepaws, my beak into a furry, saber-toothed muzzle. The transformation comes easier this time.

The Second yells in terror as I land on his side of the pool and bound toward him on all four of my powerful legs.

Mission accomplished. A little too well, in fact.

The Second's fear triggers his fight-or-flight response, and he begins hurling lightning at me with his hand. I bob and weave as I run, dodging each successive bolt.

I close the distance between us, and the wizard screams as I pounce.

"Don't kill me!" Bottom pleads as he falls beneath me.

But it's not him I've come for.

I snatch the Logos out of his hand with my jaws and make a run for the pool. I dive in, transforming into the young offspring of a great white shark while in mid-leap, the Book of Names still held secure in my razor-toothed mouth.

Milliseconds later, I leave the pool's other end, leaping into the air. From this high vantage, I can see that my friends have already begun to regain their senses, the Second's hold on them now over with the Logos out of his possession.

I release the Book of Names from my jaws, and the ancient volume falls into Eliana's now-free hands. The book is water-logged, but otherwise okay. I transform back into my humanoid form as I tumble soaking wet onto the concrete, giving myself several scrapes and bruises in the process.

"Read, Eliana!" I shout. "READ!"

Eliana opens the Logos and reads from the text. My human ears would've been unable to comprehend her strange words, but my new fairy ones understand her just fine. Rather than free the Queen, it sounds like she's decided to go with Plan B, if you know what I mean.

"Moon, eclipse the sun!"

Immediately, the blue sky above begins to hull out the sun.

The heavens darken, and storm clouds begin to form above us. Gale-force winds begin to buffet us, threatening to tear us from the roof. I see the Second climb to his feet on the pool's other side, magical energy gushing from his eye sockets, and realize that while the eclipse is Eliana's doing, the storm is Bottom's.

"You dare steal the Logos from me?" Lightning and thunder crash, punctuating the Second's words. All pretense of civility has left him. "*From me?*"

Bottom now reveals himself the violent, hate-filled monster he's always been. He raises his hands skyward, and lightning leaves the tips of his fingers to surge up into the thunderheads and come streaking down again in a hundred different sizzling bolts that pound our eardrums and shake the building.

The commotion is so much that the wizard fails to notice the break in the clouds directly above his head—one showing the last of the sun disappearing behind the moon.

Night envelops the rooftop, and the Queen, Siren, Satyr, and Gazelluride all turn to stone even as the statue that's the Boogeyman begins to stir.

"I'll kill you all!" the Second rages. "Every single last one of—!"

The Boogeyman, now alive, whole, and as frightening as ever, engulfs the Second from behind, wrapping him within the deep shadows of his cloak. The monster hunter's momentum carries the two of them down into the black depths of the pool with an enormous splash. Even after they hit the water, Bottom's rants continue in the form of angry gurgling.

Within seconds, the storm around us dissipates and the water settles, leaving no sign of either the Boogeyman or Nick Bottom.

"I wouldn't want to be the Merlin's Second right now."

I look up to see a sopping-wet Fairy Godmother dragging herself out of the pool, winded but otherwise no worse for wear.

"Here, children. Help me." She reaches for Eliana and me, and we haul her the rest of the way up.

The Fairy Godmother takes a second to wring the water from her clothes. Then her cataract-sheathed eyes find me.

She bows in a show of respect. "Well done, *my Prince.*"

When she rises, we exchange a silent nod.

The Fairy Godmother turns to Eliana. "You, too, my dear. All of Fairy is in your debt."

The three of us don't have to wait long before the Boogeyman reappears.

Bottom is *not* with him.

The Boogeyman ascends from the water like a surfacing leviathan and then glides across the pool's surface to join us on land. His shadow cloak darkles for a second, and then he's left completely dry.

I step forward. "Where's Bottom?"

The Boogeyman doesn't answer for a very long moment.

"I took the Second into the Void." The Boogeyman narrows his menacing gaze. "He wouldn't be quiet."

I think of the horrible things the sound of my own voice brought slithering out of the Void my first time there, and I shudder at the thought of what the Boogeyman is implying.

I look down at the pool's rippling water. My reflection is there on its dark, glassy surface. Only, it's *not* my reflection. Not exactly.

I more or less look the same, though I now stand several inches taller. My hair's still dark and curly. My skin is still as white as fresh milk. But now my ears, nose, and chin are all a little longer—*and a lot pointier.* My forehead is larger, and my eyebrows now slant toward my nose like the sides of an inverted arrowhead.

I slump to see my face is now that of a fairy.

I'm no longer human.

The Boogeyman places a clawed hand on my shoulder.

"You did what you had to do, Puck. Be proud. You saved us."

"Mama!"

I turn to see Eliana's mother embrace her in a loving hug. The crowd that has accompanied her onto the roof continues spilling out of the stairwell. Many of them I saw earlier, dancing beneath the disco ball.

My heart skips a beat to see Mom and Dad among them. My parents scan the roof, obviously looking for me. My eyes go hot and wet when their gaze finds me only to move on.

They don't recognize me. I'm their own son, but I might as well be an alien from Mars, now.

I look up so that I may stare the Boogeyman directly in his obsidian eyes.

"I can never go back to them, can I? Not to stay, I mean."

The Boogeyman frowns in regret and shakes his head.

"You are a true fae, now. And it is in Fairy that you must now reside."

Tears swell within my eyes.

"Then everyone else may have been saved, but I've lost everything."

34

WE BREAK IT DOWN

"So you see, Your Majesties," the Boogeyman says in his deep, Scottish burr, "the Merlin's Second was behind the plot to embroil Fairy and Earth into war from the beginning."

I stand by my mentor beneath clouds of fireflies within the purple quartz throne room of Castle Twilight, flanked by dangling banners and ornate columns of crystal as we address the King and Queen of Fairy.

His and Her Majesty are dressed in the crowns and formal, pseudo-Elizabethan clothes of their station. The Boogeyman and I are rocking our usual shades of black. The only difference today is I no longer wear the black domino mask.

There's no longer any need for it, here, within the throne room.

"The mortal Nick Bottom must have used the same book-disguising glamour to steal the Logos out from under his wizard brethren's noses as he did to fool your son, the prince," the Boogeyman continues.

I shift on my booted feet, still uncomfortable with being a prince, much less the changeling son of two fae parents.

"Sometimes the simplest solutions are the best," I mumble, echoing the words Eliana spoke back in Bottom's high-rise.

I smile at the thought of my wizarding friend. Since helping to restore Earth and Fairy, Eliana's not only been offered a place among the High Thirteen, but also an apprenticeship under Siren as the next hunter of wayward Day Lands fae.

Apparently, Eliana has fae kin somewhere near the root of

her family tree. It's enough to make her eligible for the position of Siren under the terms of the Pact.

Like me, the girl has come a *loooong* way within the past few days. Also like me, she still has some big choices ahead of her.

The Boogeyman turns his gaze directly onto the Queen. "Using your secret name from the Logos, Your Highness, Bottom was able to become your puppet master."

"It was absolutely dreadful," the Queen cries. "I've never been so humiliated. My every word and thought was his to twist and turn as he wished."

The King places a supportive hand on the Queen's. She takes it readily, and enfolds her other dainty palm over his dark, clawed fingers.

"It was through you that he brought the Duke of Night into the conspiracy," the Boogeyman says to the Queen, resuming the thread of his monologue, "causing you to seduce the King's overly ambitious brother with promises of the throne, should he aid in what was presented as a plan to bring not only Fairy under your full control, but the Mortal Lands as well."

"Why?" the King asks, his voice deep and full. "Why did the Second need my brother when he already had the Queen at his disposal?"

The Boogeyman clasps his clawed hands behind his back and begins slinking back and forth before the throne.

"That's where it gets a bit complicated, Your Highness. You see, Bottom's ultimate objective was to bring Earth and Fairy under his sole power. Quite the task. Especially if one doesn't wish to arouse the suspicion of those powerful enough to stop him. Arguably, with the Logos, the Second could have commanded you and the Queen to turn over the throne."

"But that still would've left Earth, uh, the Mortal Lands, free from Bottom's control," I interject, "and the High Thirteen at large to stop him. The wizards are mortals of free will, and so not directly subject to the Logos' power."

The Boogeyman whirls to glare at me with eyes of crystallized night, perturbed at having been interrupted.

I glare right back to him.

My mentor shakes his head and continues his lecture. "The

young prince is right. Before the Second could seize ultimate power, he had to remove those of his order from the picture, and do so without exposing himself."

The Boogeyman halts his pacing and opens his claw in a gesture of supplication.

"In short, Your Majesties, he needed someone to do it for him. And what better way, I ask you, to remove the remaining High Thirteen than to embroil them in a war with an equally powerful third party. Namely, the two of you. The first part of that was giving them cause to go after the King," I say.

The King smiles. "Please, Son. Call me Father."

I stare at the toes of my boots, embarrassed.

"You'll forgive me, Your Highness, if it takes me a while to become comfortable with that."

"Of course, my sweet boy," the Queen says. "Please carry on."

"Well, Your Highness—" the Boogeyman begins, but the Queen shushes him.

"I was talking to my son, Your Shadowiness." Her smile beams at me from her beautiful face. "Go ahead, dear."

I smile at the Boogeyman. He huffs as he folds his long, spindly arms.

"As I was saying," I continue, "the Second's plan to get rid of the rest of the High Thirteen started with giving them reason to make war on the Night Lands. Bottom used the Queen to get to the Duke of Night. The less-than-scrupulous Duke was more than willing to force his people into the Mortal Lands to make trouble. Both for Earth, and the Boogeyman."

"Now I see," the King says. "The Queen's rule doesn't extend to the Night Lands. That's why the Second used her to get to my brother. He needed someone in the Night Lands to act as his agent there."

"Very perceptive, Your Highness," I reply. "The Duke more or less launched a full-scale invasion of Earth."

"And, in the eyes of the High Thirteen," the Kings says, "blame for the Boogeyman's inability to deal with such impossible numbers ultimately fell upon me, the Lord and ruler responsible for the fairy hunter's performance of his duties."

"No doubt the Second was using his influence to steer his

brethren to that conclusion the entire time, Your Majesty." The Boogeyman glides by me, grinning from pointy ear to pointy ear for having usurped the floor from me.

Okay, I'll play your little game. Tit for tat.

"Of course, having no ethics to stop him," I say, "the Duke wiped the minds of the fairies he sent Earth-side so that the Boogeyman couldn't trace anything back to him."

The Queen stares mournfully off into space. "That was my idea, of course. Or rather, the Second used my lips to suggest it." She shudders. "Even for the elf knight who went after you, my prince. After the Duke and I wiped his mind, I sent him to the Mortal Lands myself."

The King reaffirms his hold on his wife's hands as she begins to sob. "It wasn't your fault, dear. It was that black-hearted warlock."

"Quite, Your Majesty," the Boogeyman says. "And once the High Thirteen were provoked to the point of declaring war on the Night Lands and abducting you, the Queen was more than justified in her retaliation, regardless of whether or not she was under the Second's control."

"Which I was," the Queen interjects, wiping tears from her eyes. "And so I did."

"And so the last part of Bottom's plan fell into place," I say. "With the High Thirteen out of the way, the Second had control of you and, through you, control of both Fairy and Earth."

"So, tell me if I am hearing this correctly," the King says. "The Second stole the Book of Names and used it to control my wife. Under the wizard's influence, she further twisted my already-crooked brother, the Duke. Corrupted in full, the Duke used his brainwashed minions to invade the Mortal Lands and stir up the High Thirteen. In retaliation, they magicked me away to be their prisoner, causing my wife, the Queen, to wage war on Earth and subdue the High Thirteen under the pretense of getting me back. But what this truly did was remove any opposition the Second may have encountered so he was free to set himself up as absolute ruler of both Earth and Fairy?"

"That's more or less it, Your Highness," I say. "But, though Bottom didn't allow the Queen to name names, she had to warp the truth and tell the Duke she had a warlock who wielded the Book of Names in her pocket. It was how she—or rather Bottom through her—convinced the Duke her plan couldn't fail."

"A magician never tells his tricks, indeed," the Boogeyman snarls, paraphrasing words the Duke taunted us with while we were trapped in his dungeon. "Bottom used the Logos to close off all passages from the Void into Castle Night. It wasn't the Duke at all."

I take a deep breath. "And one other thing: though it was under the Queen's invitation that the High Thirteen were lured to the high-rise in the clouds, it was Bottom himself who took them captive using the advantage of surprise, not to mention that of the Logos."

The Queen nods. "It's true."

"In summary," the Boogeyman says, unable to help himself from having the last word, "using the power of the Logos, the Second enacted a complex scheme that pitted the best of Earth and Fairy against one another. Those who could've opposed him were eliminated one at a time by their peers until the wizard's path to absolute power lay clear. But the Second failed to consider one particularly important variable."

I push back my hat and scratch my head, having no idea what the Boogeyman is talking about now. "What?"

The Boogeyman pivots on his heels to face me, his shadowy cloak swirling with the movement. I'm surprised to see a good-natured smile stretched across his ugly, long face.

I'm shocked outright when he bows before me.

"You, my prince," the Boogeyman says. "The Second failed to consider you, and the sacrifice you were willing to make, in order to see that his rule came to a quick end."

I stare at my boots, embarrassed to no end, but proud, too.

"I didn't do it alone," I say. "Siren, Satyr, and Gazelluride were all there, fighting alongside me. And it was Eliana who used the Logos to draw the moon across the face of the sun and free you from stone so you could take care of Bottom personally. And heck, if the Fairy Godmother hadn't stayed on me, and made me face my destiny, who knows what would've happened?"

"And I am thankful to no end that she did." The Queen rises

from her throne and descends the short set of steps separating us, the train of her courtly gown flowing over them as she comes. She takes my face in her hands just like the first time I visited Castle Twilight's throne room. "Otherwise, we would not have our true son with us, here and now."

I blush as I feel a large hand come to rest on my shoulder. I look up and see the King has joined us. He smiles, exposing his tusk-like lower fangs. But I can tell his expression is meant to be one of warmth.

"Uh," I say, "you're not going to send me to sleep in the tree grove, are you?"

They laugh. The King's chuckles are especially boisterous.

"No, son. The Boogeyman has educated us to the fact that such *might* not be the best way to rear a child who has already spent so much time running about. Besides, you are a knight of Fairy. One who's proved more than capable of handling himself in a tense situation."

My Vulcan-like eyebrows rise on my newly large forehead.

"You can say that again."

"You will stay with us here in the Castle," the Queen says. "The education of a prince begins at birth. And while the tree grove could whisper instruction into your mortal doppelganger's sleeping ears, you have much to catch up on."

I sigh and take a step back from the Fairy King and Queen.

"I—" I say. It takes me a moment to truly find my voice. "I'm not so sure I'm ready for that. Not yet, anyway. I mean, I've been through so much in the past few days already."

The Queen nods. "Of course. You should be given opportunity to acclimate to your new circumstances. Take all the time you need." The Queen gives me a warm smile. "As an immortal fae, you have nothing but."

"There's one more thing."

"Yes?" the King asks.

"Well, I was wondering, while I'm getting myself together, if, in the meantime, I could maybe, er, *hang out with the Boogeyman*?"

From the corner of my eye, I see the Boogeyman straighten. Now it's his turn to be surprised.

The King and Queen exchange worried glances.

"Your Majesties," the Boogeyman offers, "if I was to take the prince under my wing, I would take great pains to find him time to visit with the Lady Siren at Bright Tree. She is more than adept as a teacher, and could school him right along with the girl she is considering to take on as her *Echo*. Through this, any past mistakes could be avoided. The prince would be provided with the balance one of his royal heritage needs and deserves."

The Queen gazes at me, tears streaming down her beautiful cheeks. "Is this what you truly want, Son?"

I think a moment to be sure of my answer. "Yes, Your Highness. At least for right now."

The King's barrel-sized chest rises and falls in a reluctant sigh. "Very well. Let it be so, then. The Boogeyman shall take the prince as his ward until our son is ready to come home and resume his place at Castle Twilight."

The King narrows his gaze on the Boogeyman as if he were bringing him into focus. "Mind yourself, Lord Boogeyman, that those past *mistakes* you spoke of are indeed avoided."

The Boogeyman bows deeply. "Absolutely, Your Highnesses."

The King and Queen give me a parting hug, and then the Boogeyman and I back out of the throne room.

Once we're out of earshot of any manimal guards, the Boogeyman speaks.

"Cruel of you, Puck, not to be totally honest with the King and Queen. Wise, but still cruel."

"What are you talking about?"

The Boogeyman glides swiftly through the hall so that I have to all but jog in order to keep pace. "They may not have reacted so pleasantly if you had announced your true desire."

"And what, precisely, is that?"

"Why, to be my apprentice, of course—my *Shadow*."

"I'll have you know, I haven't made up my mind yet."

"But you *are* considering it, aren't you?"

Until that moment, I honestly couldn't have said. But once I realize the truth, I can't deny it.

"Well, yeah. I guess I am."

"Good. We must get started on your training immediately.

You need a staggering amount of work. But if anyone can whip you into shape, it's Cat and myself."

I grab the Boogeyman's forearm, forcing him to stop. "I'll play along for now. But I'm here to tell you, there's going to be some changes in how things are done."

The Boogeyman lowers his ugly, scowling face to mine.

"Changes? What sort of changes?"

EPILOGUE

I hurry down the street of my old neighborhood at night, passing a number of wizards, goblins, and fairies. There are also several cowboys, superheroes, and princesses. All of them are around my height, and carrying orange pails molded to look like jack-o'-lanterns.

Last year, the streets were a lot more crowded. The trunk-or-treat events conducted by the local churches haven't quite taken over Halloween yet, but they're well on their way. For good or bad, my favorite holiday is changing.

Everything does. I'm living proof.

"Cool costume."

I turn to see a teenage boy dressed up like a B-movie slasher looking over my black musketeer outfit. He holds a plastic machete in one hand and a roll of toilet paper in the other.

"They look so real." He reaches out a single finger to touch one of my long, pointy ears. Reflex takes over, and I slap his hand away.

He sticks out his chest, trying to appear larger than he really is. "You're going to pay for that!"

I shift my shape ever so slightly, causing my pupils to contract into twin serpentine slits and my canines to elongate into fangs.

"I don't think so." The chill of the night causes my words to come out in visible puffs of air that look like smoke and add to the overall spooky effect I'm going for.

I give a hiss, and the teen drops the roll of toilet paper and takes off down the street like his head was on fire and his butt was catching.

I watch him go, wondering if he was one of the kids I saved from the shape-shifting snake-monster—*and if it's not too late to send him back.*

"Easy," I tell myself. "You're going to have to do a better job of controlling your fairy thoughts and impulses. Especially now."

I reach down and scoop up the roll of toilet paper. I carry it with me as I walk another block and turn down a leaf-littered alley.

From here, I spot the kid I'm looking for.

My former doppelganger stands in one of the back yards adjoining the alley, unspooling rolls of toilet paper over trees and lawn furniture.

He's made up to look like the block-headed Frankenstein from the old, black-and-white, Universal Studios films.

I can't help but smile.

When the Boogeyman used his powers to copy my memories and dump them into the boy's head, I knew my love of monsters would be part of it. Still, there's something satisfying about seeing the results of our mind-meld up close and personal.

I change shape into a freckled, flame-headed boy wearing a Mummy costume. Then I walk up to Mom and Dad's replacement son and send the roll of toilet paper in my hand soaring over a maple tree. It flies fast and true and leaves a nice long streamer in its wake.

The boy whirls, shocked to see me standing here. When he sees I'm just another kid, he relaxes.

"Mind if I join you?" I ask.

"It's a free country. What's your name?"

I tell him.

"Hey," he says, "that's my name, too."

"You don't say?"

Without warning, the back door of the house we're at opens to reveal a fat, balding man dressed in a bathrobe and slippers. He is holding something in his hands.

My ex-doppelganger tenses. "He doesn't look happy."

"You kids get out of my yard!" The fat man raises what I now have no problem making out as a baseball bat and leaps off his back porch to charge after us.

"Definitely not happy," I say. "Let's get out of here!"

We sprint out of the yard and make tracks down the alley, laughing and kicking up dead autumn leaves as we go.

Once we've placed several suburban blocks between the fat man and ourselves, we duck behind a tree in another back yard to catch our breath.

"That was killer!"

"Tell me about it," I agree, and the two of us high-five.

"Want to roll some more yards?"

"Nah." I hold up my mummified hands. "Besides, we're all out of paper."

"So we are."

We sit in silence for a moment. Finally, he turns to me wearing an expression that tells me he's ready to be disappointed at my response to what he's about to say.

"Well, the candy scene's tapped out. But back home, my Mom and Dad are nuking some popcorn and baking cookies for *The Walking Dead* marathon on AMC. I don't suppose you'd want to come over and watch?"

I start to reply, but he cuts me off.

"If you don't, I understand. I guess it's pretty lame for kids our age to be hanging out with grown-ups on Halloween, huh?"

What feels like the biggest smile in the history of the world spreads across my face.

"Actually, I think that sounds like heaven."

WHEN I LEAVE MY OLD home a few hours later, the Boogeyman is waiting for me among the shadows beneath a large elm tree standing in the front yard.

"How was your visit?" he growls.

"Absolutely wonderful," I say, still unable to wipe the huge grin from my face. "I've been invited back for dinner this Sunday."

I transform back into my fairy self and join the Boogeyman among the shadows beneath the elm.

"Your parents didn't give you any indication that they recall the Fairy siege, did they?" the Boogeyman asks.

I shake my head. "Nope. The memory-suppression spell the wizards cast over Earth must be holding."

The Boogeyman growls in contentment.

A moment bloated with silence passes between us.

"So," I say at last, "shall we head back to Shadow Tower?"

The Boogeyman shakes his gruesome head. "Not yet. There's a hatchling sea serpent loose in the San Francisco Bay. It's already sunk a number of derelict barges it's mistaken for its mother. If it isn't returned to the Night Lands soon, a lot of people are going to get hurt."

"A sea serpent, huh?"

The Boogeyman nods.

"Lead the way, Lord Boogeyman."

"Please, call me Boogey."

"Only if you'll call me '*Shadow.*'"

A black rictus of a smile spreads across the Boogeyman's face.

He gives a dramatic flourish of his shadow cloak, and the two of us disappear into darkness.

TO BE CONTINUED...

About the Author

Shane Berryhill is half man, half monster, and all storyteller. His books aimed at readers both young of age and young of heart include *Chance Fortune and the Outlaws* (an official selection of both the New York Public Library's Books for the Teen Age and the Texas Library Association Lone Star Reading list), *Dragon Island, The Long Silent Night,* and others. Shane lives with his wife and son—and their pet puppy dog, Kwazii—in Chattanooga, Tennessee. Shane loves to connect with friends and fans via Social Media.

Curious about other Crossroad Press books?
Stop by our site:
http://store.crossroadpress.com
We offer quality writing
in digital, audio, and print formats.

71655476R00161

Made in the
USA
Middletown, DE